# The Surrogate Mother

a novel by

## FREIDA McFADDEN

The Surrogate Mother

For Melanie and Libby
(Or for Libby and Melanie, because I'm sure one day there will be an argument over the significance of this ordering)

## NOVELS BY FREIDA McFADDEN

The Wife Upstairs

The Perfect Son

The Ex

The Surrogate Mother

Brain Damage

Baby City

Suicide Med

The Devil Wears Scrubs

The Devil You Know

# PROLOGUE

In the next twenty-four hours, I will be arrested for first-degree murder.

I don't know how this could be happening. I'm not the kind of person who goes to jail for murder. I'm *not.* I've never even gotten a speeding ticket. Hell, I've never even jaywalked before. I'm the most law-abiding citizen who ever was.

"They have a pretty solid case against you, Abby."

My lawyer, Robert Frisch, does not sugar coat things. I've only known him a short time, but I already know he's not about handholding and gumdrops and lollipops. He has spent the last twenty minutes enumerating all the police department's evidence against me. And when I hear it all laid out for me like that, it sounds bad. If I were some neutral third party listening to everything Frisch was saying, I'd be thinking to myself, *That woman is definitely guilty. Lock her up—throw away the key.*

The whole time I was listening to Frisch, my heart was thumping wildly in my chest. It actually made it a bit hard to hear him for stretches of time. To my right, my husband Sam is slumped in his chair, a glassy look in his eyes. Sam was the one who hired Frisch. *He's your best chance, Abby,* he told me.

So if he can't help me, that means I have no chance.

"It's all circumstantial evidence," I say, even though I'm not certain that's the case or even exactly what circumstantial evidence is. But I know one thing: "I didn't do it."

Frisch lets out an extended sigh and folds his arms across his chest. "You have to understand that if this goes to court, you're going to be convicted."

"*If* this goes to court?"

"I'd recommend a plea bargain," he says. "When they arrest you—"

I imagine the police showing up at my door, snapping metal cuffs on my wrists. Reading me my rights. *You have the right to remain silent.* Is that something they really say in real life? I don't want to find out.

"*If* they arrest me," I correct him.

Frisch gives me a look like I'm out of my mind. He's been a criminal attorney for nearly thirty years. One of the best. You can tell how successful he is by the leather sofa pushed up against the wall and the mahogany desk where he's got a photo of himself shaking the hand of Barack Obama. I've got money, but the length of a full trial might bleed us dry.

"Second-degree murder is fifteen years to life," Frisch says. "Whereas for Murder One, you could get life without possibility of parole. If you plea down to Murder Two—"

"Fifteen years!" I cry.

I don't want to go to jail for fifteen years. That's a lifetime. I don't want to go to jail for one day, but fifteen years is unthinkable. I can't wrap my head around it. I can't make a plea bargain that will guarantee me fifteen years of prison. I *can't*.

I look over at Sam, hoping for an equally indignant expression on his face. Instead, he still has that glazed look on his face. He's staring at the wall behind Frisch, and even though I'm trying to catch his eye, he won't look at me.

Does he think I did it?

Does my own husband really believe I'm a murderer? He knows me better than anyone else in the world, so if he believes I'm guilty, what chance do I have with a jury?

But I'm not guilty. I didn't do it. I didn't kill anyone…

Did I?

# CHAPTER 1

## *One Year Earlier*

At this moment in time, my life is just about perfect.

A couple of years ago, I couldn't have said that. A couple of years ago, I would have rather slit my wrists than stood up in front of a room full of executives from Cuddles, "the new name in diapers," and presented them with a new ad campaign filled with dozens of pictures of cherubic babies with halos on their heads and the tagline: "Because your little angel is worth it." I would have done the presentation, of course, but the smile on my face wouldn't have been genuine, the way it is today.

But right now, everything is exactly the way I want it to be. Well, not *exactly*, but very close. I have the job I always wanted. I'm married to a wonderful man. And in a few short weeks (depending on the whims of the Labor Gods), I'm going to become a mother for the very first time.

You might say I have a glow about me.

"This new campaign," I say, as I gesture at the projected image on the screen, "has the potential to propel Cuddles into the same league as Huggies and Pampers."

I turn my gaze to Jed Cofield, the executive VP of marketing at Cuddles. Jed is in his forties with thick, chestnut hair, penetrating dark eyes, and a suit from Hugo Boss. Even though he wears a gold band on his left hand, in the two years I've worked with him, he always stands a bit closer than he needs to when we talk—close enough that I can accurately identify what he ate for his last meal. Even now—even with my impending motherhood—I notice his eyes traveling down the length of my body.

Back before I was promoted to my current position as Director of Content Strategy at Stewart Advertising, I learned a lot about how to appear confident. Eye contact is key. So I lock eyes with Jed, straighten my posture, and throw my shoulders back.

I have every reason to be confident. I know my campaign is fantastic. I worked my butt off making sure of that.

"How did this campaign perform with the twenty-five to thirty-four female demographic?" Cofield asks.

It's an excellent question. In the diaper market, twenty-five to thirty-four females are essentially *the* demographic, as far as Cuddles is concerned. Few sixty-year-old men buy diapers for babies, no matter how compelling our commercials are. Of course, I've aged out of this key demographic, yet I've got a package of newborn diapers stuffed in the closet, but no need to point that out.

Denise Holt, the Chief Marketing Officer and also my boss, opens her mouth to answer the question. Three years ago, I might have let her. But part of being confident is you don't let your boss answer questions for you.

"They love the campaign, Jed," I say before Denise can get a word out. I click on a button on my remote, bringing up a screen of data. "After viewing our campaign, they were fifty-three percent more likely to choose Cuddles over the other leading brands." I watch his eyebrows raise and add, "And in addition to your original target group, this campaign also resonated deeply with women aged thirty-five to forty-four. As you know, older mothers contribute at least thirty percent to the diaper-purchasing market."

Cofield nods, impressed. "Very true.

I make eye contact with him again. "We're going to crush it."

Cofield is smiling now, but Denise isn't. I've known Denise Holt for a long time, and I know she doesn't enjoy being upstaged. Denise was the one who hired me way back when—over a decade ago now. I still remember stumbling into her office and being terrified by her ice-blue eyes and blond hair swept back into a perfect French knot. I fiddled with my suit jacket collar as I fumbled through my rehearsed list of reasons why I wanted to work for Stewart Advertising and specifically for the infamous Denise Holt.

She hired me. Then she taught me everything I know, including how to tie my jet black hair into a French knot, which is apparently called a *chignon*. (Who knew?) It wasn't until she found out I was trying for a baby that our relationship deteriorated.

"They love it, huh?" Cofield says.

I nod. "They do."

His smile broadens. "Well, so do I. I love it. It's brilliant."

Outwardly, I remain calm, but inside, I'm doing cartwheels. *The VP of Cuddles loves my idea. He* loves *it! He says it's* brilliant!

I can't help but flash a triumphant smile at Denise, who has been nothing but negative during the entire time I've been working on this campaign. As recently as yesterday, she was urging me to postpone this meeting because "it's not nearly ready." When I insisted on going forward, she accused me of having "baby on the brain."

Denise has chosen to remain free from maternal obligations. When I started out as her assistant, she drilled into me time and again that nothing wrecked a career faster than popping out a couple of rugrats. Denise's career means everything to her, and she's been extremely successful. Back then, I thought my career meant everything to me. Then Sam came along and convinced me otherwise.

I have no regrets. Everything is working out perfectly for me.

"Tell me, Abby." Cofield raises his eyebrows at me. "Will you be purchasing Cuddles for your baby?"

"Of course," I lie. "I want the best."

Yeah, there's no way I'm putting those shoddy diapers on my own child.

We iron out a few more details, then shake hands all around. Jed Cofield winks at me when we shake, and I squeeze his fingers firmly in the way Denise instructed me years ago. His warm fingers linger on mine for a beat longer than necessary. Cofield has been my biggest fan since I started working on the Cuddles campaign, so I won't begrudge him a handshake that lasts a second or two longer than I'd like.

But if he thinks he's getting anything more out of me, he's sorely mistaken.

"Congratulations," he tells me.

I'm not sure if he's referring to my successful pitch or impending motherhood, but I simply smile and say, "Thank you."

As Cofield and his associates clear out of the room, Denise and I are left alone. There was a time when I got a thrill out of any chance to be alone with my role model, but these days, I avoid it like the plague. Given how well everything went in the presentation, it would be appropriate for Denise to say something positive or even *complimentary*, but there's a sour look on her face that tells me I will not be receiving any praise today.

"I've been meaning to speak with you, Abigail," she

says.

Denise is the only person at work who calls me "Abigail" rather than "Abby." I used to like it—the name made me sound like an executive, rather than a girl at the playground with freckles and pigtails. (I used to have freckles and pigtails.) I tried to get everyone at work to call me Abigail for a while, but it didn't stick. Now the sound of that name on her lips makes my skin crawl.

"What about?" I ask. I plaster on that fake smile I now use when I talk to my boss, although it gets harder every day. One day, I will be speaking to Denise and simply won't be able to smile. It will be physically impossible.

Denise eyes my outfit. My suit jacket and skirt are from Armani. In the month I made the purchase, Sam came to me with the credit card statement and a horrified look on his face. "Someone stole our credit card, right?" he said. "We didn't *actually* spend this much, right?"

I had to tell him that yes, we did. I absolutely did spend that much on a single outfit, and it was *worth it*. Sam claims his suits from Men's Wearhouse look identical to anything he'd get at Armani or Prada, but he's wrong. Maybe there's no difference across a lecture hall, which is all that matters to him—but close up, anyone worth their salt can tell an expensive suit from a cheap knock-off. And the executives I pitch to respect someone who dresses well—in that sense, my clothes pay for themselves.

Another lesson I learned from Denise.

"How are you doing?" she asks.

"Good," I say cautiously, because anything more positive than that is a cue for Denise to make my life worse.

"Wonderful, wonderful." Denise taps a dark red manicured finger against her chin. "Remind me how long you're planning to take for your family leave? Eight weeks?"

A muscle twitches in my jaw. "Twelve weeks."

"Twelve weeks?" Denise's eyes widen in astonishment, despite the fact that we've had this exact conversation nearly a dozen times. "That long?"

The muscle twitches again. I had my first migraine earlier this year following a particularly tense discussion with Denise—I can't let her get to me.

"Twelve weeks is allowed as family leave," I say.

"I realize that." Denise's ice-blue eyes narrow at me. "But that doesn't mean you *must* take twelve weeks, does it? It seems like an awfully long time. Your clients will be disappointed."

"I can do some of my work from home during the last month," I say. That's a compromise we've worked out. "Everyone is going to take on some of my workload. And of course, my assistant Monica will be around to help out."

"*Monica will be around to help,*" she repeats in a vaguely mocking tone. She blinks a few times. "Well then, perhaps we should give *Monica* your position?"

If I slugged her in the face, I'd get fired. I have to remind myself of that. Again and again.

"I'm just kidding," Denise says, even though she's not smiling. "Of course, you are entitled to your twelve weeks, Abigail. I was just hoping you might reconsider."

I will not reconsider. I love my career, but I have thought long and hard about my priorities. I will not rush back to work. I don't care if Denise hates me because of it. And let's face it—she wouldn't hate me any less if I took four weeks.

"Anyway." Denise pats her flawless chignon, which makes my hand go automatically to my own French knot. I feel a strand has come loose and I quickly tuck it behind my ear. Denise must use a bottle of hairspray each day to keep hers intact, but it doesn't appear that way. Her hair looks silky and perfect. "I believe Shelley has planned some sort of... *party* for you in the break room."

I'm well aware that my best friend Shelley has scheduled a baby shower for me to follow this meeting— she would have preferred to surprise me, but given my tight schedule, that was impossible. It's sweet of her, but after fifteen minutes, I'll definitely have to make my excuses and slip away. My afternoon is packed—as it is, I won't get home till eight or nine tonight.

"I'm afraid I won't be able to make it," Denise tells me, which is no surprise. She's made no secret of the fact that she does not approve of events that "waste everyone's time" such as baby showers. "But please make sure you clear away all the trash from the room when you're done."

I bite my tongue to keep from reminding her that I

am no longer her assistant, and she can't tell me to clean up garbage anymore. But I keep my mouth shut, because I'm happy. I've impressed the Cuddles people, and I'm about to go to a baby shower in my honor. A *baby shower*. For *me*.

In the time I have worked at Stewart Advertising, I have made an appearance at roughly two million baby showers. Okay, that could be a slight exaggeration. It's possible I've only been to one million baby showers. Maybe three-quarters of a million. Definitely no less than half a million.

But now, for the first time, the shower is for me. Not for Elsa in reception, who has had at least a dozen children in her time working here. Not for Shelley, who has had a more respectable two. This shower is for *me*. The finger sandwiches that will be piled in the corner will have been brought in *my* honor. The presents stacked neatly in the corner of the room will be for *me*. The first piece of chocolate hazelnut cake will be handed to *me*.

There's only one thing different about this baby shower from all other baby showers thrown for the other women in my company:

I'm not pregnant.

# CHAPTER 2

"Here's your bottle, Abby."

Shelley is thrusting a baby bottle into my hand. It's filled with… well, it's not milk. Something amber-colored. "We're going to start in another minute."

I hold up the bottle to the light. "What's in it?"

"Apple juice," Shelley says, but then she winks, which makes me worry.

"I'm not drinking whiskey at work, Shelley," I hiss at her.

"It's *apple juice*."

We've played this game… well, at least half a million times. Everyone gets a bottle of liquid, and we all chug it through the nipples. Whoever finishes first is the winner. It's just one of several inane baby shower games we've devised and perfected over the years.

Back when I first started working at Stewart, I thought the games were a real hoot. Somewhere between my third and tenth negative pregnancy test, they stopped being so much fun. Around the twentieth negative test, it became a form of torture. When I saw those big, swollen bellies, I wanted to hide in a bathroom stall and sob, not celebrate by making little Franken-babies out of magazine clippings. Usually I stayed around five minutes before excusing myself due to my heavy workload—it was true that I had a ton of work, but it wasn't the main reason I raced out of the room like it was on fire.

But today, I'm enjoying myself. Because after years of heartbreak, I am on the brink of motherhood. In about three weeks, I'm going to become the proud parent of a newborn boy, whose sixteen-year-old birth mother is currently living in Tucson, Arizona. I told Shelley I wasn't sure if an adoption warranted a baby shower, but she was insistent I get the same treatment as all the ladies with the big bellies.

The door to the conference room swings open and in walks my assistant Monica, carrying a comically large diaper cake. It's trimmed with blue ribbon, and has a blue teddy bear clinging to the side of it. Poor Monica's arms are trembling with the effort of holding it, and I rush over to grab the other end before she drops the whole thing on the floor.

"A diaper cake from Cuddles," she says breathlessly as we lower the monstrosity onto the banquet table. "It's a bit... big."

I smile to myself, imaging Jed Cofield telling his secretary to send over this giant cake. Is it terrible that I secretly hope the diapers in the diaper cake are any brand *other* than Cuddles?

I roll my eyes at Monica. "Next time, I'm going to request a diaper *cupcake*."

Monica covers her mouth with her hand as she giggles. She's been my assistant for the last six months, since my old assistant Gertie fell and broke her hip, and was not-so-gently pressured by the powers-that-be into an early retirement. And it's been amazing having Monica. Not that I didn't like Gertie, who made really incredible chocolate chip cookies, but she was just so *slow* at everything. Like, even watching her walk across the room was painful. And she didn't know how to send documents to the printer from her computer. Even faxes were a little tricky for her—I think the fax machine hadn't been invented yet when she started at Stewart. I'm not sure if phones had been invented yet. But they probably had fire and the wheel.

So yes, Monica is absolutely a breath of fresh air. She's in her early twenties, a recent college graduate with a degree in art and math, and sharp as a tack. She soaks in everything like a sponge. Having Monica as an assistant has increased my efficiency by at least… sixty-eight percent.

I knew immediately during our interview that she was going to be my new assistant. The way she looked reminded me so much of myself, from her jet black hair tied awkwardly in a bun behind her head to her ill-fitting suit to her overeager smile. And then instead of praising me for the Cuddles campaign like every other candidate I interviewed, Monica gushed in detail about a campaign I did years ago for a yogurt company—one that was less well-known but one I was particularly proud of. It showed the girl did her research.

And when I asked her what she wanted to get out of the position, she replied, "I want to learn everything you know."

I hired her on the spot.

After Monica adjusts the diaper cake on the table, she frowns at a pile of baby-sized Yankee caps on the side. I laugh at the baffled look on her face. "Shelley wanted us to wear those, but she couldn't get any takers. You'd make her day if you put one on."

Monica smiles. "Oh, no. I grew up a Red Sox fan—I went to all their games when I was a kid. I could never put on a Yankees cap. They'd never let me come home!"

"Well, I'm a Yankees fan," I say, "and yet I still don't want to put on the cap."

Shelley rushes over at that moment and thrusts a baby bottle into Monica's hands. "Ten minutes till chug time," Shelley warns.

"Oh." Monica's cheeks color and she glances at me. "I still need to type up the minutes from the meeting this morning and make copies for the—"

"No, you don't." I rest a hand on my assistant's shoulder. "You've been working so hard, and Cuddles loved our pitch today. You're allowed to take a break for a baby shower."

"Well, at least let me clean up the—"

"*No.*" I give her a sharp look. "I want you to relax. Enjoy yourself for a bit. You deserve it as much as anyone."

Shelley winks at Monica. "You're lucky, Monica. Abby is too nice to her team. If you were *my* assistant, I'd have you picking up plastic cups from the floor right now."

I survey the room, and... wow, there are a lot of plastic cups on the floor. The employees at Stewart are a bunch of slobs. Denise was right to mention the garbage situation. But we have a cleaning staff here—Monica is my personal *assistant.*

"I guess I could..." Monica glances around the room with her dark brown eyes. Sometimes when I look into her eyes, I really do feel like I'm looking into a mirror. Her jet black hair is like mine, although hers is ramrod straight while mine falls in random waves around my face. In any case, Monica and I do look somewhat similar, although she's more than a decade younger than I am. Sometimes I appreciate when people remark on our likeness to each other, but not so much when Jack in the Creative department calls her Abby Two Point Oh. "I'll stay, but just for a few minutes. Then I really should get back to work!"

Honestly, if it doesn't work out with this baby, I might just adopt Monica.

"It's so nice of Cuddles to send all those diapers," Monica says. "I've heard diapers are actually very expensive."

"Oh, Abby doesn't have to worry about that," Shelley giggles. "Her family is really rich. Her grandfather got in on an investment in this really big company on the ground floor."

I sigh. I really dislike it when she brings up my family's money—it's embarrassing and tacky. "Shelley..."

"Abby doesn't want me to tell you which company," she says. "But I'll give you a hint. You may have a product from this company in your purse right now."

"Shelley..."

"Here's another hint. It's not an orange..."

"Shelley!"

Shelley laughs. "Don't worry, Abby, I won't blab your secret." She grins at Monica. "But anyway, she's got a big trust fund, so she doesn't have to worry about the cost of diapers, believe me."

She isn't entirely wrong. I do have a small trust fund that's gotten me through some tough times. But it's not infinite money. I'm well-off, but not rich. That said, the cost of diapers is definitely not something I need to stress over.

Monica wanders off to grab a sandwich, but Shelley lingers by my side. She's got an unreadable expression on her face. I've known Shelley ten years, since the two of us were both lowly assistants ourselves, but I still have trouble knowing what she's thinking. "You getting nervous, Abby?" she asks me.

I give her a look. "What are you talking about? I nailed the Cuddles pitch."

"That's not what I mean. Are you nervous about the B-A-B-Y?"

I shake my head. "No. We'll be fine."

"How about Sam? How's he holding up?"

I can't suppress a grin. "He's *really* excited. It's adorable. He spent all of yesterday putting together the crib."

"Oh right, I forgot—Sam's perfect."

"He's not perfect…"

"Yes, he is." Shelley takes a swig from her baby bottle. What is *in* those things? "He takes out the garbage, he cleans, he does laundry… he presumably changes the toilet paper roll more than once per millennium. He even cooks now…"

"I wouldn't go that far," I say. In the last few months, buoyed by the excitement of the new baby coming, Sam decided he was going to learn how to cook. The results have been mixed. No, that's kind. He's horrible at it. You would think that just by following a recipe, he could achieve some level of competence, but no.

"Well, so what if he can't cook?" she says. "Most importantly, he's still desperately in love with you even though you've been married *forever*. And best of all, he's still really hot. He hasn't lost even one hair on his head, while Rick is practically *bald*."

I almost laugh at the expression on my best friend's face. "Rick isn't bald."

"No, I said he's *practically* bald. Bald would be better! Instead, he's pathetically clinging to those last few strands." Her jaw tightens. "One day, I swear I'll shave him in his sleep."

"I'd think Sam was just as handsome even if he went bald."

"Please stop, Abby. You're going to make me vomit."

"Well, sorry."

Shelley always pretends to be jealous of me, but the truth is, her husband Rick is a really good guy too. He's a great dad too, as far as I can tell. But yes, I have to admit, Sam is hotter and less bald. But that's not all it's cracked up to be. I like having an attractive husband, but it's not so great when that attractive husband is a math professor who works with young undergrads.

Not that I think Sam would cheat or anything, but...

Well, he wouldn't. But sometimes I wish he worked at an all-male university.

I feel my shoulders relax as Shelley and I chat. Maybe I can spend more than fifteen minutes here. I have done nothing but slave away for the last three months on the Cuddles campaign—I'm entitled to at least twenty minutes to enjoy a party held in my honor. How often do I get a baby shower?

I pick up the baby bottle in my hand and take a long

swig from the nipple. And… damn—it really *is* apple juice. Okay, I guess I won't enjoy this party *that* much.

I'm about to suggest to Shelley we get drinks after work when the door to the conference room cracks open. My mouth falls open when the familiar face of my husband appears at the door. A warm feeling of joy fills my chest like it always does whenever I see Sam unexpectedly. I can't believe Shelley invited him! She's the best.

"Hey, it's the father!" Shelley calls out when she spies him at the door. "Sam! Come get a bottle!"

Sam smiles crookedly. Whenever he appears suddenly, I always get a jolt when I notice how handsome he is. A guy like him could easily have become a player, but he's actually somewhat shy and often seems mortified by the impact he has on the opposite sex—like when his students refer to him as Professor McHottie. He wears glasses because contacts are "pointless," he's never bought a bottle of hair gel in his life, nor has he ever even set foot in an Armani store. Yet in spite of all that, he still manages to turn heads on a regular basis.

"Hey," I say. I'm smiling so wide now that it's beginning to hurt. "I can't believe you made it here. Didn't you have a lecture this afternoon?"

"Uh, yeah." Sam scratches at the stubble on his chin because he only shaves every other day, even though he really needs to shave every day. He looks ridiculously sexy on non-shaving days. "Hey, um, Abby…"

Sam lifts his brown eyes to meet mine. Sam has really

kind eyes. They say the eyes are the window to the soul, and if that's true, my husband has the best soul of anyone I've ever met. He has a lot of good qualities, but it's his kind eyes that made me fall in love with him.

And I know just from looking into those eyes that something horrible has happened.

"Is everything okay?" I ask him, even though I would bet the farm it's not.

He glances around the room, his ears turning red. "Abby, could we talk? Outside?"

The room goes instantly silent. This is really bad. I don't know what he's going to say to me and I don't want to know. I want to live in five minutes ago—when I was having a (relatively) great time at my first and only baby shower. Before my husband showed up and everything fell apart.

# CHAPTER 3

Sam takes my hand the second I join him at the door. His warm, large hand envelopes mine, and he pulls down the hallway, past a large leafy plant and the water cooler.

"Sam," I say. "What's going on?"

"Let's talk in your office."

I pull my hand away from his and grab his elbow, yanking him into the nook by the copy machine. "No, let's talk *here*."

"Okay, but…" His eyes dart around. "Maybe we should get you a chair…"

He wants me to be sitting. Oh God. I think I'm going to throw up.

"Sam," I say as patiently as I can. "Will you tell me what the hell is going on?"

Sam focuses his brown eyes back on my face. A deep crease forms between his eyebrows. "Janelle pulled out."

"What?"

"I just got the call from Steve." He rakes a hand

through his light brown hair—his fingers are shaking. "He said Janelle changed her mind. She wants to keep the baby."

"*What*?"

My legs feel rubbery. Sam was right—we should have gone to my office. Or I should have held out for a chair.

"Something about how her mother is going to help her or... I don't know." He sighs. "It all amounts to the same thing. She's keeping him."

"Is... is she allowed to do that?" I sputter. "Our contract says…"

"She's allowed to back out." Sam shuts his eyes for a moment, then when he opens them again, I notice for the first time they're slightly bloodshot. "We can't fight her in court for her baby. We'd never win."

I'm starting to get tunnel vision. The whole world is disappearing and all I can see is Sam's face in front of me. A lump forms in my throat, and I know I'm seconds away from bursting into tears.

"Abby?" His voice sounds far away. "Are... are you okay?"

"No," I whisper. "I'm not."

I fall into his arms, and even though there are still some people in their cubicles who could probably see us, I let the tears fall. Maybe "let" is the wrong word. I'm helpless to stop these tears.

At least Sam is here. When he got the news, he was all alone. I can't imagine what that must have been like for him. He wanted this baby as badly as I did. I can see in his eyes how devastated he is.

"I'll drive you home, okay?" he says. "I've got the car."

Home. Where the nursery is all set up for the baby we're not going to get. How can we go back there? I can't bear it. Also…

"The baby shower…" The thought of going back to the room with the giant diaper cake is like being stabbed in the chest. "I need to tell them."

"I'll talk to them," he says. "You wait here."

Sam is such a wonderful husband.

It's all my fault we can't get pregnant. *He's* normal. Perfect sperm. All-star sperm. I'm the defective one.

"You don't have to…" I murmur.

"I'll talk to them," he says again, more firmly this time. "But don't leave without me. Promise?"

I nod mutely. I'm not going to argue with him.

"It's going to be okay," he says. "It will."

Except I'm not sure who he's trying to convince—me or himself.

———

Sam and I don't say one word to each other on the drive home. Even Sam's car is a depressing reminder of what we've lost. Ever since I met him, Sam had driven a 1997 Honda Civic. It was old when he bought it used, and it got to the point where he had to say a prayer every time he turned the key in the ignition. I begged him to trade it in for something safer and more reliable, insisting we had the money to get him any car he wanted, but he clung to that car like it was his first child.

Then when we found out we had a baby on the way for sure, without prompting, Sam got rid of his old Civic and got a brand new Toyota Highlander. It's a big, safe SUV that has a car seat strapped into the back which we will probably never use. Just looking at that car seat makes me want to burst into tears.

I should have taken the subway home.

By the time we get to our apartment, my eyes are swollen and my cheeks are sticky with tears. Sam lets me out at the front so he can park the car. He won't let me shell out the exorbitant fee for the parking garage below our building, so he spends half his time searching the neighborhood for open parking spots. He'll drag himself out of bed at six in the morning on his day off to move his car to avoid getting a ticket. I had planned to insist on paying for the parking garage once the baby came, but that won't be an issue anymore.

I feel a surge of resentment at Sam's stubbornness about the parking garage as I trek up to our apartment all alone. I don't want to face the open door to what would have been the baby's room all alone. I catch a glimpse of the light brown wood of the crib and the yellow paint on the wall before I pull the door shut with a resounding snap.

My phone buzzes inside my purse. There's no one I want to talk to right now, but I assume it's Shelley, trying to say something comforting. I fish out the phone and see the text message filling the screen. It's from none other than my favorite boss, Denise:

*Sorry to hear about your situation. I assume I can cancel your family leave totaling 12 weeks? Also, please let me know ASAP if you will require a personal day tomorrow.*

For God's sake, couldn't the woman let me grieve for one hour? Denise used to be the woman I respected most in the entire universe, but now I hate her. I *hate* Denise. No, "hate" isn't a strong enough word for what I feel for her. "Loathe" or "abhor" don't quite do it either. Someone needs to invent a new word to describe the way I feel right now about Denise Holt.

Except none of this is Denise's fault. And an hour ago, she was no more than an annoyance in my life, instead of the object of my seething hatred. So maybe I should hold off on answering her text right now, because I can't afford to tell off my boss. My job is all I have anymore.

I glance at my watch. How long does it take Sam to park a goddamn car?

The landline next to the couch starts ringing. I don't even know why we have the damn thing, because all important calls come on our cell phones. All we get on the landline are telemarketers. Then again, I wouldn't mind yelling at a telemarketer right now. It might make me feel better.

I walk across the living room to answer the phone, but before I can make it, I trip on something and bash my knee on the coffee table. Our coffee table is one of those heavy marble tables with zero give, and *damn*, that hurts. I rub my reddening knee, searching for the object that tripped me up.

It's a bassinet. The one that arrived this morning.

Of course.

I yank the receiver off the hook, ready to scream at the voice that comes on the line. AT&T? Verizon? Progressive Auto Insurance? I'm not picky—I'll yell at anyone right now.

Except the voice on the other line doesn't sound like a telemarketer. It's a young, female voice, slightly hesitant. "Hello?"

"Yes?" I say impatiently. My knee is starting to really throb. I should probably get an ice pack from the freezer to keep it from swelling too much—that is, if I can walk. "What is it?"

"Is this… Dr. Sam Adler's residence?"

I frown. "Yes…"

"Oh, great," the girl says. She lets out a giggle. "Um, my name is April and I'm in Dr. Adler's calculus class, and I had some questions about the exam on Friday. Is he… *available*?"

I shouldn't be surprised. A few years ago, we made our number unlisted because this would happen. Girls in Sam's classes would track down the phone number of their handsome professor and call him, hoping for... well, I don't know what they were hoping for exactly. He wears a wedding ring, so I guess they were hoping for a little something on the side. But then again, if that's what they wanted, why would they call him at *home*? College girls are dumb.

If the calls he gets here are any indication, I hate to think what goes on when he's on campus. Good thing I trust my husband.

"No, he's not available," I say tightly.

"Oh, too bad..." She giggles again. "Well, I could meet him somewhere to talk more. Like, maybe on Saturday night..."

Is this girl kidding me? This is far from the first time I've fielded a call from lovestruck coed, and usually, it's funny. Sam and I laugh about it. But right now, I don't feel like laughing.

"Listen, *April*," I hiss into the phone. "This is Dr. Adler's *wife* and I would appreciate you not calling him at his home ever again."

"Oh." The girl's playful tone disappears. "Sorry, I didn't realize—"

The lock turns in the front door. Sam finally managed to park the damn car.

"And," I add, before he can come inside and stop me, "you are never, ever to bother Dr. Adler again. If I hear you have contacted him—either here or on campus—I will make sure you're reported to the dean for harassment.

Understand?"

Sam walks into the apartment in the middle of that sentence. I'm not sure how much of my little tirade he heard, but his brown eyes go wide. Enough, I guess.

"Okay," the girl says softly. "I'm sorry."

"Good," I say. And then I slam down the receiver.

That's the best part about having a landline. You can slam it down. You don't get the joy of slamming a phone down when you're on a cell phone. What can you do— press "end call" really angrily?

Sam runs a hand through his hair, but does the thing he always does where he stops midway through his scalp so that his hair stands up straight. "Uh, who was that?"

"One of your students."

His mouth falls open. "You talked that way to my student?"

"Yep."

I stare at him, daring him to scold me further. I don't want to fight with Sam right now, but I will. It would be only too easy.

But he doesn't take the bait. Instead, he crosses the room and plops down next to me on the sofa. He reaches for my hand, and just like that, all the anger drains out of me. And all that's left is sadness. And emptiness.

I can't believe we're not going to have our baby. I wanted it so badly. More than words can express.

Ironically, it was Sam who initially pushed for us to have a child while I resisted. Not that I didn't want children—I definitely did, but not until I was at least thirty-four, when my career was on solid footing. Denise had ranted long and hard about what motherhood would do to my prospects at Stewart, and it had left an imprint. I wanted to wait. *Thirty-five*, I told Sam when we got married. *Maybe thirty-four, depending on how things are going.*

Sam felt differently about it. His own father had been forty when he was born and then died suddenly of a heart attack when he was in high school. His dad never got to see him graduate high school or college, never got to see him become a professor, never got to be at his wedding. Although he's in much better physical condition than his father ever was, Sam was terrified of being an "old dad" and missing out on large chunks of his children's lives.

"I don't want to die when my kids are still in school," he said, his voice breaking.

So right after we got married, he started gently pushing for us to try for a baby. I was only twenty-seven at the time and it felt inconceivable. But when Sam hit thirty, his pleas became more insistent. And then Shelley and Rick decided to start trying, so I finally gave in.

When I first stopped my birth control pills, I was some combination of nervous and excited. I joked with Sam that I hoped it took more than a month or two to conceive. Still, I was surprised when my first pregnancy test was negative. As a healthy twenty-nine-year-old woman, I had always assumed that the second I missed even a single pill, I'd be instantly knocked up. It was a reprieve though—one extra month without worrying about the responsibility of impending motherhood. Sam and I laughed it off, saying this way we got to have more fun trying.

After six months, we weren't laughing anymore.

Sam went to get his sperm checked. His boys were perfectly fine, and due to our relatively young age, my OB/GYN encouraged us to keep trying for another six months before we got too worried. Those six months went by, Shelley gave birth to her first child, and I still didn't have a positive pregnancy test. It was time to investigate further.

And that's when it all went downhill.

My doctor told me I probably had suffered some sort of infection that left deep scarring in my uterus and especially my fallopian tubes. Natural conception, she told me, would be impossible. We went straight for IVF, even though I was warned even that had a low chance of success given my "inhospitable uterus." Sam gave me hormone injections at home to stimulate egg production, but when they retrieved my eggs, those too were deemed to be "poor quality."

I felt like an absolute failure as a woman. My uterus was damaged, my eggs were poor quality, and all our attempts at IVF were expensive disasters. I was wracked with guilt that my "normal" husband couldn't have the child he wanted all thanks to me, even though he swore again and again that he didn't blame me. Meanwhile, my boss Denise was utterly unsympathetic about my need to rush out to appointments with the fertility specialist, or about the meeting I had to reschedule when my single successful pregnancy aborted itself after three short weeks.

For a time, I was obsessed with trying to conceive. I dove into it with the same intensity that had made me so successful at my job. I went vegan for a while. I drank something called "fertility tea" that tasted like the dust from our coffee table. I visited every infertility forum in the country and became well-versed in the lingo: TTC meant "trying to conceive" as in "I've been TTC for three years with no luck." AF meant "Aunt Flo"—the dreaded monthly blood that meant another failure. DPT meant "days past transfer" after an embryo was transferred into my uterus—a countdown until the next time I could POAS ("pee on a stick").

And then every time a woman on the board would announce her pregnancy, we'd all congratulate her, but I'd get a sick feeling it would never be me.

If it were up to me, I might have kept going with IVF until we were destitute, but it was Sam who brought up the idea of adoption. *It will still be our child,* he said. I resisted, having heard horror stories from other women on the forums about adoptions gone wrong, but Sam again pushed until I gave in. He was right—we wanted to be parents and this was our only option.

Once we became immersed in the adoption process, I

grew cautiously optimistic. I had wanted a child for what felt like forever now—it was a dream come true that it would soon be a reality. Unfortunately, nothing in the adoption process was quick. After carefully deciding on an agency, we had to complete a homestudy, which was the full body cavity search of the adoption process—the agency's social worker visited us repeatedly, requesting every legal document that had ever been issued to us in our lifetime. I didn't understand how they couldn't just look at me and Sam and realize we'd be good parents, but I guess there are guidelines.

After our approval, the search began for a child to match us with. Sam was open to older children, but I was adamant about wanting a newborn. During all those years of trying to conceive, I had dreamed of a tiny little infant, and I couldn't let go of that. Sometimes I felt guilty about it, because I knew there were older children who needed homes, so we agreed our second adoption (and possibly third, if we got to that point) would be an older child. But I wanted to experience having a newborn. Just once. And it cost us a year of being rejected by multiple pregnant women until Janelle finally made our dreams come true.

Well, almost.

And now, after having it all for a very short time, we have nothing again.

"What now?" I whisper to my husband.

Sam drops his head back against the sofa, staring up at the ceiling, his eyes glazed. Sometimes I get so caught up in my own misery that I forget it means just as much to him as it does to me. He wanted a child even before I did. This is killing him—I can see it in his eyes.

"I think we should look into adopting an older child," he finally says.

I suck in a breath. "Sam…"

"I know," he says tightly. "I know you were hoping for a newborn. I *know*. But Abby, there are so many young kids out there who need a home."

I look over at the tiny bassinet that nearly broke my knee. It's trimmed in yellow ribbon with little pink flowers on it. Yesterday, when we still believed we were going to be parents, I had laid out a little outfit inside the bassinet. A blue onesie barely the size of my hand, paired with tiny yellow socks. I remember putting one of those little socks in my palm, marveling at how tiny it was. How could a *human being* have a foot tiny enough to fit into that little sock? I kissed the sock gently, knowing it would soon warm the tiny foot of my infant son.

I know it sounds silly, but I had my heart set on a newborn. I don't feel ready to let go of my dream of holding an infant in my arms—of sliding a tiny foot into that little sock.

"We bought all newborn stuff," I point out. "The clothes… the crib… the bassinet… the car seat."

"So?" He rolls his head to look at me. "We can buy all new stuff. It's just *stuff*, Abby."

Yes, it's just stuff. And it isn't the stuff that's made me

hesitant to do this.

"Everyone wants newborns," he says. "But the kids in the orphanages… they need parents so badly. I want to do that, Abby. I'm sick of waiting for a newborn. I just want for us to be parents to a child who needs us."

He's right, of course. I've got to let go of my stupid fantasies from my days of TTC. It also doesn't escape me that if Sam wanted kids so badly, he could dump me for someone like April. *His sperm is normal.* I'm the problem.

But he'd never do that.

"Okay," I say. "Let's do it."

# CHAPTER 4

The worst thing about going to work the next morning is seeing other people. If I could be magically transported into my office and not have to speak to anyone, I'd be much happier.

It's a two-minute walk from the subway station to the office building, and during that time, I pass roughly five-thousand women pushing baby carriages. I don't know what they're all doing out and about at this early hour. I try not to look, but it's hard not to. One of the babies can't be more than a month or two old—she still has that fetal look to her, with her tiny eyes squeezed shut and her minuscule hands squeezed into red fists. Her hat has fallen off her head, and I want to reach over and put it back on. If it were my baby, I would never allow her hat to fall off or her little head to be cold for even an instant. I would never neglect my hat duties.

Why would the universe take my baby away from me?

When I walk into the office, the entire room goes

deathly silent. If there were music playing, it would have come to a screeching halt. All eyes are on me as I attempt to sprint to my office. It's enough to make me wish I had taken that personal day after all.

I've almost made it to safety when I practically collide with Shelley. She's standing with two other women from the office. I've attended baby showers for all three of them within the last five years, none of which ended abruptly in tragedy.

"Are you okay, Abby?" Shelley asks me.

"Fine." I force a smile. "I'm fine. Really."

And I mean it. Well, I'm partially fine. Sam and I contacted the social worker at the agency last night and we told them we wanted to broaden our options for adoption. Sam figured there was no point in sitting around, feeling sorry for ourselves—we'd feel better if we got started on the process of finding another child to adopt. While he was saying it, it sounded stupid, but it turned out he was right.

Not that I feel all better, but that stabbing pain in my heart feels more like a dull ache.

Even so, Shelley hugs me, as do the other two women, even though I barely know either of them.

"You're going to get your baby someday," Shelley promises me.

I avoid her eyes. I'm not in the mood for patronizing pep talks. "Yep."

"Honestly, you should consider yourself lucky," a woman named Jan says to me. "Kids are nothing but work.

I mean, right now, you can go out to dinner any time you want and you don't even have to think about getting a babysitter."

"And you *never* sleep when you have a baby," the other woman, Sidney, says. "You walk around for a year feeling like a zombie. Actually, make that five years!"

"Make that eighteen!" Jan laughs.

Sidney winks at me. "You can have my kids if you want them, Abby."

I look at Shelley, who can tell how much these comments are getting to me. God knows how long these well-meaning women would have kept me there, telling me how fortunate I am to have the adoption yanked out from under me, if Denise Holt herself hadn't shown up. The heels of her Christian Louboutin pumps tap loudly against the ground with each step.

Denise Holt walks right up to us, not a trace of sympathy in her blue eyes. I wonder if she's glad the adoption fell through for me. But in a way, I'm grateful for her stony gaze. At least one person is treating me the same as always.

"Abigail," she says sharply, folding her slim arms across her chest. "I informed you that you were welcome to take a personal day. But if you are going to be at work, please don't disrupt the entire staff."

"Abby's upset!" Jan says. "We were trying to cheer her up."

"Actually, there's no need," I say quickly. "I'm

completely fine. Sorry, Denise. I'll just… be in my office."

Thanks to Denise, I'm able to escape without any more sympathetic gazes or hugs. I slip into my office, slamming the door shut behind me. Finally, I'm in my safe haven.

Except the entire corner of my office is littered with presents from the baby shower.

At least they had the good sense not to give me the diaper cake. But why would they think I want to look at this giant stack of gifts, each one covered in a different shade of pastel wrapping paper? I don't have to open them to know they're filled with tiny clothes and bibs and rattles. For a baby we won't be getting.

I pick up the present from the top of the pile. It's wrapped in blue paper, which has little teddy bears, baseball bats, and basketballs on it, interspersed with the words "IT'S A BOY." I glance at the card and see that it's from my ex-assistant Gertie, who couldn't make the shower yesterday because she was having a second surgery on her broken hip. I'm sure the box contains something tiny and cute that will break my heart.

At the time, I thought it was so sweet of her to send a gift—now I wish she hadn't bothered. I wish none of them had bothered.

And now I have to figure out how to sell *diapers*. Wonderful.

I settle into my ergonomic leather armchair. I was so thrilled the day I got my own office—the luxurious chair was just icing on the cake. Now? It doesn't matter. I'd give it all up if only Janelle would change her mind back.

I try to put those thoughts aside as I check the messages on my phone. My mother called my office line last night, after I sent her call on my cell phone to voicemail. She always calls on Wednesday nights—it's between her book club night and her ballroom dancing night. But I couldn't bear to talk to her. My mother is not the comforting type, and she was never in favor of adoption. It was her opinion that if Sam and I couldn't conceive, we were better off childless. *Someone else's child—someone else's problems.* I didn't want her to tell me about how I was better off.

I've finished sorting through most of my messages and am feeling closer to some semblance of normal when Monica inches into the office with a cup of coffee for me. She's wearing that same deep crease between her eyebrows that everyone else has. They must think I'm five minutes away from a psych admission.

"How are you doing?" she asks as she carefully places the coffee mug down on my desk.

"I'm okay," I say. "But, um, could you get all these presents out of my office?"

"Oh!" She whirls around to look at the stack of gifts. "Sorry about that! I wasn't sure what to do with them. Nobody wanted to take their present back, so I just…"

"It's fine." I force a smile. "I just… don't want to look at them."

"Of course. I'll get them out of here right away."

I reach for the mug, figuring some coffee will do me good. But then I notice it's the mug Shelley bought me last week as an early baby shower gift. The one that says "Mommy Fuel." And the ache intensifies back to a stab.

Monica notices me staring at the mug and her eyes widen. She clasps her hand over her mouth. "Oh my God, I'm so sorry!"

"It's okay," I choke out.

"No, it's not." She yanks the mug off my desk, her cheeks turning pink. "I can't believe I did that. I didn't even *notice*. I'm such an idiot."

She's biting her lip so hard, I'm afraid she's going to draw blood. This isn't her fault—she grabbed one of my dozen mugs without checking. I should have smashed the thing yesterday.

"It's okay," I say again, although my mood has darkened considerably over the last sixty seconds. "I'm fine. But… please get rid of the mug."

"Of course." Monica's brows knit together. "If you need to go home, I'm sure everyone would understand."

"No, I'd rather be here."

"Well, I emailed you your itinerary for the day if you're up for it." A smile touches her lips. "There's a lot to do."

She's not exaggerating. Now that Cuddles has given us the go-ahead on the new campaign, I've got a ton of work to do. There's no chance of a lunch break—I'll probably ask Monica to get us both salads from Chopt for the third time this week, and we'll eat together in my office.

Usually, I love busy days. I love being productive and feeling like I'm impressing my clients. But today, it's hard to muster up any enthusiasm. "It's not like I've got anything else in my life," I mumble.

"Abby…" Monica drops her eyes. "I'm so sorry about… well, what happened."

I nod. "That's life."

My assistant shifts nervously between her black heels, her dark eyes darting around the room. God, she reminds me so much of myself at her age. I was so young and eager to please back then—tripping over myself to try to make Denise happy, and then beating myself up if I brought her coffee in an insensitive mug. (Not that anything on a mug could have upset Denise Holt.) Part of me is really relieved to be past that part of my life.

And part of me is so jealous of young, carefree Monica that I want to spit.

"It's so wonderful that you're trying to adopt though," she says. "There are so many children out there who need homes. I know you'll find the right one for you. Why put more children in the world when you can take in one who needs you, right?"

"Right," I say. I hesitate, wondering if anyone has shared this piece of gossip with Monica or if I should clue her in. Oh, what the hell. "The truth is, though, Sam and I did try to have a child of our own, but... we couldn't."

"Oh." She sucks in a breath. "I didn't realize. Did you try IVF? That's what my cousin did."

I nod, not wanting to go through the whole painful story. "It... didn't work."

"That's awful..."

I shrug, as if I couldn't care less. As if I didn't cry over every negative pregnancy test.

"Aren't there women who could carry the pregnancy to term for you?" she asks. "I've heard of, like, one sister carrying a pregnancy for another? Couldn't you do that?"

I shake my head. "I don't have any sisters up for the task."

"Yes, but... what about someone else?"

A surrogate pregnancy was something I had been considering for a brief time. Sam was the one who vetoed that idea.

"It's a lot to ask of someone... I mean, we'd be using their egg *and* their uterus, so we'd be asking them to get pregnant with their own child just to give it up." I clear my throat. "We're really excited about adopting now. We've moved past that."

No, I will never have a newborn. But Sam's right—that's not important. We want to become parents. I know I'll love whatever child we'll take into our home.

"Anyway." I turn back to my computer. "Let me prep for the meeting at ten. I don't want to be unprepared. Do you have photocopies of the mockup I sent you?"

"Yes, fifteen copies."

"The projector is set up?"

"Yes, and your presentation is loaded."

I allow myself my first genuine smile of the day. Monica is incredible. Honestly, I think she might even be a little better than I was when I was her age. She's the Queen of Efficiency. I swear, nothing gets past this girl. I'm really lucky to have her.

And I'm lucky to have Sam. And this job.

There's a lot in my life that's good. And soon, we'll have a child too.

"You're the best, Monica," I say.

"Oh, and let me get you a fresh cup of coffee!"

I almost tell her to forget it—that I'll drink the coffee out of the damn "Mommy Fuel" mug. But no. I want a new mug. I don't want to look at any reminders of everything I lost yesterday. All the cuddles and burps and sleepless nights and teething and first words and first steps and preschool and…

I can't think about this anymore.

When Monica returns with a fresh white mug with steam coming out of it, she's got a funny expression on her face. She places the mug down on my desk and straightens up, but doesn't leave. She just… stands there.

I raise my eyebrows at her as I take a cautious sip of the hot coffee. She made it just the way I always take it— bitter and black. "Yes?"

She chews on her lip. "I would do it."

"Do what?"

"Be your surrogate."

I start choking on the coffee. It's very dramatic. Flecks of coffee fly out of my mouth, dotting the white papers in front of me. I'm glad I wasn't eating steak, because Monica would probably have to Heimlich me. Which I'm sure she'd do expertly.

"Wha… what?" I finally manage.

Her pale cheeks redden. "Sorry, I just… I was thinking and… I think we could help each other out."

"Monica." I self-consciously wipe my coffee-spit off the surface of my desk. "It's, um… nice of you to offer, but it would be *really* inappropriate for you to do something like that for me. I mean, we *work* together."

She squeezes her fists together, and at this moment, she looks so much like I used to at her age, it's like looking into a time machine. "Listen," she says, "I've been wanting to go back to school and get my Masters in graphic art, because what I really want is to be a creative director. That's always been my dream."

I raise an eyebrow. "What about copywriting?"

"I like it, but graphic art has always been what I love."

Somehow, that doesn't surprise me. Monica has done sketches for some of our ads and it's clear she's got artistic talent. "So why not get your Masters at night?"

"It's expensive and I'm already deep in debt from college." She shakes her head. "And you *know* what the schedule is like here. I'd never have time for both."

She makes a good point.

"Don't you see, Abby?" Her eyes are shining. "This is perfect! I can give you the baby you want, and you can help me get my advanced degree, which would be a drop in the bucket for someone like you with a trust fund and everything. It's a win-win."

Technically, everything Monica is saying makes sense. But in reality, it's insane.

"You don't want to do this, Monica," I say. "Think about what you're offering. This would be, for all intents and purposes, your baby. You'd be willing to just give away your own baby?"

"I'm not ready to be a mother." Her eyes become distant. "There are so many things I want to do in my life before I'm tied down with a child. But you—you'd be a fabulous mother, Abby. Any baby would be lucky to have you as a mother."

"God." I rub my eyes. "I know you mean well, but... it's a bad idea. We work together..."

"I'd quit."

My mouth falls open. "What?"

"As soon as I start showing," she says. "I'll leave so it doesn't become an awkward situation. If you can cover my rent, that is."

"But I thought you wanted to be a creative director..."

"Right." She nods. "But it doesn't have to be here. With my Master's degree and a strong letter of recommendation from you, I'm sure I could find a good job at another agency."

No. This is crazy. I'm not going to consider this. Sam and I are going to adopt. As amazing as this potentially could be, it's a terrible idea.

"And we look alike," she adds. "The baby would look just like you."

"I don't care about that."

"You don't?"

I shift in my seat, which creaks loudly under my weight. "I just feel like you're not thinking this through. You're only offering because you feel sorry for me."

"No," she says firmly. "I'm offering because I like solving problems. And I figured out a way for both of us to get our dreams."

She's right. This would be a way to get the newborn baby I've been dreaming about. The dream I thought was gone forever.

Am I honestly considering this? Oh God, I can't believe I'm really considering this.

"We would need to have a contract drawn up by a lawyer," I say carefully. "And I'd need access to all of your medical history. Would you be okay with that?"

Her eyes light up. "Of course. You can have access to anything you need."

I swirl around the black coffee in my mug. "I need to talk to Sam about it."

Monica flashes her teeth at me. She has great teeth. White and straight. I wonder if she had orthodontist work.

Would it be inappropriate to ask?

Yes. Yes it would.

# Chapter 5

"No. Absolutely not. No way. Are you out of your mind?"

Sam doesn't seem enthusiastic about the idea of Monica being a surrogate for us.

I brought it up in the best possible way. I cooked him his favorite dinner—pan-fried chicken with a side of creamed spinach. He seemed shocked by the food, considering the state I was in last night. But I could tell he was chalking it up to my enthusiasm over our future adoption prospects and I didn't correct him. Then I waited until he had cleaned his plate and was nursing a full belly to bring up Monica's proposal.

"You're not even going to think about it?" I say.

Sam pushes his glasses up the bridge of his nose. "If you asked me if I wanted to jump off a bridge and I said no, would you ask me if I needed to think about it?"

"Stop being melodramatic."

"Melodramatic? I'm the only one being sane."

Despite my initial reservations, I've been warming to

Monica's idea over the last ten or so hours. The more I think about it, the more I realize this is the answer to our prayers.

"You've met Monica," I say. "She's really great. I can't imagine a better person to donate eggs."

He squints at me. "Which one was Monica? The blond with freckles?"

"No, she has dark hair and dark eyes. She… uh, she actually looks a little like me."

"I don't know." He shakes his head. "I don't remember if I met her. It doesn't matter though. It's a terrible idea."

"Give me one good reason."

"One!" Sam bursts out, his ears turning red. Despite everything, I can't help but think Sam looks sexy when he's angry. No wonder his students are always calling here. "I'll give you five good reasons."

"Fine. Give me five reasons."

"One." He holds up a finger—not the middle one, thankfully. "Won't it be awkward to work with the woman carrying your baby?"

"She said she'd quit once she's showing."

He ignores me. "Two—paying for graduate school isn't exactly cheap."

"Cheaper than an adoption. And we can afford it."

"*You* can afford it."

"*We* can afford it."

He rolls his eyes, but doesn't comment further.

"Three," he goes on, "what if she changes her mind?"

"This wouldn't be a standard adoption contract," I point out. "I mean, she'd be using your sperm so you'd have a legal claim to the baby."

The red in his ears invades his neck. "Yeah, that's another thing. I'm not so crazy about the idea of using my sperm."

"It's not like you'd have to have sex with her…"

"Oh, wouldn't I?"

"Look," I say, "isn't this what you wanted? To have a biological child?"

He drops his eyes. "I wanted a biological child with *you*, Abby. This is… it's *weird*. I don't want to do it."

"Well, you *can't* have a biological child with me." I fold my arms across my chest. "Because I'm *defective*."

"Stop it. You're not defective."

"I *am*." I blink back tears. "So if you want a biological child, this is the only way it's going to happen."

"Jesus." Sam rakes a hand through his hair until it stands up. "This is a bad idea. We were going to adopt. Let's just stick with the plan."

"I can't take any more disappointments, Sam." The tears are spilling over now, rolling down my cheeks. "Monica… she's a great girl. She won't disappoint us—I *know* it."

He's still shaking his head. "Abby…"

"We could have our baby in a year. It'll never be less than that with the agency."

This is the first thing I've said that's swayed Sam. He's thinking again about being an "old dad." Even though he was thirty when we started, he's now only a few short years shy of forty. He's going to be an "old dad," like it or not. The question is *how* old?

"I don't know, Abby," he sighs. He picks up our plates from the table to bring them to the dishwasher. He does that every night without being asked. "I still think it's a bad idea."

"Will you at least meet Monica?" I plead with him. "Hear her out?"

He hesitates. And at that moment, I know I've got him.

# CHAPTER 6

Monica looks like she's at a job interview. She's dressed up in a gray suit jacket and matching skirt, and her dress shirt is so white, it's gleaming. She's wearing makeup but it's so artfully applied that her face looks bare. Her dark hair is swept behind her head in a tight bun. Her fingers are clasped together on the table of the restaurant so tightly, they've turned pale.

Sam, on his part, looks like he's conducting a job interview. He's also dressed up in a crisp white shirt and a green tie. His glasses slide down his nose as he peers down at the yellow legal pad in front of him. Apparently, he's going to be taking notes during this meal. So much for putting Monica at ease.

The whole thing would be funny if my entire life weren't riding on it.

This is Sam all over—he takes everything *so* seriously. It's adorable, except when it's annoying, like now. It makes me think of the first time we met, actually. I was still

Denise's personal assistant at Stewart Advertising, and we were putting together a campaign for the university where Sam was a grad student in the math department. My job was to meet with grad students in all the departments and gather highlights that we could use in the advertising materials.

For the most part, it was fun. The art grad student showed me some incredible paintings done by his classmates. The chemistry grad student showed me an experiment in the lab. And the English grad student took me all around campus, then offered me a joint in his office.

Sam showed up to our meeting in his office wearing a dress shirt and tie. He proceeded to spend the next half an hour teaching me math. Something about series solutions to differential equations—who the hell knows? I would have fallen asleep completely if he weren't so incredibly cute in his shirt and tie. I still remember him gesturing at a line of Greek symbols on his whiteboard and saying emphatically, "This should go in your pamphlet."

"Yes," I said and pretended to write it down. "Absolutely."

At the very first moment it wouldn't have been rude, I stood up and thrust my hand in his direction. "Thank you very much, Mr. Adler. This was really… helpful."

And then, as we shook hands, I noticed the handshake was lingering more than I would have expected. His kind brown eyes met mine and a nervous smile touched his lips. "So, uh… you wouldn't be interested in…

maybe grabbing some dinner together?"

I hesitated. I had already turned down the English grad student, who had gotten grabby after he smoked that joint. But he had a giant beard and smelled like BO. Sam smelled good. I still love his aftershave, which he applies every day without exception.

"I need to finish explaining how to solve differential equations," he added.

"I'll tell you what," I said. "I'll go to dinner with you but you have to promise not to talk about differential equations again for the rest of the night. Or any other kind of equations."

I half-expected him to clasp his chest in horror, exclaiming, "But what else could we possibly discuss?" But instead, he smiled and said, "Deal."

As it turned out, we had plenty to talk about that night. So much that we didn't leave the diner until well after midnight. So much that I was mid-sentence when Sam leaned in and kissed me for the first time.

And now here we are, over ten years later, interviewing a woman to carry our child in her womb for nine months. Couldn't have predicted that one.

Sam has made it very clear he's not excited about doing this. But he consented to meeting Monica and discussing it. If he's satisfied with the terms, then… well, he wouldn't give any promises. Sam can be very stubborn at times.

We've chosen an Italian restaurant we've never been

to before, because I don't want the staff at one of our regular establishments to overhear us asking a woman to rent out her womb to us. It's a small, dark restaurant, and Sam is squinting to see his notes on the legal pad by the light of the candle on our table.

"This is a little awkward, I know," I say to break the ice. "But I think it would be great for us all to get to know each other better."

"Uh huh, absolutely." Sam taps on the legal pad with his pen. "Monica, do you live in Manhattan?"

She nods eagerly. "Yes. I live downtown with a roommate."

"And what's your roommate's name?"

"Chelsea Williams."

He writes it down, then makes her tell him the roommate's phone number, which he jots down as well. I want to grab the pen out of his hand.

"Sam," I murmur. "You're being rude."

"No, it's fine," Monica says quickly. "I mean, I know this is a really important decision for you guys. Anything you want to know—I'm an open book."

She tugs at the top button of her white blouse. She's got her shirt buttoned all the way up to her throat, although I notice that's something she often does. Monica is not an unattractive girl, but she seems reluctant to show off her sexuality at work. She usually wears slacks or skirts that fall below the knee. I assume she's got breasts under there somewhere, but you'd never know it. That's something I respect about her. Too many girls are willing to flash a little skin to get what they want, but Monica doesn't go that route. She's got integrity.

A waiter approaches us to take our drink orders. I get a glass of red, because damn, do I need it. Sam sticks with water, and then the waiter turns to Monica: "And for you, Miss?"

She glances down at the menu. I try to send her telepathic messages: *Don't order alcohol. Don't!*

"Water's fine for me too, thanks," she says.

And Sam nods his tacit approval. Not that he doesn't drink himself, but tonight, Monica needs to be a saint.

"Do you mind if I ask a few questions about your family?" Sam asks, when the waiter's gone to fetch our drinks.

"Of course not," Monica says. "Like I said, I'm an open book. I really want this to work out."

He puts down his pen on the table and peers across the table at her. "Why?"

She blinks a few times. "What do you mean?"

"I understand you respect Abby and want her to have a baby," he says, "but if you don't mind my saying so, you seem very eager to make this happen. It doesn't make sense to me."

I kick my husband's leg under the table. "Sam…"

"No, I think it's a fair question." He doesn't take his gaze off Monica's face. "Don't you, Monica?"

Her eyes dart briefly in my direction, then she nods.

"Yes, it's a fair question."

The waiter comes by at this moment to drop off our drinks. Water for Sam and Monica, wine for me. I take a big gulp.

"Dr. Adler, Abby tells me you're a math professor," Monica says.

He hesitates, then nods.

"So I'm assuming you like math a lot," she adds.

"Yes," he agrees.

I snort. That's an understatement.

"So say you finished college and you weren't allowed to keep going to school to learn math." She takes a sip of her water. "And the cost of going to school to learn more math was more than you could ever hope to save in a reasonable amount of time. What then?"

"I'd take out loans."

"Well, what if your loan payments were *already* more than your rent?"

Sam is quiet for a moment. "There's always a way."

"Right." Her eyes meet his. "There's always a way."

He frowns at her. He picks up the straw in his water glass and stirs the ice cubes around the glass. After a minute of silence, he picks up his pen again. "So when is the last time you've had a physical exam?"

I smile to myself. Monica may not realize it, but she's swayed him. We're that much closer to getting our baby.

# CHAPTER 7

"On a scale of one to ten," Shelley says, "how much do you hate Denise?"

"Twelve," I say.

"Might I remind you, this is a scale of one to ten."

"A hundred."

"I feel like you're not taking the parameters of this question seriously."

I signal to the waiter that we're ready to order. We can't spend very long at lunch today because Denise saw us walking out. And asked very pointedly where we were going. And when Shelley replied "to lunch," she looked aghast. I don't know if I've ever used the word "aghast" before, but the expression on Denise's face when we informed her we'd be leaving the premises to eat lunch was a perfect personification of the word "aghast."

The waiter approaches our table carrying a wine glass filled with dark red liquid and places it down in front of me. I suppress an urge to roll my eyes—poor service is something I have a low tolerance for.

"I didn't order that," I inform our waiter.

"I know." He jerks his head in the direction of the bar. "That gentleman over there asked me to bring you a glass of pinot noir."

I glance over at the bar, where a man with blond hair raises a glass and winks in our direction. He's got a cocky smile and he's wearing a gray business suit. Brooks Brothers—I'm pretty sure.

Shelley giggles. "Looks like you've got another suitor, Abby."

I push the glass away from me. "It's probably for you."

"No," the waiter, a baby-faced young man, insists. "The man said it was for the woman with black hair in the white dress. He said he hoped you would join him after your lunch."

Shelley laughs harder. "I told you you've got a suitor."

My cheeks burn as I push the glass more firmly away from me. "I've also got a husband. Please remove the drink."

"And her husband is very hot," Shelley informs the waiter, who I'm sure really cares.

As awkward as that encounter was, I can't say it wasn't a boost to my self-esteem. Sometimes I think Sam just gets more attractive as he gets older while my own looks slide away. I don't get hit on nearly as much as I used to. It's nice to know a handsome stranger at a Mexican restaurant saw me across the room and found me desirable.

I look down at my watch, cursing the fact that I didn't make the waiter take our order while he was here. Shelley raises her eyebrows at me. "What time is that meeting you need to be back for?"

"It's at one-thirty. But it's fine. Monica is getting everything set up."

Shelley nods in approval. "Nice. She's really efficient."

"Actually, she's amazing. I really like her."

"Me too."

"I like her so much," I say, watching my best friend's face, "I'm asking her to be a surrogate so Sam and I can have a baby."

Shelley laughs. She thinks I'm joking. I told her after the failed adoption attempt that Sam and I would be trying for an older child. This sounds like a joke. And admittedly, even as the words were leaving my mouth, they sounded comical. Who asks their assistant to carry a fetus for them in her womb? Last month, we got a memo saying we weren't allowed to have our assistants do *laundry* for us.

I clear my throat. "That wasn't a joke."

"Yeah, right," she snickers.

I don't say anything.

Shelley's mouth falls open. "Wait. Are you serious?"

"I am."

She stares at me, shaking her head. "I… I don't understand…"

Briefly, I outline everything that's happened so far.

Monica's offer. The terms of what our contract would be. Sam's reluctant agreement to "think about it."

"I can't believe Sam is going along with this," Shelley mutters. "I thought he had more sense than this."

"So you don't think *I* have any sense?"

"Clearly not!"

My face burns. Shelley doesn't get it. When we both started here as assistants, we were single and happy about it. Then I found Sam and she found Rick, and everything changed. After Sam talked me into trying for a baby, Shelley started trying too. We jokingly talked about how they'd be the same ages so they could play together. When Shelley got pregnant before I did, we joked her daughter would be a big sister to my child. Then she got pregnant again, and I was informed my eggs were useless.

Even though Shelley and I are still best friends, she scrupulously avoids talking about her kids in front of me. We talk about work, our husbands, the latest movies—but never kids. Not until the promise of this adoption—the one that's now fallen through. Shelley knows how much I want this. She knows how much this means to me.

"You don't get it," I finally say.

Shelley lets out a sigh and takes a sip from her Diet Coke. "I know you want this, Abby. I get it. But... you really don't see why this is a bad idea?"

"I really don't."

"You're using Sam's sperm, right?"

"Uh, yeah."

"So," she says, "this pretty assistant who is over ten years younger than you will be pregnant with your husband's child. And that doesn't bother you?"

"It will be our child. Sam's and mine."

"Unless Monica changes her mind and decides she wants it." She gives me a pointed look. "And then Sam's on the hook for child support. Or worse."

"No." I shake my head emphatically. "We won't sign the contract if she's allowed to change her mind."

"Can you do that?"

"Sure, why not?"

Shelley keeps shaking her head. I know she doesn't approve of this, but I wish she'd be supportive anyway. She's got her two babies. It's my turn now.

"Stop looking at me that way," I say. "It's *not* a bad idea."

"Listen to me, Abby." She folds her arms across her chest. "I'm going to try to explain this to you the best way I can." She pauses. "I'm sure you've noticed Sam possesses some physical attributes which women find… desirable."

Yeah, no kidding. When the math department was trying to attract more female students a few years ago, their big idea was to put a photo of Sam in their brochure and mention he was one of their professors. Sam found the whole thing baffling, but he went along with it. And the crazy part is, it *worked*. Their female applications tripled thanks to him.

And he's not just eye-candy either. I've read over

some of the reviews he gets from his students, and it's obvious they find his enthusiasm for the subject just as attractive as his more superficial qualities. He gets equally revved up to teach freshman calculus as he does from his grad level courses. And it shows. *I've never had a professor as excited to teach me math as Dr. Adler,* one student wrote. Then they may or may not have mentioned his butt.

To be fair, my husband *does* have a very nice butt.

"I'm aware," I say.

"And don't you think Monica has noticed?"

I flinch. "She's not like that."

"She's *female*, isn't she? If she isn't a lesbian, she's noticed. Trust me."

"So?"

"So." Shelley gives me a look. "So what if she decides she wants him?"

"Shelley…"

"Hear me out." She lifts a finger. "Let's assume her intentions are good going into this…"

"They are."

She rolls her eyes. "Okay, we'll give her that. But even if that's true, think about how she's going to feel a few months into her pregnancy. There she is, hormones raging, parasite growing inside her uterus, getting fat—and she knows Sam is the father of this baby. They're connected by *blood*. And of course, she'll see what a great guy he is, that he does dishes, laundry, and that he's an excellent kisser…"

I can't argue with any of that. Sam does do dishes and laundry. And he *is* an excellent kisser.

"I trust Sam," I say stubbornly. "And I trust Monica."

"Sam—fine. He wouldn't cheat. But how well do you know Monica?"

"Very well," I insist. "She's been my assistant for almost six months."

"Right. So you know her for six months. Which isn't very long at all."

"I trust her." It's hard to explain that good feeling I got the first time I sat across from Monica. How I saw so much of myself in her and wanted to take her under my wing. I trust Monica as much as I trust myself.

Shelley peers at me over the rim of her Diet Coke. She's thoughtful for a moment. "You know, I've seen her listening outside the door to your office."

My heart skips a beat. "What?"

"I've seen her. She stands outside your office door when it's closed, and I think she's trying to hear your conversations."

"I..." My mouth feels dry all of a sudden. Monica is trustworthy—I know it. I don't need to hear this ridiculousness from my supposed best friend. "Maybe she was just checking to see if I was busy before she knocked on the door."

"But isn't that what knocking is for? To see if someone is busy?"

I glare at her. "So... what? You're saying Monica is

spying on me? Is that what you think?"

"No!" Shelley's cheeks redden. "Look, all I'm saying, Abby, is be careful. You can't trust anyone a hundred percent. Especially when it comes to something like this."

"Yeah," I mumble.

She's right. That's why I intend to investigate all of Monica's references before jumping into this. I'm not making a mistake. I don't care what Shelley says—I *know* Monica. I can trust her. This is all going to work out.

# CHAPTER 8

"Yes, this is Jean Johnson. Who is this?"

"Hi." I clutch my cell phone in my hand so tightly, my fingers start to tingle. "My name is Abigail Adler. Your daughter Monica…"

I don't even know how to complete that sentence. *Your daughter Monica agreed to allow my husband to impregnate her then give me the baby.* When you put it that way, it does sound a bit odd.

Thankfully, Jean Johnson knows exactly what I'm talking about. "Mrs. Adler! Yes, Monica told me all about it…"

And then there's the awkward silence.

There's a whistling sound in the background. "Sorry about that," Mrs. Johnson says. She has a pleasant, husky voice that makes her sound like a film star from another era. "I had put a pot of tea on a few minutes ago. I'm just going to turn off the oven. Sorry about that, Mrs. Adler."

"Abby," I correct her.

"Abby," she repeats. There's shuffling on the other line, the sound of boiling water being poured into a teacup. "So you work with Monica in New York, is that right?"

"Yes." I clear my throat. "And you're in… Indianapolis?"

"Yes, I am. Born and raised."

"It must have been hard when Monica moved away."

"Yes, well…" She sniffs. "Children do what they want to do. You'll find that out someday."

I analyze her tone, trying to figure out if it was a dig. I don't think it was.

"I want you to know," I say quietly, "what Monica is doing for me… it means the world to me."

She's quiet for a moment. "Well, that's Monica—she always wants to help people."

"Really?"

"Oh, yes. To a fault even." She sighs. "Whenever someone tells her their problems—she's got an open sort of face that makes people confide in her—she has to figure out a way to put it right for them."

I feel a little jab in my chest. Monica is giving me the thing I want most in the world and here I am, investigating her. But this is Sam's strict condition—he won't go through with this unless we have all the information. He's sorting through Monica's medical records while I make these calls. He wanted to hire a private investigator, but I drew the line at that.

"We're going to compensate her," I say, desperate not

to sound like we're taking advantage. "We're going to send her to graduate school in graphic arts."

"Perhaps. But you have to know, she'd do it even if you weren't paying her a penny."

"Yes," I agree. "I think she would."

"Well, anyhow." Mrs. Johnson lets out a sigh. "What information do you need about my Monica?"

I look at the list Sam scribbled out for me in his nearly illegible handwriting. "I guess… I was wondering if there are any serious illnesses that run in the family."

"My mother has the diabetes," she says thoughtfully. "But she's still living. Monica's father is healthy—well, no, a little bit of high blood pressure. Monica's always been healthy as a horse."

"Any…" I look at the next question and wince. "Any history of mental illness?"

"Mental illness?" Mrs. Johnson repeats. "You mean craziness? No, of course not! What sort of family do you think this is?"

"I, um…"

"Look, my Monica is a good girl," she says. "Always did well in school, always was kind to everyone. I have to be honest with you, Mrs. Adler, I told Monica not to do this. That we'd find another way to raise the money for her to go back to school. But she wanted to do it. And now it feels like… what's the expression? You're looking a gift horse in the mouth."

I fold Sam's notes in half and push them across my

desk. "You're right, Mrs. Johnson. I'm sorry to take up so much of your time."

I thank her again, but as I put down my phone, there's something tugging at the back of my mind. Something not entirely right. But that makes no sense. Mrs. Johnson was perfectly nice, especially given what we're proposing to her daughter. Nothing she said raised any kind of red flag.

So what is that nagging feeling that I'm missing something?

———

There's a baby in a booster seat at the table next to mine. An adorable little girl with beautiful blond curls. She's got a handful of Cheerios sprinkled all over her tray and she's picking them up awkwardly and stuffing them in her mouth. I watch her, trying to ignore the growing ache in my chest. I almost had a baby. I was so close.

"Chee-wo," the little girl informs me.

I smile at her. Why are kids so cute? Denise doesn't find children cute. She could look at a little girl like this one, shrug her shoulders, and go right back to texting on her phone.

"Chee-wo!" the girl says again, and this time she holds out a Cheerio to me with a chubby little hand dripping with saliva. She's sharing her food. What a kind, generous baby. The mother is so lucky. She's so lucky and she has no idea. She's gabbing with her girlfriend, not even *looking* at her precious child. It's so *unfair*.

Oh God. I think I have to move.

"Abby?"

I lift my eyes. The girl standing in front of me gives off a "nice girl" vibe. She has a pretty, round face, with blond hair tied back in a high ponytail at the back of her head. She's wearing a black short-sleeved blouse, which she hastily explained is part of her waitressing uniform. She has a well-scrubbed, clean-cut, American girl vibe—she's the sort of girl who you might hire to babysit your children.

"Chelsea?" I ask.

She nods.

Chelsea Williams is Monica's roommate. The two of them have lived together for the last several years, and she's the last person I'm scheduled to speak with before coming back to my husband to assure him that Monica is indeed "squeaky clean." But from the bland, pleasant smile on Chelsea's face, I know this meeting is going to go exactly as I thought.

"Please have a seat," I tell Chelsea.

She slides into a chair across from me at the table. "I'm not late, am I?"

I shake my head. "I'm early."

"Like Monica." Chelsea laughs. "She's always early."

I already know this fact about my assistant. I value promptness in an employee, and this is yet another way Monica has managed to impress me.

"So how long have you been living with Monica?" I

ask her.

"We met in college." Chelsea opens up the menu in front of her. "So we lived together two years then and now for a year in the city. She's probably my best friend."

"So you know her very well then?"

She nods eagerly. "Absolutely. What would you like to know about her?"

I don't have any notes from Sam this time. Really, there's only one thing I want to know about Monica. Is it likely she's going to change her mind and fight to keep her baby?

But I can't straight out ask that.

"Is she responsible?" I ask.

"Well, yeah!" Chelsea giggles. "Honestly, if it weren't for her, we would have been booted out of our place ages ago for forgetting to pay the rent."

I hesitate. "Does she have a boyfriend?"

"Not at the moment." She raises an eyebrow. "You think a boyfriend would be okay with something like this?"

"Probably not."

"Well, then."

I look down at my coffee cup. I just got a plain coffee—no cream, no sugar. When I was in college, I used to add about a quarter of a cup of cream to my coffee, but when I saw Denise drinking it black every day, I switched. Now that's all I'll ever drink. And like Denise, I lose respect for anyone who pours cream into their coffee.

"Does Monica take good care of herself?" I ask.

Chelsea frowns. "What do you mean? She, like, showers every day and all that."

"I mean, does she do drugs or drink a lot or…?"

That makes her laugh. "Monica? No way. She's a complete square. Like, the designated driver and all that shit."

Of course. I should have guessed. Everyone I've spoken to without exception has verified Monica Johnson is squeaky clean. She's one halo away from being a saint.

"Listen," Chelsea says as she wipes some white froth from her lips, "I just want to say I think the arrangement you've got with Monica is really cool."

I raise my eyebrows. "Do you?"

"Yeah!" She nods vigorously. "Just because you're too old to have children of your own, that doesn't mean you wouldn't make great parents, right?"

*Too old to have children of my own?* I'm thirty-six! I've got quite a bit of time left before menopause. If not for my bum ovaries, I'd have no trouble at all having children at my age.

But Chelsea here is all of twenty-three. I hate to think how old she thinks I am. I'm not even going to ask—why make this meeting more depressing?

"Thank you," I say.

She grins at me. "So are you going to go through with it?"

"Yes," I say slowly. "I think we might."

# CHAPTER 9

When I come home from work, Sam greets me with dinner.

He comes out of the kitchen, his face pink from the heat of the stove, red wine staining his T-shirt, and somehow there's white flour dotting his hair. So I have absolutely no idea what he's made. Red wine biscuits?

I glance at the kitchen, flinching at the mess inside. At least I know he'll clean it up himself—I can always count on him to clean up his own kitchen disasters without prompting. "Can I help with anything?"

"No way," he says. "You've been hard at work all day. I want you to relax and have a delicious meal. Do you want any wine?"

I look at the splotches of wine on his T-shirt and grin. "Should I squeeze it out of your clothing?"

"Ho ho, very funny."

He does pour me a glass of red wine, which is very nice indeed, because I did have a long day at work. Sam never complains about my hours—he always says he thinks it's cool his wife is a high-power advertising exec. (I'm not exactly an exec, but I don't correct him.) I've overheard him bragging about me, so I guess he means it.

A few minutes later, he emerges from the kitchen with two plates of food. He places one of them in front of me. "Ta da!" he says. "It's chicken marsala with rice."

I look down at the chicken on my plate. I chew on my lip. "Is the chicken supposed to be red?"

"Well, I used red wine."

"It's just… it's awfully red."

He looks down at his own chicken thoughtfully. "Well, it's not how it looks, right? It's how it tastes."

That's what I'm afraid of.

He watches me as I slice a small piece of chicken off the end. Well, it least it appears to be cooked. Although judging how long it took me to slice through it, I'm worried it's a bit overcooked.

"It's not pink this time," Sam points out. "Score."

I flash him a thin smile. "Wonderful."

Okay, here goes nothing.

I say a quick prayer and stuff the piece of chicken in my mouth. The taste of red wine and burnt flour mixed with chicken assaults my taste buds. Sam is still watching me, an expectant look on his face. I want to swallow the damn thing down, but it's so chewy, I can't. I'll be chewing this chicken for the rest of the night.

"Delicious," I say around bites of chicken.

He frowns at me. "Then why are you making that face?"

"I'm not making a face."

Sam regards me for a moment. Finally, he slices off a piece of chicken and pops it in his mouth. He has it in there for about two seconds before he starts coughing and spits it out into a napkin.

"Oh, Christ!" he says. "That's *awful*! Why didn't you tell me?"

I shrug. "I was just happy it wasn't raw again."

He smiles crookedly. "Thank you for pretending to like it."

"Thank you for not making me eat it."

He leans in to kiss me. "Thank you for being understanding that I'm still learning."

"And thank you in advance for cleaning up the kitchen."

He laughs and kisses me again. He probably meant it to just be another peck on the lips, but it turns into something more intense than that. He puts his hand on my back and pulls me closer to him until I start to get all tingly. He really is quite a good kisser. Back when we were dating, it used to make my knees weak every time he kissed me. I know that's cliché, but it really did.

Now we've been married a while so I don't get weak in the knees on a daily basis, but I still think our kisses are far sexier than average. They're still better than any kiss I'd had before Sam came along.

"I'm not that hungry anyway," he breathes in my ear.

"Me either."

And then he's pulling me to my feet, and at first, we're stumbling in the direction of the bedroom, but as it turns out, we only make it as far as the couch.

That's one nice thing about not having kids. Sex on the couch.

It's only when it's over and we're lying half-naked together (okay, mostly naked), entwined on the sofa, my mind wanders to Monica's offer. I have interviewed everyone on my list and found absolutely nothing concerning about Monica Johnson. There's absolutely no reason not to power through with this.

Sam toys with a lock of my black hair while I snuggle into his bare chest. Sam got a membership at his university gym a few years ago because "it lowers the health insurance premiums," but he actually started using it. He goes to the gym nearly every day to run, and I think he hits the weights twice a week. I'm proud of his determination to take better care of himself, but also, I love what lifting those weights has done for the muscles in his upper body.

"How do you get your hair so soft?" he asks me.

"Is it soft?"

"Yes. It's freakishly soft, actually."

"I'm glad you like it."

"I didn't say I liked it. I was just commenting on its physical properties."

I smack him in the arm. He laughs and hugs me closer

to him. Maybe my ovaries betrayed me, but I've been lucky in love, at least. There's no better guy out there.

"I love you, Abby," he murmurs into my hair.

I grin up at him. "I love you too."

"I was just thinking…" He toys with my hair again, his brown eyes on mine. "I think we should ask for a toddler."

Mood: killed.

I lift my head off his chest and stare at him. "*What?*"

He props himself up on the couch. "Look, Abby, I said I'd think about the… surrogate thing and… I'm not comfortable with it. I want to adopt."

I don't know how I can go from post-coital bliss to tears in five seconds, but somehow I make it happen. I can't stop it. All the pain I had pushed aside after that day Sam burst into my baby shower and told me Janelle had backed out on us comes rushing back to me. Even though Sam has stuffed the bassinet into the closet and shut the door to the would-be nursery, the pain is still there. The baby we almost had. We were so close.

And now it's never seemed farther away.

"Abby?" Sam wrinkles his brow, plainly shocked by my tears. "Why are you crying?"

"Why am I crying?" Why does he ask me stupid questions? "I'm crying because…" I wipe saltwater from my face. "This is never going to happen for us, Sam. I feel it. The next adoption is going to take forever and then something will go wrong, and… and… by the time we get a kid, we'll be fifty!"

I can't talk anymore because I'm crying too hard. A bubble of snot blows out of my left nostril and I don't even bother to wipe it away.

"Abby," he says gently, "you know I want this as much as you do…"

"You obviously don't." I glare at him. "Because if you did, you'd be willing to take this opportunity right in front of us. Not turn it down because it makes you 'uncomfortable.'"

He stares down at his hands. It probably wasn't fair of me to say that. I know how badly Sam wants to be a father. He wants it badly enough that sometimes I'm surprised he hasn't left me for a woman with two working ovaries. Yes, I know he's not that kind of man, but he's got to at least sometimes be tempted.

"I'm sorry," I mumble. "I just… I got upset. You're allowed to veto something you don't feel comfortable with." I wipe my swollen eyes and put my hand on his. "We'll try for the adoption again. It's fine."

Sam is still looking down at his hands, his brows working together.

"Sam?" I say.

He doesn't answer me right away. I don't know what that means. He sometimes gets quiet like this, and I usually assume it's because he's thinking about something math-related. That's not what he's thinking about now. Well, I suppose he could be. But probably not.

"I think we should use Monica as our surrogate," he finally says.

I suck in a breath. "Sam, you don't have to—"

"I know I don't." He lifts his eyes. "But you're right. We've wanted this for so long. I hate that we can't open up the door to the second bedroom because it's too goddamn painful. I can't even watch a diaper commercial anymore without feeling like shit—I can't imagine what it's like for you to have to pitch them." He sighs. "Maybe it's not ideal, but I want to be a dad. And I want you to be a mom. We're ready *now*."

He reaches out and gives my hand a squeeze. As he smiles at me and my chest swells with happiness, it hits me:

Mrs. Johnson lives in Indiana. Her phone number was an Indiana area code, and she told me she was "born and raised" in Indianapolis.

*I grew up a Red Sox fan—I went to all their games when I was a kid. I could never put on a Yankees cap. They'd never let me come home!*

That's what Monica said at the baby shower when I tried to give her that baby Yankees cap. But the Red Sox is a Boston team. Every Yankees fan knows that. I'd suspect nobody in Indiana is going to give you *that* a hard time for being a Yankees fan. But maybe they would. It's not like I've ever been there before.

So why is Monica a hardcore Red Sox fan if she's from Indiana?

It doesn't make sense.

I turn to Sam, about to tell him what I just realized, but then I shut my mouth. He's already having reservations. If I tell him I'm worried Monica was lying to me, that will shut everything down for good. And maybe I'm remembering wrong. Maybe someone else made that comment about the Red Sox. Could it have been Lily, from accounting?

It's such a small thing. It can't be important.

# CHAPTER 10

## *Three Months Later*

There are five plastic containers of baby food laid out on my desk: apple, pear, peach cobbler, sweet potato, and autumn vegetable turkey.

Recently, Cuddles has decided to branch out into the baby food market. I'm supposed to be writing copy for the website they're developing to display and sell their baby foods. Specifically, they want a catchy slogan. Considering I have little experience with baby food, I thought I would buy a few containers of them and hopefully it would inspire me.

I have learned one important thing about baby food:

It tastes awful.

I can't believe people feed this crap to helpless infants. Well, the apple and pear were okay. Tolerable. The peach cobbler sounded good, but tasted too sweet. The sweet potato made me gag, but I successfully got down a bite of it. But the autumn vegetable turkey... I don't use the word "sickening" too often, but wow. That could have been the worst thing I've ever put in my mouth.

Oh, and I learned one other important thing about baby food:

It's a very powerful laxative.

And I didn't even try the *prune* baby food.

Maybe there's a slogan in there somewhere. *Cuddles Baby Food—as good for the bowels as it is for the soul.*

Maybe not.

A fist raps on the door to my office. Monica is standing at the doorway, in her modest outfit of black slacks and a crisp white blouse buttoned up to her throat. She smiles when she sees me.

One month ago, we finalized our contract for Monica to serve as our surrogate. Sam spent forever going through it with our lawyer, and the terms are very strict. We will pay for Monica's entire graduate school tuition, but she gives up all rights to the baby at the moment of conception. There is no option for her to change her mind at any point after that. I worried the terms might scare her, but it didn't. She signed with a flourish.

Then a few weeks ago, Sam went to the doctor's office and gave a sample of his sperm. Since I know Monica so well, we certainly didn't have to go through the doctor— we could have gotten a sample on our own and given it to her. But he insisted on doing it this way.

And now… we're waiting. Obviously, this is only our first try so the chances of pregnancy aren't huge, but I'm still excited. If it doesn't work this month, then it will next month or the month after that. Monica is only twenty-three and her doctor declared her to be in excellent health, so there's no reason this shouldn't work.

"Have you ever tried baby food?" I ask Monica.

She makes a face. "No, should I have?"

"No. You definitely shouldn't." I notice Monica is clutching her purse under her arm. "Is everything okay?"

"Well," she says thoughtfully, "sort of."

"Sort of?"

She reaches her hand into her purse and digs around a bit. When she pulls her hand back out, she's holding a white plastic stick in a clear Ziploc bag. She lies it down on my desk so I can see it clearly.

There are two blue lines on the stick.

"You're pregnant?" I breathe.

Monica nods, her eyes shining. "There are no false positives."

Monica's pregnant.

Sam's sperm knocked up my assistant on the very first try. We tried for so many years without any success. It's not like I ever doubted that I was the one responsible for our infertility, but I've never seen the evidence smacking me in the face like this.

First try. Pregnant.

After a second of silent self-deprecation, the impact of the news hits me. Monica is pregnant. Which means in less than nine months, she will give birth. I'm going to be a mother. After all this time of waiting and trying and wishing, this is finally going to happen for me.

I can't believe it.

"This is incredible!" I exclaim.

She nods happily. "I didn't think it would happen so fast. I guess I'm really fertile, huh?"

Her words are a quick jab in the gut, but I push it aside. She's doing this for me—she's just excited at how quickly it all happened. "I guess so. Hey, I'm going to text Sam, okay?"

"Of course."

I whip out my iPhone, which of course doesn't recognize my thumbprint because my fingers are all sticky from baby food. I punch in my passcode, which is my birthday. Yes, I know—it's not very secure. But I don't think anyone is plotting to steal information from my phone. Half of what's on there are text messages with my coworkers. Mostly between Shelley and me, complaining about Denise.

I type a quick text to Sam: *Monica's pregnant!*

After I type the words, the iPhone suggests a pregnant lady emoji, which I add in, even though I know Sam is not a big fan of random emojis. Oh well.

"What did he say?" Monica asks, casually leaning over my desk to see the screen of my phone.

Sam's reply comes a second later: *Wonderful.*

It's hard not to imagine a touch of sarcasm in his response. Even though Sam has been on board throughout this process, he's been noticeably reluctant the whole way. When he left to give the sperm sample, he gave me this look and said, "Here I go." And then he waited, like he was hoping I might tell him to forget the whole thing. I didn't.

"He said, 'Wonderful!'" I say.

Monica beams. She doesn't need to know I inserted the exclamation point myself.

I look down at her stomach, which is flat as a board. We agreed she'd work until she was showing, but it doesn't look like that will happen any time soon. "How are you feeling?"

"Good!"

"Any nausea?"

"Not at all."

"Tired?"

"Just a bit." She holds her thumb and forefinger a centimeter apart. "But not too bad."

She doesn't look like she feels tired or nauseous. She looks… great, actually. Like she's glowing.

"You're taking the prenatal vitamins, right?" I ask.

She nods.

"Two a day," I remind her. "The recommended dose is two pills per day."

She smiles. "I know."

I squeeze my hands together. "And you have to avoid cold cuts. And sushi. And, well… alcohol is supposed to be okay in moderation, but—"

"Don't worry, Abby," Monica says in that calm voice

of hers. "I'm not going to drink at all. I promise."

I hear a knock on the door, and before I can say anything, Denise is standing in the doorway. She never waits for a reply before barging in. She peers at me, a noticeable lack of a smile on her lips, but that's nothing new. She regards Monica briefly, but chooses not to even acknowledge her with a greeting.

"Abigail," she says. "Have you found a slogan yet for Cuddles? I just got a call from them."

"Um…"

*Cuddles baby food—tastes fifty percent less sickening than the other leading brands.*

"Not yet," I say.

Denise eyes the baby food containers on my desk. Too late, I notice Monica's pregnancy test is still lying there. I put my elbow in front of it, hoping Denise doesn't notice. Aside from Shelley, I haven't told a soul here about my arrangement with Monica, and I don't intend to. Nothing good can come of that. She's going to leave the company before she's showing, so really, it's none of their business.

"We're meeting with them tomorrow," Denise reminds me. "I hope you'll have something by then."

"Absolutely."

She frowns at me. "Don't disappoint me, Abigail. This is an important account."

Yes, I *know* this is an important account. Despite my success with the diapers campaign, you're only as good as the last thing you've done. If I screw this up, I'm finished.

Why else would I be sitting here, eating this disgusting baby food?

"Don't worry," I say. "I'm on it."

I let out a breath when Denise breezes out of my office. I'm dreading the conversation where I have to tell her I need twelve weeks of family leave after all. But what can I do?

Wow, this baby thing is really going to happen.

I'm going to have a baby.

I can't believe it.

"I better prepare for this meeting," I say to Monica, who kept her head down the whole time Denise was berating me. "But… well, I know I've said this before, but I can't say it enough: thank you. This is… incredible."

She smiles, showing off a row of pearly white teeth. "I'm happy to do it for you."

She looks down at the positive pregnancy test lying on the table in front of me. She starts to reach for it, but I shake my head. "I can throw this away for you."

"Oh, *no*." She snatches it off my desk and holds up it, admiring the two blue lines. "I want to save it. You know, as a keepsake."

She wants to *save* it? She wants a keepsake from a pregnancy she's going through just to get a ticket to art school? Is it just me or is that odd?

If anyone should want to save the pregnancy test, it should be me. And I don't want it. I mean, it's got *urine* on it. But I don't want to make a big thing of it. So I don't say a word as Monica carefully tucks the pregnancy test back in her purse.

# CHAPTER 11

Today, Sam and I have been married for eight years.

We're going out tonight to celebrate, to a nice Spanish restaurant in midtown that serves really good paella. Most nights we stay in and cook or else get takeout, because I'm always so busy, but we always go out on our anniversary.

Sam finds parking a few blocks away from the restaurant, which is something of a miracle. The major bonus of his refusal to lease a spot in a parking garage is he has become amazing at parallel parking. I'm certain he'll never squeeze the Highlander into that tiny little spot, but he insists he can do it. As he attempts to maneuver his car into the space, a small crowd of pedestrians gathers to watch.

"You'll never make it, buddy!" one guy yells out.

"Watch me!" Sam yells back.

When he makes it into the spot (as if there was any doubt), he's met with a smattering of applause. I'm still not sure how he did it. There's no more than a couple of inches of give on either end of the vehicle. Sam always says the eternal goal is to have zero space on either end of the car.

As we walk the short distance to the Spanish restaurant, Sam reaches for my hand. He always holds my hand when we walk—he did it when we were dating, and he does it now, after eight years of marriage. It's sweet.

"I'm glad we're married," he says as he squeezes my hand.

I laugh. "Good to know."

He's not just saying it because it's our anniversary—it's obvious Sam is truly glad to be married. The first couple of years we were together, before the fertility stuff went off the rails, he would say it constantly. *I'm really glad we're married.* Or, *I'm so glad I have a wife!* Or sometimes, *Thank God we're finally married.* I don't think he liked dating very much. He said it was exhausting.

That's probably why we got married relatively quickly after we started dating. Shelley started dating her husband Rick at around the same time I met Sam, but Rick was always squeamish about commitment. Sam was the polar opposite. We quickly fell into an exclusive relationship with an implied date every Saturday night and several weeknights too. While Rick had a freak out when Shelley left a toothbrush at his apartment, Sam—unprompted—cleaned out a drawer for me in his bedroom and made me a copy of his key, and soon after, said, "Wouldn't it be easier if you just moved in with me?" Shelley and I were both in our late twenties with marriage on our minds, and she was dying of jealousy.

Then when we were living together, he started making comments that began with, "When we're married." For example, "When we're married, we can file our taxes jointly." Or, "When we're married, we should get a two-bedroom apartment." Granted, they weren't super romantic statements (like, "When we're married, we should honeymoon in Paris" or "When we're married, we should buy a villa in Milan") but there was something sweet about his assumption we'd end up together. Eventually, I started making "When we're married" statements too.

One day, we were passing a Zales, hand-in-hand, and I commented, "When you propose to me, you better get me a ring from Tiffany's."

Sam got this odd look on his face and my heart sank. He'd been making so many statements about marriage, I'd thought it was okay. This was entirely his fault!

Finally, just when I was about to stammer an awkward apology, he leaned over and murmured in my ear, "And what if I got it from Kay's?"

I frowned at him. "Huh?"

That's when he reached into his pocket and pulled out the little blue box. My mouth fell open. We'd only been dating a year and a half, and even though we were living together, I hadn't expected this. "Oh," I breathed. "I didn't expect…"

He blinked at me. "Well, I love you. Why wait?"

Why, indeed.

"Hang on, let me get down on one knee," he said. And then he did, like he was following some proper procedure for proposing to one's girlfriend that he read in the relationship manual. He opened up the blue box and the ring was... well, I'm not going to lie. It was tiny. Sam had only recently finished his doctorate and wasn't making the big bucks in his postdoc program. But still. It was perfect. "Will you marry me, Abby?"

I said no.

I'm just kidding. Obviously, I said yes. A very vehement yes. Because otherwise, why would we be sitting at table, waiting to enjoy paella, going into our ninth year as husband and wife. I have never for one moment regretted my decision to marry Sam Adler.

Although sometimes I wonder if he feels the same.

But there's no trace of regret on Sam's face as he watches our waitress place the large pan of piping hot rice and seafood down in front of us. He grins at me over the steam rising off our food.

"What do you think?" the waitress asks us.

"Looks great," I say.

She places a white hand with red nails on my husband's shoulder, "And what do *you* think, *cariño*?"

Our waitress has been flirting shamelessly with Sam since we arrived. This sort of thing always happens—I hardly even notice anymore. And he *never* notices. You'd think his wedding ring and the fact that *he's here with his wife* would be deterrent enough, but apparently not.

"Yep, looks good," he says, but his smile is directed only at me. It's amusing to see women try to flirt with him while he completely ignores them. That will never get old.

The waitress gives up and leaves us to our paella. It's really good. It's costing us a fortune, but money has never been something I worry about. I've always felt a need to strike out on my own, even with my trust fund sitting in the bank, but between my salary and Sam's, it would be hard to live in Manhattan without that nest egg.

"This is really good," I say as I pop a piece of sausage in my mouth.

"I don't know," Sam says. "I think the paella I made last month was pretty good too."

It wasn't. It really wasn't. Sam is not getting any better at cooking.

"Well, that wasn't technically paella," I say. "It was Spanish rice with pieces of sausage and shrimp in it."

"Yeah, and what is *this*?" He digs some of the *socarrat* off the pan. "Same thing. Rice with sausage and shrimp."

"You don't have the crackling part at the bottom."

"Sure I do."

I grin at him. "Burning it at the bottom is not the same thing."

"It was just a *tiny bit* burned."

"It was black."

"Hmm. I think it was brown."

I roll my eyes. "I will say, I do like that you put fresh

tomatoes in yours. Tomatoes are my all-time favorite vegetable."

He gasps. "Abby! Tomatoes aren't vegetables! They're fruit."

"No way."

"Way," he says firmly. "It's got seeds on the inside. That makes it a fruit." He winks at me. "It's a *savory* fruit."

"That doesn't sound right."

"It's right. Trust me."

No… is it?

I whip out my phone to Google it and… wow, it turns out tomatoes really are fruit. Damn. "I can't believe it! How could tomatoes be *fruit*?"

"What I can't believe is you didn't *know* tomatoes are fruit."

"Yeah, well." I give his shoe a gentle kick under the table, which makes him smile. "*You* didn't even know Brad Pitt and Jennifer Aniston broke up."

"So I don't follow the recent tabloid news. So what?"

"That's not recent—their divorce was over a decade ago! Since then, he got married to Angelina Jolie, they adopted a bunch of babies, and then *they* broke up! You're one full marriage behind."

"You sure know a lot about Brad Pitt's love life," he says as he kicks me back under the table.

And then we're kind of playing footsie under the table. I slide off my shoe and get it up his pants leg, and he reaches down to grasp my bare calf. Our eyes meet across the table, and the smile he gives me makes me tingle all over. Shelley always talks about how her husband doesn't "excite" her anymore, but I can't relate. Sam still gets me all hot and bothered. I can't imagine that ever changing. I'm even looking forward to him getting old because I think he'll be sexy with lines around his eyes and silver hair.

As soon as we're done eating, Sam wants to exchange presents. He's more excited over this than an adult should rightfully be. I've got his present stuffed into my purse, and presumably, my present is in his jacket pocket. Which means it's something small. Maybe jewelry.

I hope it's jewelry.

Sure enough, he pulls a rectangular box from his coat and slides it across the table to me. He smiles when he sees the square box I hand him. He lifts it, evaluating its weight.

"This doesn't feel like electronics," he says.

"It's not."

"Is it… socks?" He grins. "You know how much I like socks."

He's joking—referring to a time when we went to my parents' house for Christmas, and their gift to Sam was a pair of fancy socks. This was, I suspect, my mother's not-so-subtle way of saying she wasn't excited about our upcoming nuptials. I was mortified by that one, but he thought it was funny. He still wears them. He calls them his Christmas socks.

"Yeah, but they're nice socks," I say. "Prada socks."

"Ooh, Prada socks. This I gotta see."

He rips off the wrapping paper and pulls off the lid to the box. His eyes widen when he sees what's inside. "It's… a tank top?"

"It's an apron!"

"Oh…" He pulls it out, holding it up in the light. The apron contains a bunch of mathematical symbols, including the square root of negative $i$, two to the third power, a summation symbol, and pi. I would never know this, but the website assured me that this reads… "I ate some pie?"

"Right." I beam at him. "Cool, right? For all the… you know, cooking you do."

Not that I want to encourage him in his cooking or anything. But since I can't *dis*courage him, I may as well buy him an apron so he doesn't have stains on every last piece of clothing in his closet.

"Yeah, this is great," he says, although it's hard to tell if he means it. "I'll be like Euclid meets Martha Stewart."

"You hate it."

"I don't hate it."

"You obviously do."

"No, I don't. I *love* it."

"You definitely don't love it."

"I do!"

"Liar."

"I love it so much," he says, "I'm going to put it on right now, because I can't wait to wear it."

"Okay, okay…"

"No, watch…" And then he stands up, and in front of the whole restaurant, puts the strings of the apron over his head. He makes a big thing of tying it, until I'm laughing into my palm. People are starting to stare at us, but I don't care. "How do I look?"

"Sexy as hell."

"Well, that goes without saying." He grins at me. "Okay, now you open yours."

I pull the lid off the box of what is clearly jewelry. Sam doesn't buy me jewelry much, but when he does, he's actually decent at picking it out. For a guy.

But this isn't jewelry. It's a long silver object with diamonds on the handle and the name "ABBY" engraved on the blade.

"It's a letter opener," he says. "I got sick of listening to you complain about all your papercuts."

I do complain about papercuts a lot. "It's beautiful," I say, and I mean it. The handle is absolutely exquisite. I can't say I wouldn't have liked a necklace, but this is thoughtful. It's something I don't have and that I need, and whenever I use it at work, I'll think of Sam. He always gets me really thoughtful presents.

"I'm really glad you like it," he says. "You're not going to impress the Cuddles people if you've cuts all over your hands, right?"

I pull it out of the box, admiring the design. It really is beautiful. The blade catches the overhead light and I notice how sharp it is. Well, I shouldn't have any problem opening letters anymore.

An hour later, we're walking hand-in-hand back to the Toyota. He's removed the apron, and he looks really handsome in his dress shirt and slacks. He only had one small glass of wine because he's driving, but I've had two, and somehow it's enough to make me tipsy. What can I say—I'm a lightweight. So holding hands quickly degenerates into me hanging onto his arm, and then he's got his arm around my shoulders, pulling me close to him as we walk.

I stumble over a crack in the pavement, which is more a symptom of my high heels than the amount I've had to drink, but Sam thinks it's hilarious. "Are you drunk on two glasses of wine, Abby?"

"*No.*"

"You kind of seem like you are."

"Listen, Mister." I grab him by the arm. Ooh, nice biceps. Thanks, Gym Membership. "You be nice."

We stop walking and just stare at each other for a moment. He leans forward until I can smell the wine and paella on his breath. He almost certainly would have kissed me except a voice from my left-hand side calls out, "Abby!"

Damn.

I swivel my head to the side. I'm shocked to see none other than Monica Johnson standing only a few feet away from us. We're nowhere in the vicinity of work. What is she *doing* here?

"Um, hi, Monica," I say as I back away from Sam, who on his part looks properly disappointed.

She doesn't seem at all cognizant of having interrupted us as she clutches her purse to her chest and steps closer to us. "I'm so surprised to see you two here!"

Sam barely acknowledges her, glancing down at his watch then at a streetlamp. He's not the most social guy in the world under the best of circumstances, but he's made no secret of how uncomfortable this situation makes him. Monica is pregnant with a child who has half his DNA. It's an odd situation.

"It's our anniversary," I explain. "We were just having dinner."

"Oh, that's wonderful!" She clasps her hands together. She's still wearing the same blouse she had on at work this morning, and I can't help but notice that while her stomach hasn't gotten any bigger, her boobs definitely have. She had fairly unremarkable breasts before, but now she's stacked.

I glance at Sam to see if he's noticing, but he's got his hands shoved into his pockets and is looking everywhere but at Monica. At least he hasn't taken out his phone.

"What are you up to?" I ask.

"Just dinner with some old friends." She shrugs. "And now, you know, trying to snag a taxi on a Friday night. I've heard it helps to show a little leg, but it's not working."

"Oh." I glance down the street, where Sam's

Highlander is parked. "We could give you a ride home, if you'd like."

Sam's eyes fly open, but thankfully, he keeps his mouth shut. This woman is pregnant with our child—I'm not letting her wander the city late at night.

Monica's cheeks color. "Oh, I don't want to take you out of your way."

"No, we insist," I say. "You don't live that far from us. It's no trouble."

I look at Sam for confirmation and he reluctantly nods.

So instead of making out with my husband on the streets of Manhattan on the night of our anniversary, we all trudge back to the Toyota to head back home. Which is fine. I guess.

But here's the weird part: when Sam unlocks the doors to the car with his key fob, Monica immediately jumps into the shotgun seat. Considering we're giving her a ride, that seems odd to me. I'm Sam's wife—*I* should be the one sitting next to him. Technically this is his car because it's in his name, but he bought it with money from our joint bank account. And since I earn way more money than he does, that means, in a way, this car is more mine than his. In any case, it's more mine than *Monica's.*

How could she sit in the front seat?

I fume about it for a minute, but there's nothing I can do. Sam is the one driving, so I have no choice but to get into the back seat. I know it's a small thing, but it makes me uncomfortable. When I look at Sam and Monica sitting up in front, they seem very much like they could be a couple. On top of that, she's pregnant with his child. On so many levels, Monica and Sam make more sense than Sam and I do. Yes, she's over ten years younger than he is, but so what? Men marry much younger women all the time.

I'm beginning to feel like a third wheel back here. I hope Sam drives fast.

We drive in awkward silence for about five minutes. I'm good at small talk, but what sort of conversation do you make with the woman who's carrying your baby in her uterus? *Have you thought of any names for the child you're giving us?* Nothing brilliant is coming to me. It isn't until we're stopped at a red light in front of a movie theater that Monica exclaims: "Oh my gosh! The new Quentin Tarantino movie is out!"

Sam's eyebrows shoot up. Quentin Tarantino is one of his favorite directors and we've already made plans to see the movie this weekend. "You like Quentin Tarantino?"

"Uh huh." She nods eagerly. "My favorite is *Pulp Fiction.*"

*Pulp Fiction* is Sam's absolutely favorite Tarantino movie. Without exaggerating, I would say he's probably seen it ten-thousand times, and those are just the times we've watched it together.

He snorts. "You probably weren't even born yet when that movie came out."

It bothers me that she doesn't contradict him on that

point. "It's still a great movie. Samuel L. Jackson? Classic." She grins. "Do you know what they call a quarter pounder with cheese in Paris?"

A smile twitches at his lips. "A Royale with Cheese."

"Right," she giggles. "Because of the metric system."

And then they spend the rest of the drive quoting lines from *Pulp Fiction*. I've seen it almost as much as Sam, so I could get in on the fun, but because I'm in the back, it's difficult. By the end, Sam's smile has become genuine. When he pulls over at the curb next to her building, he seems disappointed that the fun has come to an end.

"So are you seeing the new Tarantino movie this weekend?" Monica asks.

"Yep," Sam says, looking at me as if for confirmation. I nod.

There's a long silence, and for a scary second, I think Sam might invite her to come along. Not that it would be awful, but… well, I don't want her to come along. In any case, he doesn't offer, and Monica gets out of the car without further fanfare.

Once Monica is out of the car, I unbuckle myself and get into the front seat next to Sam. He gives me a funny look. "You didn't have to move," he says.

"I didn't want to sit in the back like you're my driver."

"Why not? It could be one of those roleplaying games where I'm a taxi driver and you're the mysterious, beautiful woman I picked up at the airport."

I laugh. "Is that what you want?"

"Actually, I mostly just want to get home so we can… you know, *celebrate*."

"Sounds good to me."

Sam starts up the car and turns onto Third Avenue, heading back to our condo. I look at his profile in the light of the moon. He's clean-shaven now, which means he shaved just before we went out. For me.

"Hey," I say, "didn't you think it was weird Monica sat up in front?"

He pushes his glasses up the bridge of his nose. "Yeah. A little."

"I mean, she was the passenger. She should have sat in the back."

"Yeah, I guess."

Sam doesn't seem particularly upset about it, so maybe it's better not to push the issue. Yes, it was weird. I'm sure Shelley would agree with me. But Sam doesn't get bothered by stuff like that. And anyway, it looks like he had lots of fun talking about *Pulp Fiction* with Monica.

It isn't until we've been driving for several minutes that I remember a conversation we had at a conference table a few months ago:

"Just watched *Django Unchained* again on Netflix last night," I said.

Monica, who was arranging coffee on the table, shuddered and said, "Oh God, Tarantino is so violent."

I laughed. "Yeah, but my husband loves his movies. Especially *Pulp Fiction*. We've seen that movie more times than I can count."

I close my eyes, trying to remember what Monica said to that. Did she say she'd seen the movie? I can't recall. But still. Saying that Tarantino is "so violent" is a far cry from calling him her favorite.

Yet somehow, now it's not only her favorite movie, but she's memorized every line of it.

I bite my lip hard enough that it hurts. Sam is still driving, whistling to himself. He had a good night tonight—he has no clue what I'm thinking about.

I'm probably being irrational. Maybe I'm remembering the conversation with Monica wrong. Yes, she said the movies were violent, but she didn't say she didn't like them. Maybe she was saying it in a complimentary way, like, "Tarantino's the only director who satisfies my thirst for violence!" And she never said she didn't see *Pulp Fiction*. Most people have seen that movie—it's a very popular film. A classic, like she said.

Hey, maybe our conversation inspired her to revisit his movies.

I'm definitely making too much of this. So what if Monica sat in the front seat? So what if she shares movie taste with my husband? I'm the one who's married to Sam. And thanks to Monica's generosity, we're going to be parents soon. I don't know why I'm getting so paranoid.

# CHAPTER 12

This is Monica's first OB/GYN appointment since her positive pregnancy test.

Based on her last menstrual period, she's ten weeks along, nearly eleven. Her stomach is still flat as a board and her boobs are huge. She's wearing a hospital gown, but has nothing on from the waist down. I came with her to the examining room and offered to wait outside while she changed, but she insisted it was "no big deal."

I turned away when she was undressing, but I couldn't help but take a tiny peek. And then I wished I hadn't. I never thought of Monica as particularly attractive, but she's twenty-three years old, and her body is absolutely perfect. Not that mine is terrible or anything, but everything on her is so tight and… well, like I said, perfect.

"This is exciting," Monica comments.

"Yes," I agree. "It is."

She squeezes her white hands together. "They said on the phone we might be able to hear the baby's heart today."

The thought of it brings tears to my eyes. Yes, Sam and I almost had a baby before, but Janelle lived across the country and I never got to go to any appointments with her. I never got to experience anything like this.

Monica has been really wonderful, honestly. That night we drove her home was a little weird, but since then, she's been so sweet. She updates me every day on how she's feeling, she helped me brainstorm about baby names (all of which Sam promptly vetoed... what's so wrong with Worthington?), and she offered to let me come to this appointment. I never would have asked, but I was thrilled by her offer. *It's your baby, Abby. You should be there.*

I can't believe I was being so petty about her sitting in the front seat in our car. Who cares about that? Maybe she was feeling nauseated and needed to be in front. That was probably it.

"By the way," I say to Monica, "Sam and I want to have you over for dinner next week. Are you free on Wednesday evening?"

"I am." She brightens. "That would be great. Thanks!"

"It's our pleasure. You're our hero, after all."

She rests a hand gingerly on her abdomen. "Too bad Sam couldn't make it to the appointment today."

Okay, full disclosure: Monica invited me *and* Sam to the appointment today. And I told her I'd ask him if he wanted to come, but I didn't end up doing it. I'm sure he wouldn't have wanted to come. It would have been really awkward with both Sam and me here. This is just easier.

"Maybe he'll come to the next appointment," she says.

"Maybe," I say vaguely.

Or not.

Dr. Selena Wong came highly recommended, although it's not like Monica needs a high risk OB/GYN like I would have if I had ever managed to get knocked up. But I still feel reassured when Dr. Wong enters the room with her broad smile and intelligent eyes. There's an air about her that makes me trust her instantly.

"Hello." She holds a hand out for Monica to shake. "I'm Dr. Wong. You must be Monica Johnson."

Monica nods and takes the doctor's hand.

Dr. Wong then turns to me. "And you're… Monica's mother?"

Oh God. She did *not* just say that to me. Monica's *mother*? Really? Yes, I'm thirteen years older than she is, but I'm not old enough to… well, I suppose technically I *could* be her mother. It's not like we're one year apart in age. But since people in this country don't generally have babies at thirteen years old, this is highly insulting.

"Abby is going to adopt the baby," Monica explains, because I'm too flustered to speak. "I'm serving as her surrogate for the pregnancy."

"Oh." Dr. Wong's eyes widen. "Sorry… I thought I saw a family resemblance."

"It's fine," I mumble. If she saw a family resemblance, couldn't she have guessed "sister"?

Okay, I'm not going to obsess over this.

"So is it Abby's egg?" the doctor asks.

Monica shakes her head. "No, Abby's eggs are no good. We're using my eggs and her husband's sperm."

"Oh!" Dr. Wong gives me a strange look, which I probably deserve. Monica is essentially having a baby with my husband. It's not like I would have considered this if I weren't so desperate to become a mother. "Well, that's great."

Dr. Wong proceeds to go through Monica's medical history, which is fairly unremarkable. She's barely had anything more than a cold in her life. Of course, I always thought I was perfectly healthy until I was unable to get pregnant.

After the questions, she does a pelvic exam, which I insist on stepping out for, even though Monica doesn't seem to care. Then Dr. Wong comes out to bring me back into the room.

"We're going to try to listen for the heartbeat with a Doppler," she explains. "Monica thought you'd want to hear."

My own heart is pounding in my chest. "Yes, that would be great."

Monica has her pants on again so that she can lift her gown without revealing her nether regions. Her belly is completely flat. I had no idea it was possible to be nearly three months pregnant and have a belly that flat. *I* look more pregnant than she does.

Dr. Wong dabs gel on her Doppler probe and places it

gingerly on Monica's tummy. Monica shivers and giggles. "Cold!"

"Sorry about that." Dr. Wong smiles at her. "Okay, now let's see if we can find that heartbeat. Remember that it's still on the early side, so I wouldn't panic if we can't hear it. We'll do the transvaginal if that's the case."

But then Dr. Wong shifts the probe and we hear it:

*Whoosh, whoosh, whoosh, whoosh…*

It's really fast, but I've heard fetus's hearts are faster than adult hearts. It sounds… well, it sounds normal to me, but what do I know? Actually, it sounds perfect.

That's my baby's heart.

"Perfect." Dr. Wong smiles up at us. "One-hundred-eighty beats per minute, which is normal for ten weeks. It will slow down a bit in the second trimester."

I feel a lump in my throat and my eyes are tearing up. All of a sudden, I'm sorry I didn't invite Sam to come along. I wish he could be here to hear this with me. Our baby.

Monica is gazing down at her belly, her mouth hanging open. "That's incredible," she breathes.

And then her eyes start to water. She swipes at them quickly, before the tears can fall, but she's definitely on the verge of crying. Except why is *she* crying?

"Can we get a recording of this?" Monica asks.

*She* wants a recording of this? What the hell?

"Well, you can record it with your phone," Dr. Wong says.

And she does. She gets out her cell phone and records the sound of the heartbeat for much longer than I feel is necessary. Like, a minute. A minute doesn't sound very long, but after ten seconds, it's a bit repetitive, isn't it?

It makes me think of when she first got the positive pregnancy test, and how she wanted to save the pee stick. I wonder if she still has that stick. She wouldn't really have saved it, would she?

"Are you planning to do the First Trimester Screen?" Dr. Wong asks, after the recording is (finally) finished. "That's a blood test to look for signs of chromosomal abnormalities and an ultrasound to look at nuchal translucency, which is the fluid beneath the skin behind the baby's neck. It's pretty accurate in screening for birth defects. We could do it in a few weeks."

"Oh." Monica laughs. "Well, I'm only twenty-three. I'm sure the baby is fine. It's not like we're using Abby's eggs."

Gee, thanks.

"The risk is lower," the doctor admits, "but not nil. I'd recommend the test. Plus you get to have an ultrasound, so you can see your baby."

Monica's eyes widen. At first, I think she's going to ask me what I think, but instead, she blurts out, "Yeah, that sounds great."

She should have asked me. *I'm* going to be the mother of this child. But I suppose she's the one carrying the baby. Anyway, I'm not going to make a big thing of it. I *do* want her to get the screening test, so there's no need to intervene. She's doing exactly what I want her to do.

So why do I have a sick feeling in the pit of my stomach?

# CHAPTER 13

"So how is *that woman* doing?"

My mother stubbornly refuses to remember Monica's name. She only refers to her as "that woman." Needless to say, she's not entirely on board with using Monica as a surrogate. I believe her words were: *Abby, have you completely lost every bit of your common sense?* Or something along those lines.

"She's doing great!" I say into the phone with enthusiasm I hope doesn't sound forced. "The pregnancy is going really well. And everything is going according to plan."

"The plan being a beautiful young woman is pregnant with your husband's child."

"Yes," I say through my teeth. "*That* plan."

"Mmm."

My right hand squeezes into a fist. That always seems to happen when I'm speaking to my mother. "You told me you weren't going to be judgmental."

"I'm not! I just said 'mmm.' You're the one who interpreted that as me being judgmental. It must be because you're insecure that a beautiful young woman is pregnant with your husband's child."

The fist tightens. One day when I'm talking to my mother, I'm going to punch a wall and break my hand. "You know Sam and I can't have a child on our own and the adoptions keep falling through. This is the only way."

"Yes, so you say," she murmurs. "And how is Sam doing, anyway?"

"He's fine."

"Yes, I'll bet he is."

My mother's dislike of Sam was almost instant when they met. Sam quickly agreed to drive up to Long Island to meet her and my father when we had been dating about three months, which I thought was a great sign of his commitment to me. He was adorably nervous about the whole thing—he wore a suit and tie, and he purchased both flowers *and* a box of chocolates. He spent ten minutes in the mirror, trying to get the knot on his tie perfect.

I would say the moment things went wrong was when my parents' housekeeper Imelda opened the door, and Sam mistook her for my mother. I am still baffled at how he messed that one up, given Imelda is a dark-skinned Mexican and my complexion is about as pale as they come. When I asked him about it later, he muttered, *Sorry, Abby, I don't come from a house where we have servants opening the doors for people.*

After that, it was all downhill. Sam called golf "boring" before being informed it was my father's all-time favorite sport. He offered to carry the carrots to the dining table, then dropped them all over the floor. His finale was backing into the mailbox on the way out of the driveway and knocking it over. *He's lucky he's good-looking,* my mother told me on the phone the next day.

She eventually warmed up to him though. Well, sort of. Mostly, I try to keep them from getting together very often, a strategy that everyone seems happy with.

"Listen," I say. "You know, Sam has been great through all of this. Not every guy would be so understanding about… everything."

"So I'm supposed to be thrilled he didn't dump you when he couldn't get you pregnant?"

I let out a huff. "That's not what I'm saying, Mother."

"Listen to me, Abby," my mother says, her voice suddenly very serious. "Life lesson—you can't trust men. None of them."

"I can trust Sam."

"Especially not Sam."

"Mother!"

"Fine," she grumbles. "Sam is no less trustworthy than other men. Happy?"

Not really. But I'm not going to belabor the point.

"All I'm saying," she continues, "is you don't want to leave him alone with *that woman*. He's a man and he won't be able to help himself."

"Oh *God.*"

"That's simply the way men are."

"He's not an *animal,*" I snap at her. "He's a decent person. He's not going to cheat on me because the opportunity arises. He wouldn't do that."

"Wouldn't he?"

"No! He wouldn't!"

And I believe that. I really do.

"Fine, Sam's a saint," my mother snorts. "But… all I'm saying is be careful, Abby. Don't tempt fate."

Maybe I won't mention to my mother that we invited Monica to have dinner with us. I get the feeling she won't approve.

# Chapter 14

"Do we really have to do this?"

Sam is being his usual antisocial self and kicking up a fuss about having Monica over for dinner tonight. I called to remind him to put the lasagna I made in the oven, and he's taking the opportunity to piss and moan about how he doesn't want to do this. I'm sure he must realize it's futile though—Monica is coming, whether he likes it or not.

"Yes, we have to," I say.

"Do I have to wear nice clothes?"

"Yes."

"And by nice clothes, you mean…?"

"I mean if you open the door in sweatpants and that T-shirt with the rip in the sleeve, I will murder you."

"Okay. Gym shorts then. Got it."

I roll my eyes at the phone. "I'm going to trust you're joking."

"Relax, Abby. I'm putting the lasagna in the oven as we speak while wearing my tuxedo."

"Sam…"

"I just don't understand why we have to do this," he sighs. "We're paying for her to go to grad school. We're going to cover her expenses when she quits your company. Why do we have to have *dinner* with her?"

"You don't like to have dinner with anyone."

"I like to have dinner with *you*."

Well, that's true. But he's averse to most social interactions, except with his closest friends. He's okay with having dinner with his mother, but he's thrilled with the arrangement where we only get together with my parents a couple of times a year.

"I'll be home by a quarter to six, okay?" I say to him. "Just… please try to be good."

"I'll try to try."

I don't know what he's so worked up about. He seemed to like Monica enough when we gave her a ride home that other night. Although I have to admit, there's a small part of me that's glad he isn't all that excited about having dinner with the twenty-three-year-old girl who's pregnant with his child.

I've got a few letters on my desk that Monica brought for me this morning that I never got around to opening. I grab my ABBY letter opener that Sam got me and slice open the first letter. But before I get it open, the letter opener nicks my finger, which immediately starts bleeding.

Damn. That thing is sharp. It's supposed to open letters, not perform surgery.

"Abby?"

I look up from my wounded finger and see Monica standing at the doorway of my office. She's got on another of her outfits of black slacks paired with a white shapeless blouse buttoned up to her throat. In the last week or so, I've noticed a tiny bulge in her midsection, but she's still probably got a smaller waist circumference than I do.

"Hey." She beams at me. "I'm so excited about tonight. Six, right?"

I grab a tissue off my desk to ease the flow of blood from my finger. "That's right."

"Are you sure I can't bring anything?"

"Just yourself."

She nods happily. "Would it be all right if I head out now? I need to go home first."

I glance at my watch—five o'clock. "Sure, sounds good! I'll see you at six."

She claps her hands together. "This will be so much fun! I can't wait!"

As Monica races off down the hallway, I smile to myself. As long as Sam isn't too cranky, this should be a nice night. I'm glad I invited her.

My finger seems to have stopped bleeding—guess I don't need stitches or even a Band-Aid. I spend the next fifteen more minutes answering emails, then I shut down my computer. I'm about to head out of my office when I practically slam right into Denise. Even though it's the very end of the day, Denise's suit is as crisp as it was this morning and she doesn't have a hair out of place. How does she do that? She must spritz herself with some sort of glaze every morning.

"Abigail." Her cool, calculating blue eyes look me over. I'm sure I look as rumpled as I feel. "You never sent me the new website copy for Cuddles."

"Oh." I frown. "Sorry, I thought I did."

"You did not." She frowns at me. "I'd like to see it now. A printed copy, if you can."

"Um…" I glance at my idle computer. "Can it wait until the morning? I've sort of… got to be somewhere…"

"It absolutely *cannot* wait until the morning." She folds her arms across her chest. "Our meeting with the executives from Cuddles is tomorrow at eight!"

It is?

I'm usually so on top of these meetings, but I've had a lot on my mind lately. How could I not have realized I've got a meeting tomorrow morning?

"Any time now, Abigail," Denise sighs.

"Right." I go over to the computer to turn it back on. I glance at my watch—five-twenty. Plenty of time to get back for dinner with Monica. "Let me get this printed for you."

While I'm waiting for the computer to boot up, I slip my phone out of my purse and check my calendar. And there's the meeting: eight in the morning, just like Denise said. How did I miss that?

It takes several minutes to boot up and load the

document Denise wants. I send it to my printer as I feel a vein throbbing in my temple.

"It's not printing," Denise observes.

Damn it. Monica's the one who knows how to troubleshoot the printer. I don't know what to do now. I try printing again, but nothing happens. I flash Denise an apologetic look, and she simply sighs loudly.

"Could I just email it to you?"

She sighs again. "I suppose that's fine."

I look at my watch again—five-thirty. It takes me twenty minutes to get home by taxi if traffic isn't too bad. I should be okay. Well, unless traffic is killer. But even so, Sam will entertain Monica until I get home.

Denise stands in front of my desk, her phone held up to her face. She taps on the screen, obviously opening up my email. I hold my breath, watching her face.

"Okay?" I ask.

She shakes her head. "This is really what you're going to present at the meeting tomorrow to Cuddles?"

"Um…" Admittedly, it's not entirely finished because I hadn't realized the meeting was first thing tomorrow morning. But I didn't think it was *that* bad. With a few finishing touches that I could come in early to do tomorrow morning…

"I thought we were going to emphasize the nutritional value of the baby food," she says.

"I did."

"I don't see it."

"It's right here." I read off the screen: "Cuddles baby food is made with only the healthiest and most wholesome of ingredients."

"Yes, but that's the only place." She frowns at me. "I said *emphasize*. Mentioning it *once* is not emphasizing, Abigail."

"So… I should mention it twice?"

"It should be everywhere!" Her cheeks turn pink. "The apple puree should be made from apples harvested from a pesticide-free orchard! The pea oatmeal should be created from peas picked from a natural pea ranch!"

A pea ranch? What the hell is a pea ranch?

"You need to fix this, Abigail."

"I'll fix it first thing tomorrow morning," I promise. "I'll come in at the crack of dawn."

"Unacceptable." She arches an eyebrow at me. "Tomorrow morning, the clock will be ticking. This needs to be fixed before you leave for the day."

Great. If only I had known about this a few hours ago, it would have been fine. I can't believe I forgot I had a meeting tomorrow morning. What's happening to my brain?

"I'll be in my office," Denise says. "Please send me a more appropriate draft as soon as you've completed it, then we'll discuss if further changes need to be made."

I shoot daggers with my eyes at Denise, but they bounce harmlessly off her back as she exits my office. Fine. I can fix this draft in fifteen minutes, then I'll grab a taxi home. I'll be late, but not too late.

I shoot a text to Sam: *Denise making me fix something. Should be leaving within 15 minutes.*

Sam replies almost instantly: *What????? She's going to be here soon! Get your butt back home!*

Poor Sam. I can almost picture him freaking out. I write back: *Really sorry. Start dinner without me. Should be back soon. I promise.*

*You better be.*

And at the time, I really believe I will.

———

When I stumble home over two hours later, I have a throbbing headache in my left temple. I fixed the draft for the meeting in fifteen minutes, sent it to Denise, but it was still unacceptable. So was the next draft. At one point, she gave me an exasperated look and said, "Honestly, Abigail, I feel like I'm talking to an *intern*."

If it had taken even five minutes longer to fix the document, I swear I would have strangled her with my bare hands. She never treated me this way before I started trying to have a baby.

It feels like an icepick is jabbing me in the side of the head while I fumble in my purse for my keys. Whenever I get a headache, it's always in my left temple. Why is that? Is it a sign of a tumor? Christ, where are my keys? Sam is going to kill me for being so late.

And then I hear it:

Laughter. Coming from inside the apartment.

My fingers make contact with my keyring. I yank it out and when I get the door open, I see Sam and Monica sitting together in the living room. They've got two empty plates on the coffee table, which means they ate in the living room, which Sam knows I hate because I'm worried about the floral-patterned couch getting stained. There's a bottle of white wine open on the table that is half-full, and Sam's got that flushed look he always gets when he's had a bit too much to drink.

And Monica…

In the time I've known Monica, I've always thought of her as being somewhat plain. She has some nice features, but she doesn't wear makeup and she dresses like a choirgirl, which makes her look fairly average. But tonight she looks very different. She's got on mascara that makes her dark eyes pop, dark red lipstick that compliments her jet-black hair, and a low-cut blouse that shows off her now impressive cleavage.

Monica isn't just attractive—she's really *hot*. Much more attractive than I am, if I'm being completely honest. Especially right now, when I'm rumpled and exhausted from my twelve-hour workday.

"Abby!" Sam exclaims when he notices me staring at them, probably for far too long. "You're home!"

He gets up off the couch and stumbles in my direction, nearly tripping on the carpeting. Oh my God, how much has he had to drink? He plants a wet, sloppy kiss on my face. "We missed you. The leftover lasagna is in the kitchen."

At first, I think he's going to go get me some, but instead, he returns to the sofa next to Monica and falls back down with a plop.

"Are you drunk?" I ask him, eyeing the half-empty bottle of wine. Sam rarely has more than one drink, so that's more than enough to put him over the limit. And presumably, Monica wasn't helping him make a dent in the bottle.

"No!" He blinks a few times and pushes his glasses up the bridge of his nose. "I barely had anything. We're just having fun here. Right, Mon?"

"Abby." Monica smiles up at me. I still can't get over how much makeup she's wearing. "You didn't tell me how funny Sam is."

I didn't, because he *isn't* funny. Well, sometimes he is. But certainly no more than average. Nothing worth commenting on. "Oh," is all I can muster.

"He's been telling me all these math jokes," she says. "They're *really* funny."

Okay, I have heard Sam's math jokes and they are *not* funny. The only thing funny about them is how incredibly *un*funny they are. Like how something is so bad that it's good? Although I think the math jokes might have circled around and gone back to being unfunny again.

"Monica was a math minor in college," Sam informs me. "Isn't that incredible?"

Yes. Incredible.

She grins at him. "Do you have any other jokes, Sammy?"

*Sammy*? She's calling him *Sammy*? And he's apparently calling her *Mon*. When did they get nicknames for each other? How long was I at the office?

Sam scratches at his chin, thinking for a moment. "Um... why did the chicken cross the Mobius strip?" When she doesn't answer, he says, "To get to the same side."

Monica laughs louder than anyone should rightfully laugh at a joke about Mobius strips. And as she laughs, she grips his arm. "Oh my God, you are *so* funny."

Sam notices me staring at them blankly. "Abby, a Mobius strip is a surface with one continuous side that—"

"It's okay," I say quickly. "You don't need to explain it to me."

There's an awkward silence. Monica's eyes dart around and finally land on the two plates on the coffee table. She reaches for them. "Let me bring these to the kitchen."

"Hey, no way," Sam says as he brushes her aside. "You're our guest, and also, you're pregnant. You let me take care of that."

He's being a gentleman like I told him to. I wish he would cut it out.

He seems steadier as he brings the plates into the kitchen. Monica gets up off the couch to follow him, but I step in front of her. "Hey, Monica," I say. "Did you know there's a meeting tomorrow morning at eight?"

"Uh huh." She nods. "It's on the calendar. The Cuddles people, right?"

Damn, even Monica knew about the meeting. What's wrong with me?

"That reminds me," she says. "I'll need to take off for a few hours next week to do that ultrasound and the blood tests. Is that okay?"

Sam drops the plates in the dishwasher and lifts his head. "Ultrasound?"

Monica arches an eyebrow. "Abby didn't tell you? I'm having this screening ultrasound next week."

He frowns. "Is something wrong?"

"Not at all!" She clutches her chest. "I would tell you if there were. This is something everyone gets. But it's a chance to see the baby. Do you want to come?"

"Uh…" Sam glances in my direction, then back at Monica. He seems like he's looking at her abdomen, but he could also be looking at her boobs. Not that I would blame him, because they're pretty spectacular right now. "Yeah, of course I would. That would be incredible."

She brightens. "Hey, I recorded the heartbeat at my appointment last week. Do you want to hear it?"

He nods vigorously. "Yeah, definitely."

Monica and Sam go back to the living room and sit together on the couch, while I take the loveseat. She gets out her phone and scrolls to the recording she took last week. Then she presses "Play."

*Whoosh! Whoosh! Whoosh! Whoosh!*

His eyes widen. "That's the heartbeat?"

She nods.

I wouldn't have expected it from Sam, because he's not an emotional sort of guy, but his eyes start to get misty the same way mine and Monica's did in the examining room. He listens to the whole thing, then he makes her play it a second time.

"That's amazing," he breathes.

She grins at him. "That's our baby."

Her words hit me like a punch in the gut. *Our* baby. No, it's not *our* baby. This fetus inside her is *my* baby. Mine and Sam's. Even if she's using a general "our" to include me too, it's still inaccurate. This is *not* her baby. We have a contract. What the hell is wrong with her?

And why is she sitting so close to my husband? This is a very large couch. She's got the whole couch to spread out on, but somehow, she's so close to him, their knees are nearly touching.

I want this girl out of my house.

"Anyway," I say. "I'm so sorry I couldn't make it here sooner, Monica, but it's been great having you."

"Well, thanks for inviting me," she says. "The lasagna was really delicious, Abby."

I'll have to take her word for it. I've lost my appetite.

"Not as good as mine though," Sam says with a grin.

Her eyes widen. "You know how to cook?"

"Uh…" He offers a crooked smile. "I'm… learning."

She claps her hands together. "I'd love you to try something you've made sometime."

"Sure," he says. "That sounds great."

Great, now they're setting up *another* dinner? I've got to get her out of here ASAP. Before she moves herself in.

But before I can say anything else, Sam heaves himself to his feet. "Well, it's late. You should probably get going."

My shoulders relax. He's making her leave. Thank God. But I don't even have a chance to celebrate before he adds, "Let me give you a ride home."

The other night he didn't want her near his car, but now he's apparently willing to drive her home *drunk*. I've never seen him try to drive before when he's had more than one drink. *Never*. What has she done to his brain?

"You're not getting in the car," I say through my teeth. "You're way over the limit, Sam."

Sam's ears get red as he realizes what he was about to do. "Yeah, Abby's right," he mumbles. "I shouldn't be driving. Let me call you a taxi."

"Thank you." Monica grabs her purse from the end of the couch. "And Sammy, I'll text you the time for the ultrasound appointment, okay?"

He gives her a thumbs-up, and all I can think is, *When did they exchange phone numbers?*

And also, *Why does she keep calling him Sammy?*

I take a deep breath. I need to calm down. It's not Monica's fault I got delayed at work by Miss Oxford. It's not Monica's fault Sam drank too much and is acting like an idiot. And it's not Monica's fault that she's more attractive than I thought she was. It's also not her fault that she's pregnant with Sam's seed.

That last one is entirely my fault.

God, I can't wait for this pregnancy to be over so things can get back to normal.

# Chapter 15

If there were any justice in the world, Sam would have a whopping hangover the next morning. But maybe he didn't have as much to drink as I'd thought, because he seems fine. So fine, actually, that I catch him whistling in the bathroom while he's shaving his face.

What the hell is he so happy about?

I say as much to him while he's putting on his tie, and he blinks a few times, surprised. "Uh, I don't know. It's a nice morning."

"I thought you might be hungover."

He rolls his eyes. "I told you I didn't drink that much."

"You were acting like you did."

He doesn't respond to that, but while he's putting on his shoes, he starts whistling again. I've never known Sam to whistle before, but after one evening with Monica, suddenly he's a goddamn teapot. Did he whistle like this when we were first dating?

"Do you think Monica is pretty?" I blurt out.

"Pretty?"

"Yes."

"No way." He smiles crookedly. "She's not pretty at all. Just the opposite. She's really horrible to look at. I didn't want to be mean or anything, but I had to squeeze my eyes shut all night like this." He scrunches his eyes closed in a demonstration. "I hope she didn't notice."

"Haha, very funny."

"I don't know much about women, but I know there's only one right answer when your wife asks you if another woman is pretty."

Fair enough. "You just seemed to be having a really good time with her last night."

He lets out an exasperated sigh. "Abby, you're the one who wanted to have her over for dinner last night. And you're the one who showed up two hours late. You made me promise to be 'well-behaved.' So she shows up and I'm nice to her, and now I'm in trouble?"

"Well, there's nice and there's *nice.*"

"It's not like we were making out, Abby. We were just talking."

He's actually making some reasonable points. So why can't I get rid of that tight, awful feeling in my chest?

"She called you Sammy," I say.

"So?"

"It seemed a little… familiar. Also, you hate being called Sammy."

"I don't hate it."

"You told me you hate it."

He yanks his keys off the dresser. "Fine, I hate it. I hate it and I hate her and I don't want you to invite her here ever again. Okay? Happy?"

I lower my eyes. There's part of me that realizes I'm being ridiculous, but I can't help it. Something isn't right. "Are you going to that ultrasound appointment?"

He doesn't hesitate. "Yes, I am."

I bite my lip.

"Look, this isn't about Monica," he says. "I want to see the baby. It's my baby too, and I think I should be allowed to go." He frowns at me. "I didn't say anything about the fact that you *never even told me* about the other appointment, but from now on, I want to go."

I was afraid he was going to say that. And he's right— he deserves to be there as much as I do. Or admittedly, more than I do. I'll be adopting this baby, but it's *his* biological child. And I want to share this with him because I love him. I just wish *she* didn't have to be there.

Of course, that's impossible since the baby is literally inside her.

"Abby." His voice softens. "I get why you're upset, but you shouldn't be. It's like you said—this is what we've always wanted. You should be happy."

His kind words help, but not completely. I take a deep breath, trying to put my finger on the exact source of my misery.

"She said it was 'our baby.'"

Sam wrinkles his brow. "What?"

"That's what Monica said when she was talking about the baby. She called it 'our baby.'"

"Right. It *is* our baby."

"Yes, but she didn't say 'our' meaning yours and mine. She said 'our' meaning, presumably, hers."

He shakes his head. "So what are you saying?"

"I'm saying, what if she wants to keep the baby?"

"That's what our contract is for, right? We can take her to court."

*Except what if she wants to keep* you *too?*

Sam isn't even thinking that way though. He's not worried about falling under Monica's spell. I wouldn't have worried about it either, except I saw the look on his face when he was listening to that heartbeat. His child is in *her* womb. That's got to be messing with his head.

"Come here, Abby." Sam holds out his arms and I fall into them, nuzzling my head in his shoulder. Despite everything, being in his arms makes me feel warm and safe. "Don't worry so much. It's going to be fine."

I don't know what I'd do if I ever lost him.

# CHAPTER 16

Monica is having her ultrasound today at two.

She had to get her blood drawn too and some other stuff, so she ended up taking a personal day. Sam is coming too, obviously, but all three of us will be arriving separately, and then meeting up. It's an awkward situation, but there's not much we can do about it. I want to be there for the ultrasound, especially if Sam is going to be there.

I eat lunch at my desk just to ensure I'll make it there on time. At one-thirty, I grab my purse and head for the door. But I swear to God, Denise must have cameras in my office to know when I'm trying to leave, because she heads me off before I can get to the elevator.

"Abigail." She narrows her ice-blue eyes at me. She's the only person here who has the ability to make me feel terrible with a single gaze. "Where are you going? You're not *leaving*, are you?"

"I've got…" I swallow. "I've got a doctor's appointment. I'll be back soon."

I'm going to be here till ten o'clock tonight. I just know it.

"Are you ill?" Denise says the words with utter contempt.

"No." I look away. "It's just an appointment."

That's vague enough. No way can she get an inkling of my arrangement with Monica. In another few weeks, Monica will be resigning, before she starts to show. If Denise found out what we were up to... well, I don't even want to think about it. It wouldn't be good.

Thank God, Denise seems to accept this explanation. In any case, she doesn't physically stop me from leaving. Which is what she'd have to do to keep me from going to this ultrasound.

"By the way," Denise says. "When you get back, I'd like you to catch up with your correspondence. When Cuddles sends you an email, I expect you to answer within twenty-four hours, if not within the hour."

"I do." I glance at a clock on the wall—one-thirty-five.

"They told me several of their emails have gone unanswered."

What? That can't be right. I'm obsessive about answering all my emails. Missing one—possible. But several?

I'll have to check my spam folder when I'm at the doctor's office.

"I'll take care of it," I assure Denise, then I push past her to get to the elevator. I'm not missing anything else because of her. I'm still upset about that dinner I missed last week.

I hail a cab quickly outside the building and make it to the hospital in record time. It's ten minutes to two, which means I've got time to spare.

The waiting area for maternal-fetal medicine is populated with several women in various stages of pregnancy. In the past, seeing a bunch of pregnant women like this would have made me burn with jealousy. I probably would have gone home and sobbed into my pillow, thinking about how unfair it all was. But it's okay now. I'm part of it.

Monica and Sam are nowhere to be found—I guess I'm the first to arrive. I settled into one of the plastic chairs to wait. A receptionist gives me a funny look. "Can I help you, ma'am?"

I smile, but it feels crooked. "I, uh… I'm meeting someone here."

The woman arches an eyebrow at me. "Meeting someone?"

"Yes, she's my…" God, I don't want to explain this to a stranger. "Monica Johnson."

"Oh!" The receptionist's face relaxes as she smiles in recognition. "Yes, she's just about done."

Just about… done?

Before I have a minute to mull this over, Sam and Monica burst out of the back. She's holding a string of black-and-white images, and he's grinning ear-to-ear. My mouth falls open. What. The. Hell?

"Abby!" Sam waves at me. "You missed it, but we've got pictures."

I jump out of my seat and rush over to them. I don't want to lose my temper in this waiting room, but I'm furious. How did I miss it? I'm on time! I'm *early*! What is going on here?

"How could you be done?" I hiss at him. "The appointment is at two!"

"No," Sam says patiently. "The appointment was at one."

I look at Monica, who is no longer smiling. "You told me it was at two," I say.

She frowns. "I told you one, Abby."

"You told me *two*." Damn it.

She shakes her head. "I know I told you one. You put it in your calendar—I saw it."

Bullshit. I reach into my purse and yank out my phone. I bring up the calendar and…

*Monica ultrasound – 1 PM.*

Oh my God, how did I get it wrong? I had in my head the whole day that it was at two. Did I really manage to screw that up? What's the matter with me?

"Why didn't you text me?" I say to Sam, desperate for this to be someone else's fault but mine.

He shrugs helplessly. "You've been so busy lately with that Cuddles baby food stuff. I didn't want to bother you. I figured you couldn't make it."

I feel like bursting into tears. I can't believe I missed the ultrasound. I wanted to be there so badly. And the worst part is that Sam and Monica don't seem to care in the slightest. I wouldn't expect Monica to care necessarily, but Sam doesn't seem to feel all that bad about it either.

"Everything looked good, they said," Sam adds.

I guess that's all that matters. The point of this ultrasound was to make sure the baby is okay, not for entertainment purposes. "Well, that's good."

He holds up the row of images. "Do you want to see?"

I snatch the pictures from his hand. My anger fades slightly at the sight of them. The images are mostly black, but in white is an outline of the baby's face—a tiny nose, a tiny chin, and the curve of the baby's skull.

Sam grins at me. "Great, right?"

"Can…" I look up at them. "Can we keep this?"

Sam and Monica exchange looks. "That's mine, actually," she says. "But they're printing out a second copy. They just had an issue with the printer."

"Oh." I don't say what I'm thinking, which is that if there's only one copy, why does *Monica* get to keep it? After all, it's *our* baby. "Our" meaning mine and Sam's.

Before I can get worked up, the receptionist calls out, "Mrs. Johnson?"

Monica smiles at us and walks over to the reception table, where the woman is holding another set of images. She hands them over to Monica. "Here's an extra copy for your husband."

"Thank you," Monica says.

"Enjoy! And congratulations, you two!"

Wonderful. This woman just referred to Sam as Monica's husband and nobody felt a need to correct her. The best thing I can say about Sam is he's looking down at the images of the baby and not really paying attention. He probably didn't hear the receptionist call him Monica's husband. But still.

Monica flashes us both a big smile. She's wearing lipstick again. She's been wearing makeup a lot more lately, and dressing less like a nun. Today she's wearing a low-cut black blouse that clings to her breasts. And of course, she's still barely showing.

"We should celebrate," she says. "How about coffee?"

"I've got to get back to work," I mutter.

She doesn't seem surprised or perturbed by my refusal. "What about you, Sammy?"

No. She didn't just ask my husband out for coffee without me. That didn't really just happen. *And why is she still calling him Sammy?*

"Um," Sam says, glancing in my direction, "I actually also need to get back to work."

She raises her eyebrows. "I thought you said you were done for the day?"

"Done with classes." He smiles awkwardly. "But I've got, you know, research."

"Oh, really? What sort of research?" she asks with what appears to be genuine interest.

Sam brightens the way he always does when someone asks him about his research, which doesn't happen too often in social situations. "I'm studying random integral matrices and the universality of surjectivity and the cokernel."

She looks thoughtful. Did she actually understand that? "So what specifically about the cokernal?"

"Well," he says, "I'm looking at the probability that the cokernel is isomorphic to a given finite abelian group."

"And how about when it's cyclic?"

He nods eagerly. "Yes! That too."

"Wow, that sounds fascinating," she says. "I would *love* to hear more about it."

Sam glances at me again. I can tell he's dying to talk to her more about this, but he doesn't want to upset me. "Abby," he says, "are you sure you don't have time for a quick coffee?"

That lump in my throat returns. "No, I don't. But if you really want to go, Sam, it's up to you."

"Oh." He looks between the two of us, unsure of what to do. Except isn't it obvious what he's supposed to do? He's supposed to say "no" to the attractive twenty-three-year-old woman asking him to coffee! Any idiot would know that! I'd like to tell him as much, but I don't want Monica to see me forcing him to turn down what would probably be an entirely innocent coffee.

Probably.

"Maybe just like twenty minutes," Sam says. "Then I

really need to get back to work."

"Wonderful!" Monica beams at him. "I know the perfect place."

We walk out together to the lobby, then Sam and Monica go together to the coffee shop while I hail a cab. I watch them walk down the street together, getting farther and farther away from me. They seem to be standing awfully close to one another. Isn't there some rule that you're supposed to stand at least one foot away from someone you're walking with? Or did I just entirely make that up?

All right, I need to stop driving myself crazy. I trust Sam. And that's all there is to it.

# CHAPTER 17

If I didn't need to go back to work after this lunch, I'd definitely be getting drunk right now.

Even so, I'm sorely tempted. Shelley and I managed to sneak away to the Mexican place down the block for lunch, and this place has the *best* margaritas. But I'm already skating on thin ice with Denise—I can't afford to be performing at any less than my best. Also, if she smells alcohol on my breath, it won't be good.

"You don't look so good, Abby," Shelley says. "No offense."

Shelley is the queen of the "no offense" remarks. The game is you say something super offensive, then mitigate by adding "no offense" (but not really). For example, "No offense, but that dress makes you look like you should be jumping for fish at SeaWorld." Or, "No offense, but you look like you're old enough to be Monica's mother." But this time, it's hard to take offense.

"I don't feel so good," I mumble. I stare down at my

Diet Coke, wishing it would magically morph into a margarita.

"But I thought things were going well." Shelley takes a chip from our communal bowl. "Monica got pregnant on her first shot, and you said that ultrasound was normal. So… good?"

I chew on my lip. I haven't voiced any of my anxieties to Shelley, partially because I haven't had a free moment to talk to her in person and this was a little too heavy for text message, but also because I know she's going to say, "I told you so." And I don't need an "I told you so" right now.

But on the other hand, I need to talk to someone about this.

"Things have been weird lately," I admit.

"Weird in what way?"

"Like…" I run a chip through the salsa, even though I'm not terribly hungry. "Sam and Monica have gotten to be… friendly."

Shelley raises an eyebrow. "Friendly?"

And just like that, the whole story comes pouring out. The night we gave Monica a ride and she stole the shotgun seat. The dinner I was late for, where Monica and Sam bonded big time over math jokes. The way she calls him "Sammy." The ultrasound I missed, followed by the two of them getting coffee after.

"He said he was just going for twenty minutes," I say, "but I texted him and he didn't get back to me for two hours. So."

"Wow," Shelley breathes. "That's intense."

"And haven't you noticed how she's been wearing more makeup lately and dressing more seductively?" I add. "She always used to dress like she was in church, but now she looks… you know, *hot*."

"Monica's really attractive," she agrees. "I always thought so. And she's Sam's type."

I frown. "His *type*?"

She smiles crookedly. "Well, she looks like you. So I'm assuming that's his type."

Good point. I never thought of Sam as having a "type," because he rarely comments on other women or talks about old girlfriends. I've never even seen photos of the women he dated before me. But he asked me out so quickly after we met, there must have been something that drew him to me immediately.

And yes, Monica looks like me. Except younger. And curvier. And pregnant with his kid.

"Also," I say, "they're texting each other."

"They are?"

I nod. "I saw a text from her pop up on his screen this morning."

"What did it say?"

"Um." I think for a minute. "I think she was thanking him for sending her a math paper she liked."

"Well, that's pretty innocent."

"But how is she so into math all of a sudden?" I stir the ice listlessly in my Diet Coke. "She wanted to go to school for graphic art to become a creative director, and now somehow she knows all about matrices and cokernels, whatever the hell those are."

"I don't think Sam is going to be overcome by passion while talking about *math*." She snorts. "Actually, I take that back. Maybe he would."

"Haha."

"I don't know, Abby." She shrugs. "It sounds like the texts are pretty innocent. But if you're not sure…"

I frown at her. "What?"

"Do you have the code for Sam's phone?"

My mouth falls open. "I'm *not* going to spy on my husband!"

"It's not spying. It's snooping."

I do have the code for Sam's phone. But I don't intend to do anything with it. "I'm not doing that, Shelley."

"Well, then you really don't know how innocent it is, do you?"

I don't like the direction this conversation is going in.

"I mean, really, Monica hasn't actually done anything wrong, has she?" I crunch miserably on a chip. "After all, it's my own fault I messed up the time for the ultrasound."

"Maybe. Maybe not."

"What does that mean?"

"Well," she says thoughtfully, "doesn't Monica have access to your calendar? Couldn't she tell you the wrong time, wait for you to put it in your calendar, then swap it out for the correct time so you look like an idiot when you show up?"

My mouth falls open. "Do… do you really think she'd do that?"

Shelley shrugs. "Maybe. Maybe not."

And then there's that morning meeting I was supposed to have with the Cuddles people that I didn't know about. Is it possible Monica could be responsible for that?

"I don't know, Shel," I say. "That's a little too diabolical. I can't imagine Monica doing that." I pause. "Can you?"

She's quiet for several seconds while I hold my breath. Finally, she says, "I guess not."

I let out my breath. I'm glad she doesn't think so, because I couldn't possibly take away Monica's access to my calendar. She's my assistant—a large part of her job is making sure my calendar is updated and accurate. I have to trust her.

And I do. I trust her.

But maybe I'll change the password on my phone. My birthday isn't very secure.

"But still," she says. "It's an emotional situation for everyone. Monica is pregnant, so she's got all these hormones. And then Sam—he's wanted a baby for a long time, and now here's a woman who's pregnant with his child, but she's not his wife. That's got to be messing with his head."

"Yeah," I mumble. "We should have adopted. This

was a mistake."

Shelley is silent.

I sigh. "Go ahead. Say it."

"Say what?"

"You know what."

"What?"

"Tell me you told me so. You said this was a mistake before we even got started."

"I'm not going to say 'I told you so' when you look like something the cat dragged in." She shakes her head. "What kind of friend do you think I am?"

The kind who tells me I look like something the cat dragged in? Never mind.

"Anyway," I say, "Monica will be leaving work soon, so I'll probably hardly see her until the baby comes. Just at the appointments. And then in less than five months, we'll have the baby."

She grins. "And I promise—no baby showers this time."

"Please no," I say. "I can't imagine anything worse."

Except that's not true. I *can* imagine something worse.

———

Sam is sitting across from me on the couch, quietly working on his computer. That's something we do—sit next to each other in the living room, both of us working. Sometimes we don't say a word for an hour or more, but it still makes me feel close to him. Especially when I put my legs up on the couch, and he puts his hand on my calf, absently stroking it. And whenever I look up at him, he smiles.

Sam's phone breaks the silence by buzzing with a text message. He picks it up and grins at the screen.

"Who's texting you?" I ask, as casually as I possibly can.

"Monica."

Of course. Prior to Monica entering our lives, Sam only got texts from me and from work. Now she's his new text buddy.

He nudges me. "She found out the gender of the baby."

"Oh." I slide my laptop off my lap. "I thought we decided to wait until the birth to find out."

He frowns. "We did?"

"Yes! We did!"

"Uh…" He looks down at his phone, then back at me. "So… she already sort of… told me."

My mouth falls open. "She *told* you?"

"Well, I didn't realize we were waiting to find out!"

I shake my head. "You knew I wanted it to be a surprise."

"I didn't know that." He's typing something into his phone as he talks, which is incredibly irritating. What is he saying to her? That his wife is being a bitch? "Seeing what the baby looks like will be enough of a surprise, don't you think?"

I don't know what to say. It's too late to change the fact that Monica blabbed to him. Also, why would she text *him* and not me? *I'm* the one she works with. I knew her before he did. It's because of me that all of this is happening.

"So what is it?" I finally ask.

"I thought you didn't want to know."

I let out an irritated huff. "If *you* know, then I want to know."

"Are you sure?"

"Yes!"

He grins crookedly. "It's a boy."

"Oh."

"We're going to have a son!" His brown eyes are wide and excited. "Isn't that incredible?"

His enthusiasm is contagious. I was feeling upset about Monica blowing the secret but he's right—the important thing is we're getting a healthy baby. A healthy baby boy! This is really happening—we're going to be parents soon.

"I love you so much, Abby." Sam puts down his computer on the coffee table and climbs on top of me. He kisses my neck until my body starts to tingle. "I'm so glad you're my wife."

I smile to myself, giving into the wonderful sensation of my husband's lips on my body. I try to ignore the buzzing of the text messages still coming in on Sam's phone.

# CHAPTER 18

Today is our big meeting with Cuddles, and I'm so nervous, I could throw up.

The last time we met with Cuddles, I was nervous but in an excited sort of way. I knew my campaign was incredible, and I felt one-hundred percent confident. Today I feel none of that confidence. My only hope is I can fake it.

Somehow I haven't been on my game lately though. Ever since the night of that dinner I missed two months ago, it's like I can't keep anything straight. Earlier in the week, I completely missed an important meeting even though it was right in my calendar. I misplaced an entire folder of baby photos and had to ask Cuddles to fax them to me again. Denise had to come in to scold me on two separate occasions for not responding to Cuddles's emails. Also, I became violently ill from some banana pudding baby food I sampled.

I could use another week for this meeting, but that's

not happening. It's today—like it or not.

Monica has loaded up my presentation on the laptop connected to the projector in the conference room. I have to say, Monica has been a rock star lately. Given how scatterbrained I've been lately, she's doing an amazing job picking up the slack. Ever since I missed that meeting on Monday, she's started printing out daily itineraries to leave on my desk in the morning, she's been highlighting important emails in my inbox, and she's arranged a gourmet lunch for the Cuddles execs at the meeting.

Yes, she's still friendly with Sam. He swears they haven't gotten together again for coffee, but I still see her text messages popping up on his cell phone. Also, her last OB/GYN appointment coincided with a meeting I absolutely couldn't miss, so Sam ended up accompanying her by himself. I tried not to let it bother me how happy he seemed after that appointment. It's about the baby—not about Monica.

I'm sitting in the conference room, chugging coffee as I chew on my fingernails, when Jed Cofield and his minions arrive. I'm worried Cofield is going to be cool to me after I missed answering several of his emails, but he comes right over to me and shakes my hand. Although I notice he doesn't hang onto my hand any longer than necessary.

"Good to see you again, Abby," he says. He flashes his teeth at me. "I expect you're going to dazzle me yet again today."

I do my best to return his smile. "Naturally."

*Confident. Act confident.*

I usually don't even have to tell myself that. It's become automatic to follow Denise's lessons to project an image of complete confidence. Even when I start to suspect I'm wrong about something, I'll plow forward with my shoulders squared, and you would be amazed how often that's effective. But today I'm not sure I have it in me.

"I always tell everyone," Cofield says, "that Abby Adler—she's the best. You want to sell your product, she's the one."

"I appreciate that, Jed," I say.

And I smile confidently. I should be confident—I have an excellent track record. There's no reason to doubt myself.

My confidence doesn't waver again until Denise enters the room. She strides right up to me, her ice-blue eyes regarding me with barely repressed disdain. She's been witness to every single one of my screw-ups lately, and she's not impressed.

"Abigail," she says. "I'll be in the back to lend my expertise if needed."

The subtext is painfully obvious: *I'm going to stay in the room in case you mess up.*

The last person to enter the room is Monica, carrying a plate of gourmet sandwiches. She's wearing a vivid red blouse paired with a black skirt that shows off what are some really very nice legs. Between her boobs and her legs, every red-blooded male in the room swivels around to stare at her. Cofield's mouth is hanging open. I wonder if Sam were here, he'd be staring too.

Monica is now close to six months pregnant, but she's still able to hide it with creative clothes pairings. For example, her red blouse hugs her breasts, but is loose around her midsection. I expect in another couple of weeks, she won't be able to hide it anymore at all. Which means that as painful as it will be, I'm going to have to give up Monica. Nobody at work can know about our arrangement.

When everyone is seated and has chosen a sandwich, I can begin my presentation. With their product information and the baby photos, we've written the copy for and designed a website to display their baby food. We've been going back and forth on it for months, and now I'm showing them the near-final version. Even as late as last night, Monica and I were going over a list of slogans to find the best one.

"Obviously the real website will be interactive and we're working with our tech people on that," I say, "but I just wanted to show you what we expect it will look like."

I give everyone in the room a chance to look at the image I've flashed on the screen. In spite of my issues recently, I worked very hard on this website. I hope they appreciate it.

Jed Cofield is the first to speak. I was hoping he'd say something enthusiastic, but instead he frowns at me. "Um,

Abby?"

"Yes?"

"This isn't what we talked about at all."

All eyes in the room are suddenly staring at me. *This isn't what we talked about at all.* What does he mean by that? I incorporated absolutely everything he told me. How could he say something like that?

"What do you mean?" I ask carefully.

Cofield shakes his head. "These weren't the babies we discussed using. Remember—I said we needed a more diverse selection. Also, I said I wanted to have the toddler foods at the top and the stage one foods at the bottom."

He's right. He did say all that to me. And I made the changes. Except when I look at the screen displayed overhead, I realize the image does not reflect any of this. I see the first baby in the image is the kid with red hair that sticks up, which I specifically remember Cofield saying was an "ugly baby" because I got offended by his calling any baby ugly. But here is Cofield's "ugly baby," staring me right in the face.

Oh my God, did I put the *old* images in my presentation?

Oh no.

I can't believe I did that. What a stupid mistake. And to not even double-check it before a major presentation in front of the Cuddles executives... what is *wrong* with me? I must be losing my mind.

"Um..." I shift between my feet, trying to figure out

how to play this like it isn't a huge mistake. I'm not sure if there's a way. "Right, so these are the first images I used, so I could show you how much better our new design is."

"Okay…" Cofield says.

And now everyone is waiting for me to show them the new design.

"I need a few seconds to load it," I say. "Sorry."

I'm not fooling anyone. Monica has to come to the front of the room to help me load the correct images, and it's a complete mess. I can feel the anger emanating off Denise, who is doing her best to placate the Cuddles people while I attempt to salvage the meeting.

It takes twenty minutes, but I finally get the right image on the screen. Okay, fine—it was a bit of a snafu, but the important thing is, I've got a great website for their product. That's all that matters.

"I don't know, Abby…" Cofield is saying.

Jesus Christ, now what?

"Yes?" I say, as calmly as possible.

"I don't love that slogan." He shakes his head. "Cuddles Baby Food—nothing is more important than your baby's tummy."

"What's wrong with that?" Aside from the fact that it's terrible. I couldn't come up with anything better.

"It's clunky," he says.

"Clunky?"

"I want something that rolls off the tongue," he says. "You know?"

Denise is giving me the stink eye from across the room. I wrack my brain, trying to remember the list of slogans I had saved on my computer. There are others they might like better. If only I could remember…

"How about," Monica says suddenly, "Cuddles Baby Food—because your baby deserves the best."

The slogan rings a bell. It's from the list of rejects from last night.

Cofield turns to stare at the woman who's been serving him coffee and helping with the projector. A slow smile curls across his lips. "Actually, I like that."

Monica beams. "Really?"

"Yeah!" He nods vigorously. "It's clean, simple… and it guilt trips the parents into paying a little more for our baby food." He leans over to grin at Denise. "This girl here is a gem."

"Well, I can't take credit," Monica says quickly. "It was on Abby's list. She's really the one who came up with it."

"Yes, but you're the one who knew it was right for us," Cofield says. "That's half the battle."

"Very true." Denise smiles warmly at my assistant. "You know, Monica is one of our rising stars here at Stewart."

She… is?

The meeting is salvaged, but I don't feel good about any of it. Cofield was supposed to love my presentation. Instead, somehow Monica stole the spotlight with *my* slogan. When the meeting ends, the people from Cuddles are chatting her up like *she's* the one in charge. Meanwhile, Denise grabs me by the arm so hard, it feels like she might yank it out of the socket.

"What was *that*, Abigail?" she hisses in my ear so the Cuddles people can't hear us. "You almost blew it. Are you on *drugs* or something?"

"It was an honest mistake," I mumble.

Her ice-blue eyes meet mine. "People get fired over honest mistakes."

"It all worked out okay."

"Yes, thanks to your *assistant*." Denise shakes her head. "I don't know what's going on with you lately, Abigail. Perhaps something in your personal life." That's an understatement. "But you need to turn it around. Fast."

"It won't happen again."

"No. It won't."

Denise gives me one last ice-cold look, then turns on her heel to speak with Cofield, a bright smile now transforming her face. I can't remember the last time Denise has smiled like that at me. She's right that I'm the one who screwed up today, but it's not like she's making things any easier.

Monica goes to the back of the room to clear away the coffee and I join her. If things keep going the way they are now, soon my only responsibility will be bringing coffee to these meetings.

No. That's not true. I'd be fired first.

"I hope I wasn't out of place speaking up just now," Monica says as she wipes a coffee stain off the table.

"Of course not." I force a smile. "You saved the meeting."

She smiles back. "You think so?"

"Sure," I tell her, even though it kills me to say it.

"Monica!" Denise calls to her. She's standing by Cofield and the other men from Cuddles. "Come here and join us for a moment!"

"Uh…" Monica glances at the leaky coffee pot and the cups scattered everywhere. "Let me just get this cleaned up."

"Nonsense," Denise says. "Abigail will clean up. We'd like to speak with you."

I watch in disbelief as my assistant goes to speak with the executives while I tidy up the coffee. I feel sick. I'd been grateful to Monica for rescuing me during the meeting, but now I wish she'd just left me to flounder.

# CHAPTER 19

I can't sleep.

I tried reading. I downloaded three separate books onto my Kindle, but none of them held my attention. I peed twice. I watched a few videos on YouTube, but I heard screen time is bad for sleep so I shut it off.

And that's when I got out of bed and started pacing.

Unsurprisingly, this pulls Sam from sleep. He sits up in bed, rubbing his eyes and yawning. He turns on the lamp by the bed and stares at me in disbelief. "Abby, it's two in the morning."

"I can't sleep."

"Yeah, I gathered that."

There was a stressful time I had at work four years ago, which coincided perfectly with the peak of our infertility issues. I had a lot of trouble sleeping then too. I'd routinely be up at two in the morning, pacing our bedroom.

I have to give it to Sam—he was great about it. He

used to get up with me, and the two of us would sit in the kitchen together, talking and drinking warm milk. That's how I knew he'd be a great dad to a newborn. He didn't mind getting up in the middle of the night to make me milk. And somehow, that made it even worse. Because I wanted a child not just for me, but also for him.

"I screwed up a meeting today at work," I say, as I perch down at the edge of the bed. "A really important meeting. I put up the wrong images. It was a disaster."

"Oh." Sam rubs his eyes again. "So… what? Are you unemployed now?"

"*No.*"

"Then you'll make it right again. You always do."

"What if I don't?"

He shrugs. "Well, we're going to have a baby soon. You can stay home if you want."

"You know I don't want to do that! I've worked really hard to get where I am!" I put my hands on my hips. "Anyway, you don't earn enough money on your own. We'd have to start going through my savings."

"I earn enough for us to get by."

"Not really."

He gives me a look. Sam rarely seems resentful of the fact that I earn twice as much as he does or that we had to use my trust fund to put down money on our condo. But sometimes I get the feeling it bothers him more than he lets on.

In any case, this isn't making me feel any better. I

pace across our small bedroom, my heart pounding in my chest. Why can't I shut down my thoughts? What's *wrong* with me?

"Don't you have those sleeping pills?" Sam says. "From when you were having trouble sleeping before?"

"Maybe…" I think they're still in the medicine cabinet. "But they're four years old. They've probably expired."

He yawns. "Maybe tomorrow you should call your doctor to get another prescription."

"I don't want to rely on pills to sleep."

"Yeah, you just want to spend the night pacing the apartment."

He has a point. "Okay, I'll call my doctor tomorrow."

Sam rubs his eyes again. He looks so sexy right now, his dark hair disheveled, the stubble on his chin—also, he sleeps shirtless. So there's that.

I can think of *one* thing that might relax me…

"Hey." I climb back onto the bed, but this time onto Sam's side. "You feel like fooling around…?"

"Uh…"

I frown at him. Is the answer not yes?

He looks a little uncomfortable. "I mean, yes, of course I do. But… well, I've got an eight a.m. lecture tomorrow and…"

Oh my God, is Sam blowing me off? He's *never* blown me off! Not in all our years of dating and marriage has he ever refused a request for sex. Never. It's made me feel guilty in the past because there have been times he's wanted it and I turned him down because of (ironically) an early meeting. But Sam always says yes. Even when he had an early lecture, he was always willing to trade sleep for sex. *Always.*

Why isn't he interested anymore? Does it have anything to do with the text messages he's still getting regularly on his phone?

"Okay, fine," I say as I roll off him. "Whatever."

"I'm sorry, Abby."

Now he's apologizing to me for blowing me off. If anything could make me feel worse, it's that.

"Don't worry about it," I say.

"Tomorrow night," he promises.

"Yep."

He looks at me for a moment, then shakes his head and shuts off the light. He rolls over, trying to get back to sleep, and after a few minutes, the sound of his soft snoring fills the room.

Sam's phone is plugged in and resting on the windowsill. I know his password by heart. It would be very easy to go over there and check his text messages. See what he and Monica have been discussing so enthusiastically these last several weeks. But that would be a major betrayal of his trust.

I couldn't do that.

Or could I?

Sam isn't interested in sex with his wife. Isn't that a

sign of another woman in his life? I've certainly got probable cause here.

But I can't do that to Sam. I trust him. He wouldn't cheat on me. He *wouldn't*.

I'm still staring at his cell phone when I eventually drift off to sleep.

# CHAPTER 20

Monica's got an OB/GYN appointment today and I'm going to this one. Somehow she's managed to schedule every single appointment at times I couldn't manage. But this one is first thing in the morning, and Sam and I are driving there together, just to make sure I don't mysteriously have the time wrong.

"I'm glad you could make it today," Sam comments as he drives uptown to Dr. Wong's office. "It sucks the last two appointments didn't work with your schedule."

"Yeah," I mutter. "Too bad Monica doesn't have access to my calendar. Oh, wait."

He gives me a sideways glance. "What is that supposed to mean?"

"I'm saying it's a bit of a coincidence, that's all."

He comes to a stop at a red light. "Are you saying you think Monica is purposely scheduling her appointments at times you can't make?"

"No." But I'm heavily implying it. "It's great that *you*

could make all the appointments though."

"Well, my schedule is a little more flexible than yours."

It's true, although I have a feeling she checks with him before she schedules anything. For some reason, Monica wants Sam at those appointments. He even drove her to the last appointment, and at work she couldn't stop gushing about the amazing job he did parking his car in some tiny little spot. He must have eaten that up.

"What is she always texting you about, anyway?" I ask him.

He pushes his glasses up the bridge of his nose. "Mostly math stuff."

"*Math*?"

"Yeah." He nods vigorously. "You know, Monica really knows her stuff—she's got a brain for it. I know she's set on going back to school for graphic art, but I'm trying to talk her into a math degree. She could do it."

"And what does she say about it?"

"She's thinking about it." A guy cuts Sam off and he curses under his breath, but doesn't honk. "She wants to apply to our program, but I thought that might be awkward because… well, you know."

"Gee, you think?"

Sam lets out a sigh. "Look, let's not talk about Monica anymore. Okay?"

"Sure. What do you want to talk about?"

"I don't know." He grins at me. "How about baby

names? We don't have much time left to decide."

I can't help but return his smile. "I'm not going to cave on Adam."

"What's wrong with Adam? It's a great name. Biblical."

"Adam Adler? It's a little too much alliteration. Sounds like the civilian identity of a Marvel superhero."

"What about Jacob?"

"No. I dated a guy named Jake."

"So?"

"So it would be weird!"

"Fine." Sam rolls his eyes. "What about Richard?"

"I also dated a guy named Richard."

"Matthew?"

"I also dated a Matthew."

He snorts. "Maybe we need to look to more international names to find one that you haven't already dated."

"Okay, but keep in mind, I spent a semester abroad in Italy."

"Yeah, I don't want to know."

It's sort of odd in a way how Sam and I haven't discussed our prior relationships much. I know he's had girlfriends before me—it would be weird if he hadn't since we didn't start dating until we were in our mid-twenties. If I ever asked him about it, he'd say something vague about it being in the past, then ask me why I wanted to know so badly. Or he'd make some comment about them, like, "The relationship wasn't a big deal." It irked me because I worried someday he'd be talking to a future girlfriend about me, and say, "Abby wasn't a big deal."

Of course, then when we got engaged, I recognized our relationship *was* a big deal to him, so I put that particular worry out of my head. But I was still curious about his previous girlfriends. Maybe because I couldn't imagine any girl breaking up with a great guy like Sam, but at the same time, it's hard to him imagine him dumping anyone. I can't picture him having a conversation like that.

We arrive at Dr. Wong's office with enough time for Sam to find parking and then walk over together. I can't help but notice that while we walk to the doctor's office, he doesn't hold my hand like he usually does. But I suppose this isn't really a hand-holding type of atmosphere.

When we get into the waiting room, Monica is already there. She stands up when she sees us, and my jaw falls open. She usually makes an effort to hide her baby bulge when she's at work, but now she's wearing a blue maternity shirt with a string that ties just below her large boobs, and… God, she looks *so* pregnant. I shouldn't be surprised because she's nearly seven months along, but wow, she's big. There's no question of there being a baby in there.

Sam's baby.

Monica's face lights up at the sight of us. As we get closer, she rushes over and throws her arms around Sam's shoulders. If my jaw weren't already hanging open, that would have done it. I had no idea Sam and Monica had a hugging type of relationship. Sam especially is not much of a hugger. He's very affectionate with me, but he's ranted before about how he dislikes random displays of affection from friends or relatives. *The only person I want to hug or kiss is my wife. And maybe my mother.*

And Monica, apparently. Because he is definitely *not* pushing her away.

Monica waves at me—I don't warrant a hug. I can't stop staring at her midsection. I can't get over how big she is. Whatever she's been doing to hide it at work is admirable, but it's clearly not going to work for much longer.

Sam seems equally mesmerized by her stomach. He keeps looking at it and finally feels compelled to comment, "The baby's getting big."

She nods eagerly. "And active! He's been kicking up a storm today."

He smiles. "Oh yeah? That must be something."

"It is." She returns his smile. "Here, feel."

And then she picks up his hand and places it firmly on the bulge of her abdomen. To his credit, Sam looks embarrassed, but he doesn't pull away from her. He allows her to hold his hand on her belly. After a few moments, his eyes widen. "Oh, wow! That's incredible!"

"Isn't it?" she laughs. "It's like he's always keeping me company."

Monica removes her hand, but Sam doesn't move his.

He's still got his palm pressed to her midsection, feeling the baby shift. He's got a silly grin on his face. "Abby," he says, "you've got to feel this!"

I don't want to touch Monica any more than she wants me to touch her. Fortunately, we're saved by a nurse calling out Monica's name.

The three of us are heading to the back, but the nurse stops us. "I'm so sorry," she says, "but we only allow one other person in the room during pregnancy checks. It's just a rule we have."

What kind of stupid rule is that? Monica's eyes immediately go to Sam, and it's obvious who her preference is. But Sam quickly says, "Abby, you should go. I was already at the last two appointments."

Monica's lips set into a straight line. "Are you sure?"

"Yeah, it's fine." He smiles crookedly. "I'll just wait out here. I got to feel the baby, so that's the best part."

Monica doesn't speak to me at all on the way to the examining room, clearly pissed at me for being here when Sam is not. She makes a point of walking several steps ahead of me, so she doesn't even have to look at me. And when we get to the examining room, she regards me coolly and says, "Would you mind stepping out so I can change?"

"Sure," I say, not mentioning the fact that she was fine with me being there when she changed during the first visit.

I step outside the room, but it's clear she's not going to call me back inside until the doctor arrives. Which is fine because the last thing I want is to be standing awkwardly in that room with her.

Dr. Wong comes walking down the hall, her white coat hanging loose on her shoulders. She sees me standing outside the room, and her eyes widen in surprise. "Oh!" she manages.

"Hello." I give her a half-hearted wave. "I'm Abby. I don't know if you remember me from the first visit…"

"Yes, yes, of course." Her smile is strained. "Sorry, I just… somehow I didn't realize you were still involved."

I blink at her. "What do you mean?"

"Well." Her cheeks color. "Monica's husband has been here for the last couple of visits, so I thought…"

"Monica's… husband?"

Dr. Wong nods. "Yes. He's maybe in his thirties, brown hair, glasses, fairly, um,… attractive."

"Sam?"

She snaps her fingers. "Yes, that's right! Sam."

"No, Sam is *my* husband," I correct her.

"Oh!" She laughs. "Well, I suppose that makes more sense, doesn't it? I could have sworn they said he was her husband though."

I want to tell Dr. Wong she's got it wrong, but I can't quite get the words out. All of a sudden, I get this horrible feeling in the pit of my stomach. I can imagine Monica telling the doctor that Sam is her husband—that seems consistent with her recent behavior. But Sam would never have gone along with it. If the doctor had asked him, he would have told her that he wasn't Monica's husband. He would have corrected her.

Wouldn't he?

# CHAPTER 21

When Monica comes into my office this morning with my coffee, there's no denying it anymore—she is really visibly pregnant. People at work are going to start noticing very soon, if they haven't already.

It's not surprising. She's now seven months along. It's amazing she's managed to hide it this long, even with her creative fashion choices. I heard some snarky secretaries in the ladies' room whispering about how Monica needs to "cut back on the chocolate." I've heard still others joking about who the father might be. The gig is definitely up.

"How are you feeling?" I ask her carefully.

She rests her hand gently on her belly. "A little tired, but generally pretty good."

"That's great." I chew on my lip, considering my next words carefully. "Do you, um… want to have a seat?"

Monica gives me a funny look, but she settles into the seat across from me. I get up and close the door so we can have some privacy.

"Listen," I say to her as I settle down into my leather chair. "I'm sure you realize that it's becoming very obvious that you're pregnant."

"I guess so," she says.

She bows down her head. I notice for the first time that even though Monica has jet black hair like I do, her roots are pale. One of the selling points when she suggested being a surrogate for me was our similar appearances, but now I'm not sure anymore she's a natural brunette. Does Monica dye her hair black?

Why on earth would she dye her hair black?

I clear my throat. "So per our arrangement, I think it's time to resign. I can start looking for replacements for you right away."

Her eyes fly open. "Resign?"

"Yes," I say tightly. "That was the agreement. When you started showing, you would resign."

She stares at me for a moment, her mouth hanging open. "Is this because I came up with a better idea than you at that meeting with Cuddles?"

Ouch. Admittedly, I've felt a smoldering resentment toward Monica because of that meeting. Ever since then, Denise has been acting like Monica's the new office prodigy. I can barely remember the last time I got that kind of mentorship from Denise. At a meeting yesterday, Denise told Monica that she was "really going places" at Stewart Advertising.

"It's not because of that," I say quietly. "This was our

agreement from the beginning, Monica."

"But it's not in the contract."

"Excuse me?"

"It's not in the contract," she repeats. "I said maybe I'd leave, but I didn't sign anything saying I would definitely leave."

Now it's my turn to stare. "But we agreed…"

She shrugs. "Yes, but I changed my mind. I like it here. I want to stay."

I feel like she just punched me in the gut. I don't even know what to say. This was our agreement and she's backing out. It raises the question, what else will she back out of?

"Monica." I'm trying to keep my voice even. "If you keep working here, I could get in a lot of trouble for our arrangement. It could look like I… that I pressured you into it."

"Well, maybe you should have thought of that beforehand." She sticks up her chin. "I don't want to give up my job, Abby. I shouldn't have to."

I want to leap across the desk and shake her, but that would be a bad idea for so many reasons. I have to stay on Monica's good side. There is so much riding on her.

"If this is really what you want," I say quietly, "we'll figure out a way to work it out. We can go to HR and explain the situation. As long as you back me up that I didn't coerce you into anything."

I watch Monica's face. I'm terrified she's going to

refuse to go along with it, but then her lips curl into a smile. "Sure, Abby. Of course."

Thank God. This is still going to be a total disaster, but maybe there's a way to mitigate the damage.

———

I don't know why I'm so bad at getting envelopes open. Considering how much snail mail I get every day, you'd think I'd have acquired reasonable skill at this. But it feels like every envelope I open results in a twenty-five percent chance of a serious paper cut.

Where the hell is that letter opener Sam got me?

The top drawer where I usually keep it only has papers in it. I rifle around, trying to find it. Wow, my desk is getting to be a mess. I always used to be so organized, but somehow, the top of my desk has become a hurricane of papers. I don't know how I let that happen. I've got so much on my mind…

I'm still searching for my letter opener when Denise strides into my office without knocking. I look up, and the expression on her face unsettles me. It's not like Denise doesn't always seem a little pissed off at me, but right now, she's got a pink circle on each of her cheekbones and there are veins standing out on her neck.

"Abigail," she says as a vein pulses in her neck. I hope she doesn't burst an aneurysm right in front of me.

Well, I mostly hope that.

"Yes, hi," I say. "What's up, Denise?"

She glowers at me. "I was hoping you could explain the meaning of this email to me."

She holds out her phone in my direction and I take it from her. I immediately recognize an email I *thought* I had sent to Shelley, asking her opinion on the latest copy I had written for Cuddles. Except it turns out I accidentally cc'd the message to Denise Holt.

Also, I prefaced the message by writing: *Let me know what you think. Of course, no matter what, Denise will probably be a bitch again and make me redo everything.*

"Uh…," I say.

This is fantastic. I called my boss a bitch in an email, then accidentally cc'd the email to her. Of all the stupid things I've done recently, this has got to take the cake.

Denise yanks her phone out of my hand. She places her fists on her hips and stares at me, waiting for an explanation. Her face is noticeably pink under her concealer. I wonder how old Denise is. Shelley and I have debated it countless times and we can't figure it out. She looks mid-forties, but she looked mid-forties when we started working here ten years ago. So… mid-fifties? Sixty? Seventy? Who can tell?

"I'm really sorry about that," I say, trying to sound as genuine as I possibly can, considering I very much meant what I wrote to Shelley. "I was just blowing off some steam and… well, obviously, I didn't intend for you to see it."

"So you didn't intend to send me an email calling me a bitch?" she snaps at me.

I lower my eyes. Is she going to fire me? Oh God, I can't be fired right now. Or ever. No time is a good time to be fired.

And then just when it seems like this situation can't get any worse, Sonia Watson from Human Resources taps on the door to my office. At first, I'm certain Denise called her here to deliver my pink slip, but it quickly becomes obvious Denise had no idea Sonia was coming.

"Hi, Abby," Sonia says, her hands clutched in front of her. "Denise. I'm glad you're both here. Would it be possible to speak in the conference room?"

My stomach sinks. Sonia from HR wants to speak with me and Denise together in the conference room? This morning is not getting any better.

Denise narrows her eyes. She doesn't like surprises. "What's this about?"

Sonia tugs on her cream-colored pencil skirt. "It's best if you come with me."

I feel like I'm following Sonia to my own execution. And I don't feel one bit better when I see none other than Monica Johnson already sitting in the conference room. For the very first time, she's wearing maternity clothes to work. She's got on a light blue top that cinches below her breasts and stretches comfortably over the swell of her belly. She looks beautiful, actually.

Denise sees her, and her eyes fly open. It would be comical if it weren't all so, so horrible.

"Monica," she gasps. "You're… pregnant?"

"Yes," Monica says. "I am."

This must drive her crazy, considering the way she's taken Monica under her wing lately, and as we know, Denise hates pregnant ladies and children and probably also animals and flowers and Christmas snow.

"Please take a seat," Sonia says to me and Denise.

Denise is clearly very confused. It's interesting to watch her off her game, because she's always so damn composed. "What's this about, Sonia? Do we need a meeting to discuss pregnancies now?"

"No, we don't," Sonia says, patting her cornrows self-consciously, "but I think we need to have a meeting to discuss the circumstances of Monica's pregnancy."

Denise's eyes dart around the room, trying to figure it all out. "Circumstances?"

Sonia nods. "It's come to my attention that Monica and Abby have an arrangement in which Monica is acting as a surrogate for Abby, and Abby will be adopting her baby."

The look of surprise on Denise's face is absolutely priceless. I wish I could photograph it. I couldn't have imagined her being more upset than she was when I called her a bitch, but here it is. Well, it's been nice working here.

"Abigail," Denise gasps. "You... you..."

"The arrangement has nothing to do with the company," I say, my voice surprisingly firm considering I'm about eighty percent sure I'm going to be fired. No, make that ninety-five percent sure. "It was something

Monica and I arranged outside of work and we have a signed contract."

"Granted, that may be true," Sonia says, "but given Monica is your assistant, she is in a compromised position here in terms of entering into any agreements."

"She doesn't work for me," I point out. "I don't pay her salary. I wasn't even the one who hired her."

"But she is your assistant," Sonia says.

"That's her job title, yes," I admit. "But practically—"

"I can't believe this," Denise sputters. "How could you force Monica to do something like this, Abigail?"

Everyone in the room is staring at me. I'm at a loss for words. I could point out that I thought Monica was going to quit prior to this point, but I don't think that would make things better.

"Monica," Denise says gently. I don't think she's ever talked to me that nicely in all the time I've known her. "I am so sorry about what Abigail did to you. If there's anything the company could do—"

"It was my idea," Monica says suddenly.

Sonia blinks a few times, taken aback. "What?"

"It was my idea to be a surrogate for Abby," Monica says. She crosses her legs slowly, adjusting the weight of her belly. "I felt terrible for her after everything she went through, so I offered to help her out. She didn't ask me. I mean, you know she's been trying to have a baby for a long time…"

"It still wasn't appropriate," Denise snaps, her eyes

flashing.

"I had an attorney look over the contracts," Monica says. "We have a very fair arrangement. Like I said, it was my idea. I wanted to do it. Abby in no way coerced me. She shouldn't be punished for something that was my idea."

Sonia and Denise are exchanging looks, but I don't know what that means. However, I'm beginning to have a tiny shred of hope that I might not lose my job today.

"Monica," Sonia says carefully, "you don't need to defend her."

"I'm only telling the truth." She sticks up her chin. "If you're going to fire someone today, then I'll be the one to leave."

Wow. I did not expect that.

"Nobody is going to be fired today," Sonia says hastily, although Denise shoots her a look. It's clear Denise would like nothing better than to say goodbye to me forever. And keep Monica instead.

Sometimes I worry Sam feels the same way.

"I'm so sorry about all of this," I say. "Honestly, I didn't mean to involve the company in our arrangement."

"Didn't mean to involve the company!" Denise bursts out. "How could you possibly think that—"

Sonia holds up her hand. "If Monica insists the arrangement was made fairly and is willing to sign paperwork to that effect, I think it would be in our best interest not to pursue it further. Monica, are you comfortable signing some documents for me?"

She rests a hand protectively on her belly. "Of course."

Denise is glaring at me like she wants to reach out and strangle me with her bare hands. This probably isn't the best time to discuss my upcoming maternity leave.

# CHAPTER 22

"So it sounds like Monica saved the day then."

I glare at Sam, who is wearing his "I ate some pie" apron and attempting to cook meatballs. He's got them in a pot on the stove, simmering in tomato sauce, but he's babysitting them too much. Every thirty seconds, he lifts the lid of the pot to stir them.

While he's been cooking, I told him the whole story about what happened today, about how I got called into HR thanks to Monica. But he doesn't seem to get it.

"Yes, she 'saved the day,'" I admit. "But she wouldn't have had to save the day if she had left the job like she was supposed to. It really got me in a lot of trouble. Denise *hates* me."

A smile twitches at Sam's lips. "Maybe you shouldn't have emailed her that she was a bitch."

I groan. I'll never live that down. I told Shelley what happened, and she couldn't stop laughing. This isn't funny. This is my *career*. Maybe we've got enough money to get by without my salary, but that doesn't mean I want to give up everything I've worked for.

"I just feel like this is a bad sign," I say. "If she's going to go back on our agreement about work, what else will she back out on? Giving us the baby?"

Sam opens the pot and peers down at his meatballs. "She won't."

"How do you know?"

"She said she wants to focus on her career right now. And maybe go back to school at night after all. Possibly to study graphic art or maybe math—maybe both. Either way, she can't do that with a baby."

I narrow my eyes at Sam. "And when did she say all that to you?"

Any trace of a smile fades from his lips as he quickly busies himself with the pot again. "What?"

"It just seems like you know a lot about her plans for the future, that's all."

Sam fiddles with the knob on the stove. "We had lunch a couple of days ago."

Well, great. My husband is having lunch with a young, attractive woman who happens to be carrying his baby. And he's lying to me about it.. "Were you planning on telling me about it, *Sammy*?"

"It wasn't a big deal," he mumbles.

"Then why didn't you tell me?"

"Because I knew you'd make a big thing of it." He shakes his head. "Look, Monica is at a crossroads in her career and I want to help her, you know? That's part of what I do—advise students."

"Yes, but she's not your student! She works at *my* company. Don't you think if she really wanted advice, she'd come to *me*?"

He lowers his eyes. "I think you intimidate her a little."

"I *intimidate* her?"

"Yes, that's what she said."

"Oh, Lord." I roll my eyes. "That's the horseshit she's been feeding you?"

"It's not horseshit. You *can* be intimidating, Abby."

"Oh, really? Do *you* find me intimidating?"

"The first time I met you, I did," he admits. He smiles crookedly. "You had on that power outfit of yours with the matching black skirt and short jacket and your hair up in that elaborate knot. It was so goddamn sexy. You got me so nervous. I didn't even know what I was saying."

I can't suppress a smile. "You mostly started talking about math."

"I know—that's what I do when I'm nervous. I thought I'd made a complete idiot out of myself. I couldn't believe it when you agreed to go to dinner with me. I almost didn't bother asking."

My anger from earlier is starting to fade. "I'm glad you did."

"Me too." He lifts the lid from the pot one more time and fishes out a meatball with his fork. "Want to taste?"

"Um, you first."

He clutches his chest with his free hand. "Are you afraid to try my meatballs?"

I peer at the lopsided gray blob hanging off the fork. "What is in them?"

"Well, ground beef, obviously. Um… breadcrumbs, parmesan cheese, an egg…"

Bread crumbs, parmesan cheese, and an egg. How could he mess that up?

I lean forward and take a bite from the meatball on his fork. And…

"Sam!" I cry. "This has eggshells in it!"

"It does?" He looks down at the meatball, baffled. He takes a tentative bite. "Oh. It does. Damn."

He looks down at the pot of meatballs, crestfallen. I want to tell him I'm willing to eat them anyway, but I'm not. Crunchy meatballs are not pleasant to eat. Even to spare my husband's feelings. Plus I'm pretty sure he doesn't want to eat them either.

"Pizza?" I say.

He sighs. "Sure."

But before I can grab my phone, Sam reaches out to take my hand. "Hey," he says.

"Yes?"

His brown eyes meet mine. "I just wanted to say… I'm sorry. I shouldn't have gone to lunch with Monica."

"Oh…"

He squeezes my hand in his. "I figured… well, I didn't

think it was a big deal when she asked me, and honestly, she's doing so much for us, I felt like I owed her. But then when I was there, I realized it was a mistake. I knew you'd be hurt if you found out, and I felt terrible about it. I felt like an asshole."

Sam is really good at apologizing. He's harder on himself than I would ever be on him.

"It's okay," I say. "You're right—it wasn't that big a deal. I mean, it was just lunch."

"I won't do it again. I promise."

And now I feel guilty for giving him a hard time. "It's fine."

I suppose I'm making too big a deal out of all of this. Lunch is lunch—not an affair. Sam wouldn't do something like that. If there's one thing I know for sure, it's that my husband isn't a cheater. And he's right—Monica stuck up for me today and saved my job. If she wanted, I could have been clearing out my office as we speak. I suppose it's not crazy that she might want to keep her job. At age twenty-three, you're allowed to change your mind about your career path.

Everything is going to be fine.

# CHAPTER 23

"Knock, knock!"

I look up at my office door and see a face peeking in. It takes me a second to recognize Gertie, my old assistant pre-Monica. She hasn't been back once since she fell on those stairs and broke her hip. She limps into the office, holding a plate of chocolate chip cookies that I can smell all the way across the room. She's got a cane in the hand that isn't holding the cookies, and she leans on it heavily as she walks.

I miss Gertie's cookies. I miss Gertie. I miss having an assistant I'm not worried is making a play for my husband. I don't care that she didn't know how to use the fax machine and sometimes even seemed confused by the phone. Right now, I'd give my right arm for another Gertie.

"How are you, Abby?" Gertie beams at me over the plate of cookies. "It's so great to see you again! You look like you're hard at work!"

I am hard at work. At this point, I can't afford any

more screw-ups. I've been showing up early, taking lunch in my office, and staying later than anyone else. It's still a little hard to focus, since my sleep is still not great, even with my new prescription for sleeping pills, but I'm doing the best I can.

"Yeah," I say. "What can I say—I'm lost without you, Gertie."

Her face softens. "I heard what happened. About, you know… the adoption falling through. I'm so sorry. That must have been awful."

"Yes," I agree. If only Janelle hadn't changed her mind. We'd have a baby right now, and I'd probably be exhausted like I am now, but a good kind of exhausted. "I'm okay though. We're… uh, adopting from someone else."

No need to get into the details.

She places the plate of cookies down on my desk and clasps her hands together. "Oh, that's so wonderful to hear! You're going to be a great mom, Abby. I just know it."

"Thanks." I manage a smile. "Anyway, have a seat. How is your hip feeling?"

Gertie settles gingerly into a chair in front of my desk and rests her cane against my desk. "Good days and bad days. I'm on my feet again, and that's what's important."

"Absolutely. You look great."

She laughs and pats her puff of white hair. "Well, aren't you sweet?"

"Any chance you might come back?"

This time when she laughs, she throws her whole head back like I made a hilarious joke. Except it wasn't a joke. "Oh, I don't think so, Abby. I'm done living in the fast lane. Done rushing to make deadlines and getting pushed down the stairs."

I start to say something else, but her words stop me. "Pushed down the stairs?"

She waves a hand. "Just a joke. It was an accident, obviously."

"But…" I grip the edges of my chair, my heart pounding. "You were pushed down the stairs?"

"No, no!" She shakes her head. "There were a lot of people in the stairwell and… well, it *felt* like a push, but it was obviously an accident. Who would push little old me down the stairs?"

Maybe someone who wanted her job.

I stare at Gertie, my mouth hanging open. I know she thinks it's all a big joke, but I'm not so sure. She said it felt like someone pushed her down the stairs. And then almost immediately after the accident, Monica appeared to take her place.

It's got to be a coincidence.

It's *got* to.

"Abby, are you okay?" Gertie asks. "You look downright pale! Are you eating enough cookies?"

"Uh, I guess not."

"Well, take one! I made you a whole plate. For you and that lovely husband of yours."

Right. Me and my lovely husband.

I reach out and take a cookie from the plate. It tastes like cardboard.

# CHAPTER 24

I'm in the ladies' room, dabbing extra concealer under my eyes. I'm absolutely exhausted because I haven't been taking my sleeping pills for the last week. They're doing the annual drug screens today and I didn't want there to be any chance that stuff would show up. I've got a note from my doctor and all, but I can't give Denise any ammunition to get rid of me.

I look really tired. Like I'm ten years older than I actually am. Sam came into the bathroom this morning while I was brushing my teeth, and when he kissed me, I couldn't help but wonder how he could be attracted to me when he's got a younger, prettier version of me texting him every five minutes. But I'm not going to say that to him. Don't need to give the guy any ideas.

Shelley walks in on me mid-dab. Her eyes widen. "Abby," she says. "Are you okay?"

I snap my compact closed. "Yes, I'm fine."

"You look *really* tired."

"Gee, thanks a bunch."

She winces. "Sorry. I didn't mean it that way."

My shoulders sag. "No, I'm sorry I snapped. It's just… it's been a rough month."

That's an understatement. Monica's belly has really popped in the last few weeks, and everyone is oohing and ahhing over her. Only a few people know the whole story about her being my surrogate—I've noticed she's not volunteering that information, which is just as well. I'm sure I'll get lots of weird looks when the truth comes out.

But the good news is, Monica's pregnancy will be over soon. And then I won't have to deal with her anymore. I'll leave the company if I have to—it's not like I'm getting anywhere fast with Denise as my boss. Maybe I'll just stay home with the baby. At least money won't be an issue.

"It's okay," Shelley says. "I get it. And Monica… well, she's acting weird. I don't blame you for being worried."

I frown. "Acting weird?"

"Well…" She hesitates. "I didn't want to say anything…"

"Oh my God, please just tell me."

"It's just… I know it's uncomfortable for her to admit she's giving the baby up. But if you talked to her, you'd never guess in a million years. She really acts like she's keeping the baby."

I feel a lump in my throat. "What do you mean?"

She lowers her voice a few notches. "Like I overheard her having a long discussion with Mia about baby names.

She told Mia she was all but decided on David."

That one hits me like a punch in the gut. Especially since David is one of Sam's favorite baby names—it was his father's name. He's been pushing hard for the name, even though I told him I dated a guy named David who was a bit of a jerk.

"And then she was asking for advice from Lucy on cribs," Shelley continues. "Like, they were really getting into it. They went to a website and everything."

"Do… do people think she's married?"

Shelley shakes her head. "I heard her telling someone she has a serious boyfriend."

A serious boyfriend? No way. One thing I know for sure is Monica doesn't have a serious boyfriend. For starters, her roommate Chelsea told me she didn't have one and…

Chelsea.

An idea takes root in my brain. Maybe I should call Chelsea. She seemed nice enough and clearly she knows Monica really well. Maybe I could get an idea from her what the deal is with her roommate. Like she could tell me if Monica's apartment is filled with baby apparatus or if she's saying inappropriate things about Sam. Chelsea might be reluctant to betray her roommate, but I can be fairly persuasive. I can put it in the context of trying to help Monica.

"I'm sorry." Shelley winces at the look on my face. "I probably shouldn't have said all this. You've got enough to worry about without my putting ideas in your head."

"No, it's good to know," I say. "If Monica plans to back out on us, I want to know in advance."

I've got to give Chelsea a call.

———

I wait until I get home to try Chelsea's number, remembering how Shelley told me she'd seen Monica listening at the door to my office. Plus I don't have her number handy. Thankfully, Sam files all our paperwork away in the second drawer of his desk, and he's ridiculously organized. He has everything about Monica in a file labeled "Monica Johnson." Chelsea's number is still in there.

I go into the bedroom while Sam is cooking dinner and dial Chelsea's number on my cell phone. My heart is pounding as I hit the green button to send the call.

Before the phone even rings on the other line, I hear an automated voice: "You have reached a nonworking number."

I stare at the phone. Chelsea's number is no longer functional. That's... interesting.

Sam comes into the bedroom in his "I ate some pie" apron, which is dotted with pesto sauce. He's also got some pesto on his chin that I'm guessing he doesn't know about. He looks very proud of himself.

"Dinner is served," he says.

I don't budge.

"I tasted it this time," he assures me. "And it's definitely edible. I swear."

I can't even manage a smile.

Sam frowns and looks at the phone in my hand. "Who were you talking to?"

"Monica's roommate Chelsea," I say. "Or at least, I was trying to. Her phone was disconnected."

"Oh," he says.

"Don't you think that's odd?"

He shrugs. "Maybe she forgot to pay her phone bill."

Maybe. But somehow I don't think so.

"Why were you calling Monica's roommate anyway?" he asks.

"Because." I shift on the bed. "Shelley told me that Monica is talking about the baby like she's planning for after he's born. She even has a name picked out."

"Oh yeah? What name?"

"David."

He grins at me. "Hey, she's got good taste!"

I glare at him. "I feel like you're not taking this seriously. This is our *baby* we're talking about. It's not funny."

Sam sits down beside me on the bed, leveling his kind brown eyes at me. "I'm sorry. It's not funny—you're right. But I genuinely don't think there's any chance Monica will keep the baby. It's all just talk."

Just talk. He seems so sure of himself, but I'm not so confident.

"Hey," I say.

He raises his eyebrows.

"Did you tell Monica you wanted to name the baby David?"

"Uh…" His ears turn red. "I guess I… must have mentioned it to her."

"I see. I thought you said you only talk about her *professional development*." I fold my arms across my chest. "So what else do you talk to her about?"

"Look, she's carrying my baby. It would be weird *not* to ever talk about it."

I drop my eyes. "*Your* baby."

"I meant *our* baby."

"Then why didn't you say that?"

"I don't know… it just… slipped out."

"Because that's how you think of him. As *your* baby."

Sam rakes a hand through his hair. "Abby, I'm going to remind you again that this was all *your* idea. I wanted to adopt, remember?"

"Actually, it was Monica's idea."

"Fine." I can hear the anger growing in his voice as he stands up off the bed. Sam rarely gets angry. "Monica is the bad guy here. She's the worst."

I look up at my husband with his tousled hair and his sexy five o'clock shadow. We haven't had sex in a week, which has got to be some kind of record for us. I've been so stressed out with work, and he hasn't initiated anything. And when I look up at him now, I know nothing will happen tonight either.

"Do you want to have dinner or not?" Sam says impatiently.

I nod and follow him to the living room.

# CHAPTER 25

I've got to find Chelsea Williams.

Calling her is obviously out, given she no longer has a working phone. But she lives with Monica. As I head up in the elevator to my office, it occurs to me that I could look up her address on the computer and pay ol' Chelsea a visit. Maybe I'll do it during lunch, at a time I'm sure Monica won't be around.

Except as I'm walking to my office, Denise is standing in the doorway, a grim expression on her face.

Christ, what now?

"Abigail," she says sharply. "Can I speak with you in my office?"

"Now?" I say.

She looks at me like I'm an idiot. "Yes, now."

I wordlessly follow Denise down the hall to her office. Her heels click loudly on the floor, echoing through the relatively quiet room. I look around and notice everyone seems to be staring at us. What's going on here?

"Please have a seat," Denise tells me, gesturing at the chair in front of her desk.

I settle into the chair, my heart now pounding audibly in my chest. There is no way this is good news. She's definitely not telling me I just got a promotion and a huge raise.

"As you know," she begins, her ice-blue eyes on my face, "yesterday, we completed company-wide urine drug testing. I was informed this morning that your test came back positive for methamphetamines."

My... *what*?

"That... that's got to be some sort of mistake," I gasp.

"Is it?" Denise arches an eyebrow at me. "Your behavior has been increasingly erratic in the last several months. I've been suspecting drugs were involved for some time now. This only confirmed my suspicions."

I feel like someone punched me in the gut. How could there have been *meth* in my urine? That's not possible! I don't take meth. I don't even know *how* to take meth? Do you snort it? Smoke it? Chew it? Mix it in a blender with bananas and yogurt?

The only thing I've been taking is an occasional sleeping pill. But I haven't had one in a week... and anyway, I'm pretty sure sleeping pills don't have meth in them. It would defeat the purpose.

"I don't take meth," I manage. "This is a big mistake."

Denise rolls her eyes. "Well, in any case, the laws in New York State allow us to dictate our own policy for positive drug screens, and Stewart has a zero-tolerance policy. So as of now, you are terminated."

I'm… fired?

I can't believe this is happening. I've never done drugs in my life. I've never even smoked a joint! I'm too square for any of that. I know there are rumors about businesspeople doing coke and then there's that opioid epidemic, but I never do any of that! Hell, I've never even smoked a cigarette.

"I swear to you," I choke out, "I never… I mean, I would never… you *know* me, Denise…"

"Do I?" The woman who hired me right out of college more than a decade ago raises an eyebrow. "I gave you an incredible opportunity, Abigail. I put my trust in you. You're the one who chose to throw it all away." For a moment, her voice breaks. "I'm very, very disappointed."

I think back to the day when I got the call from Denise Holt herself, telling me I was her new assistant. As soon as I put down the phone, I started jumping around the room and shouting like a crazy person. She was my idol. And those first few years, she was so good to me—she taught me everything she knew. Not just about the advertising business, but about life. She listened when I admitted things were getting serious with my mathematician boyfriend. *He sounds like a keeper, Abigail.* She taught me how to dress, how to smile, and how to be confident.

I still remember standing in the ladies' room with

Denise, the two of us giggling like schoolgirls while I attempted to twist my hair into a chignon. I doubt many people besides me have seen that side of Denise Holt. I haven't seen it in years.

"*Please*, Denise." I'm ready to get down on my knees. "You have to believe me."

When she raises her blue eyes, that twinge of emotion has disappeared. "I'm sorry, Abigail."

I'll have to go over Denise's head. I'll have to talk to *her* boss, and figure out if there's anything I can do. But it can't be now because a security guard has arrived to escort me out of the building. They don't even let me go back to my office. The guard marches me right out to the elevators, in front of everyone. I can hear them whispering.

Everyone knows.

I realize at this moment that I can never return to Stewart Advertising. My reputation has been irreparably tarnished. And what sort of job will I land with this in my history?

As soon as I get out of the building, I hail a taxi back home even though I usually take the subway. I need a taxi. I don't think I can keep from crying for the length of a train ride. As it is, I sob in the back seat the entire way home. The taxi driver doesn't comment.

When I get back to the condo, I can hear the water running in the bathroom. Sam must still be home. Thank God. I need someone to talk to about this. He'll know what to do.

He comes out of the bathroom, his hair still damp from the shower, his face smooth and smelling of aftershave. His eyes light up when he sees me. "Abby! What are you doing home?"

It takes him another half-second to notice the tears in my red, swollen eyes. He sprints across the room, his brow furrowed. "What's going on? What happened?" Before I can answer, he says, "Is Monica okay?"

"Is *Monica* okay?" I practically scream at him. "Is that the first thing you ask when you see me crying?"

"Well, I… I just thought…" His face turns bright red as he stammers out the words. "I thought maybe it was something with the baby…"

"No, Monica's fine," I snap at him. "The baby's fine. But I…"

His brow creases, looking down at me. "What?"

"I… I got fired!" I sob.

He pulls me close to him, even though I'm ruining his dress shirt with my tears and snot. He doesn't seem to mind. He holds me until my shoulders stop shaking.

"That Denise is unbelievable," he says. "You need to fight this. Take them to court for wrongful termination. What was the bullshit reason they gave for firing you?"

I pull away from him, wiping my eyes. "My drug test came back positive for methamphetamine."

Sam's mouth falls open. He drops his arm from my shoulder and takes a step back. "*What*?"

"Denise told me this morning," I say. "They did this

urine drug test yesterday and apparently it was positive for meth."

He takes another step back, shaking his head. "You're not serious."

Oh my God, does he think I was actually doing meth? He can't possibly. "It's a false positive, Sam. I'm not doing meth!"

But he doesn't say anything. He just keeps staring at me.

"Sam!" My heart is pounding. "You don't really think I'm a meth addict, do you?"

"No…" He squints at me through his glasses. "But… you have to admit, it does explain a lot of your behavior lately. The way you're up pacing every night. The paranoia."

"Yes, but the insomnia is from stress." I frown at him. "And I'm not paranoid."

"You're definitely paranoid."

"No, I'm not!"

"Abby." He shakes his head at me again. "You went on a long rant last night because you were trying to get through to Monica's roommate on the phone and couldn't. You thought something terrible was going on."

"You don't think that's at all suspicious?"

"No, I don't! And you can't seem to keep track of any of your meetings. You mixed up the times for Monica's appointments. Plus you're constantly talking about how you think Monica is up to something…"

"She almost got me fired!"

"No." He takes another step back. "You got *yourself* fired."

My stomach sinks. "Sam, I swear to you: I'm not taking meth."

He doesn't say anything.

"Please." The tears spring to my eyes again. "You've got to believe me. You're my husband. If *you* don't believe me, then…"

Sam blinks a few times. "I… I've got to get to work, Abby."

"Do you believe me?"

He lets out a long sigh. "Yeah. I guess so."

I try to reach for him again, but he jerks away. It's obvious that in spite of what he says, he doesn't really believe me. My own husband thinks I'm a meth addict.

# CHAPTER 26

I spend most of the day wandering the city aimlessly. I walk to all my favorite shops, looking at clothes and bedding and perfume, but I buy nothing. I don't even eat lunch. Shelley texts me a bunch of times, but I don't want to feed her gossip. I just want to be alone.

Sam comes home after nine, which is unheard of for him. Usually he's home by five, and if for any reason he's later than that, he texts me. I texted him to ask where he was, but he never responded. He just shows up after the sun is already down, his hair disheveled, smelling slightly of alcohol. And—maybe this is my *paranoia* talking—he also smells like Monica's lavender-scented perfume.

"Do you want dinner?" I ask him when he walks through the door. "I got pizza."

"I already ate," he mumbles.

"Where?"

He shrugs.

"Monica's apartment?" I say pointedly.

He glares at me. Maybe I shouldn't have said that, but what else am I supposed to say when my husband comes home late and smelling like another woman's perfume? I didn't do anything wrong. I don't take meth, and he should know that.

"I'm going to go to bed," he says as he pulls off his tie, which is already hanging loose around his neck.

"But it's only nine-thirty."

"Yeah, well."

Except he doesn't go straight to bed. He goes in the bathroom and I hear the shower running for about half an hour. I turn the television to the news because it's about all I can focus on right now. This has been one of the worst days of my life. That day we lost the baby was bad, but this is right up there. At least when that happened, I had Sam's support. I don't know how he could possibly believe I'm a meth addict. I haven't been acting *that* weird.

Have I?

Just as I'm about to get up to go to bed myself, Sam stomps out of the bedroom, his hair damp, dressed in boxers and an undershirt. He's holding a plastic bag in his hand.

"What the hell is this?" he says.

I stare at the object in his hand. It's a Ziploc bag that appears to be filled with small, white crystals. "Is it jewelry?"

"Are you fucking kidding me?" He's nearly shouting now. He shakes the bag in my face. "Are you honestly going to tell me you don't know what this is?"

I take the bag out of his hand. It looks like crystals. Like rock candy or something. I have no idea what this is. Except…

"Oh my God, is this *meth*?" I breathe.

"You tell me," he snaps. "I found it in *your* drawer!"

"You were snooping through my drawers?"

"Yes, I was." He glares at me. "You just failed a drug screen at work and you've been acting insane lately, so yes, I looked through your drawers. But I don't think that's the most important issue here."

"I swear to you, Sam," I say. "I've never seen this before."

"Well, why was it in your drawer?"

"I don't know."

"You and I are the only two people who live here. *I* didn't put it there. So if it wasn't you, who did?"

"I… I don't know." I flinch at the anger on his face. "But you've got to believe me—it's not mine."

"Right," he snorts. "So it's in your urine and in your drawer, but it's not yours. You can see why this is a little hard for me to believe."

"Someone must have put it there."

"Who? Santa Claus?"

I squeeze my fists together. "I don't know. But I've never seen that bag before in my life."

Sam plucks the bag out of my hand and looks at it in disgust. "I'm flushing this down the toilet."

"Don't do that!"

He shakes his head. "Why not?"

"Because it's evidence. There might be fingerprints on it."

"You've got to be kidding me." He rolls his eyes. "You know what will happen if you get caught with this? You'll go to jail. I'm flushing it. Sorry—you'll have to get your next high somewhere else."

I stare after him in disbelief. I look down at my hands, which are shaking badly. I don't know what's going on here. Is it possible I'm a meth addict and don't know it? Maybe I have one of those conditions where I black out and have a whole other life on the side. Is that possible? Because he's right—there's only one logical explanation for all of this.

And it doesn't make me feel very good about myself.

# CHAPTER 27

For the first time in a long time, I sleep like a rock. It's surprising, given how anxious I was all day. I thought I'd be awake until two in the morning with thoughts racing through my head, which has become the norm lately. But instead, the second my head hits the pillow, I'm out like a light, even though I didn't take a sleeping pill. I don't even wake up during the night to pee, which is practically a miracle.

When I get up, Sam isn't in the bed anymore. He didn't sleep on the couch or anything, but he slept as far on his side of the bed as possible without being in an entirely different bed. I've never fought like this with him in the entire decade we've known each other. It's depressing.

I stumble out of bed and hit the bathroom. When I see myself in the mirror over the sink, I almost gasp. I look *awful.* My hair has that Bride of Frankenstein look it always gets when I've slept too long, and there are a few new gray hairs that weren't there the last time I looked at myself. There are deep purple circles under my eyes and my cheeks are hollowed out. Honestly, if someone held up a photo of a woman who looked like me and said she was a meth addict, I'd believe it. No wonder Sam was suspicious.

I forgo a shower because I'm suddenly starving. I pad out to the kitchen to get some food… and stop short at the sight of the couple sitting on my couch.

Sam and Monica.

What is *she* doing here?

"You're awake," Sam notes, a clearly forced smile on his lips.

Sam is dressed for work, wearing a crisp white shirt with a tie, and he's clean-shaven. Even though he might not be wearing Prada or Armani, he looks very good right now. This is the version of Dr. Adler that makes all the undergrad girls fall in love with him. Monica is wearing a blue maternity dress that shows off her substantial cleavage, and her hair looks luscious and silky. The two of them are a really attractive couple. I think of the reflection of myself in the bathroom mirror and wince. Also, I'm wearing pajama shorts and an oversized T-shirt, neither of which is doing me any favors.

"Um, what's going on?" I say.

"Can you sit down for a minute, Abby?" Sam says.

I finger the rat's nest on my head. "Can I shower first?"

"No, I've got to get to work, and we really need to talk to you." His brown eyes meet mine, but the usual affection is absent. "This won't take long."

I don't know what they have to say to me, but it's clearly nothing good. Still, I settle down in the armchair across from them. Monica crosses her legs, smiling kindly at me. I want to punch her in the face.

"Monica and I had a long discussion yesterday," Sam begins. Ha, I knew he smelled like her perfume! What the hell was that woman doing with my husband the whole evening? "And she has some very valid concerns."

"Concerns?" I echo.

He glances at Monica, then plows forward. "She's worried about the adoption, given your recent problems with… you know, drugs."

"I don't have a drug problem!" I burst out. "This is all just a huge mistake!"

The two of them exchange looks. I really dislike these meaningful looks they're giving each other. Monica barely knows him! I'm his *wife*!

"I think Monica's concerns are really valid," he says. "And… well, we've come up with a compromise. We'd like you to attend an inpatient drug rehabilitation program."

My mouth falls open. "You want me to go to *rehab*?"

He nods. "Yes. There are a lot of great programs. I called up a bunch of them yesterday and—"

"I'm *not* going to rehab!" This is insane. I'm not going to rehab when I haven't done drugs even once in my entire life!

Monica puts her hand on Sam's. I want to reach

across the coffee table and strangle her with my bare hands. "I told you she wasn't going to want to do it."

"This is not negotiable, Abby," Sam says. "If you don't do this, I'm going to allow Monica out of her contract."

I can't believe this is happening. How could I be in this situation? I don't do drugs. The only way it could be in my urine is if someone slipped it to me. But how could that happen? I can't even think of a time when...

Wait a minute...

"My coffee!" I gasp, pointing at Monica. "You bring me coffee every morning. You must be slipping it in my coffee!"

Monica's eyes widen. Sam, on the other hand, turns bright red. "Abby, please, you're embarrassing yourself," he says.

"Don't you see?" I cry. "It's the only explanation!" I glare at her. "And she probably grabbed my keys out of my purse and made a copy, then planted the meth in the drawer."

Sam drops his head into his hands. "Abby..."

I stand up off the chair, my legs trembling underneath me. "Search her purse, Sam. I bet you'll find a copy of my keys in there."

Sam stands up too. "Are you *out of your mind*, Abby? I'm not searching her purse!"

"I don't mind if you look through my purse," Monica speaks up.

"No." Sam folds his arms across his chest. "You're out

of control, Abby. I mean it. I want you to think about what I said about going to rehab, because if you don't… well, I just don't know."

I stare at him. "What does *that* mean?"

He's quiet for a moment, the silence heavy between us. He finally looks down at Monica. "Mon, could you step outside? I need to talk to Abby alone."

"Of course, Sammy," she says softly. "I'll… um, see you later."

*Mon. Sammy.* Oh, and *later.* What does "later" mean?

Monica leaves our apartment, closing the door quietly behind her. She doesn't lock it though, although she could have, because I'm a hundred percent sure she's got our keys in her damn bag. She knew Sam would never agree to search her. She's smart, that one.

It's very quiet when we're alone. Despite everything, Sam looks really good in his shirt and tie. I wish we could put all this drug business aside and he would kiss me. But I'm beginning to wonder if he'll ever kiss me again.

"Abby." He takes one of my hands in his. That's promising. "Monica is gone now. It's just us. Please tell me the truth."

"Sam…"

"Please." He blinks a few times like he's trying to hold back tears. "I won't be angry with you. I want to help you, Abby. Just… be honest with me. I deserve that after all these years."

Wow. He's almost making me wish I were a meth

addict.

"I'm telling you the truth," I say. "Monica has been drugging me."

"Goddamn it," he says under his breath. He drops his head. "You understand the position I'm in, Abby, right? This isn't just a regular adoption. This is *my* kid."

"*Our* kid."

"No," he says. "*My* kid. This is half my DNA. *My* son. If you decide you don't want to do this or if Monica backs out, which she has every right to given the circumstances, I still have an obligation to be there for her. I'm not going to walk away from this."

I feel like I'm going to throw up. "What are you saying?"

"I'm saying," he says, "please think about this rehab program."

"Sam…"

"Think about it," he says again. He lets out a long sigh. "I've got to go to work. But we'll talk more about it later. Okay?"

I nod, not trusting myself to speak. I realize at this point I can't convince my husband I don't have a drug problem. I don't see any way out of this.

# CHAPTER 28

Nobody believes me about Monica. Nobody.

Sam adores her. He believes everything she says unquestioningly.

My ex-boss Denise thinks she's a prodigy. She's probably going to get my job soon.

I have to figure out some way to prove Monica isn't as great as she said she is. I need some sort of evidence of wrongdoing on her part. But what? Absolutely the only person she's targeted is me. Well, except for…

Gertie.

When my former assistant came to visit, she mentioned she felt like she had been pushed down the stairs. She claimed she was joking, but I'm not so sure. What if Gertie really was pushed down the stairs? What if Monica wanted to get her out of the way so she could take the role of my new assistant?

It's a long shot, but then again, it's not like I've got anything better to do today.

I find Gertie's home number in my cell phone. When I call her, the phone rings several times, and I start to get worried maybe Monica finished her off to eliminate any loose ends.

Wow, maybe I really am getting paranoid.

"Hello?" Gertie's voice shouts into the phone. When Gertie is on her cell phone, she seems unable to modulate the volume of her voice. It was something that used to drive me crazy about her, but now I miss it desperately. I'd take Gertie's shouting over Monica's clipped efficiency any day. "Who is this?"

"Hi, Gertie. It's Abby."

"WHO?"

That's another thing. Gertie can't seem to hear anything coming out of the phone. Which could explain why she shouts. "ABBY ADLER! FROM WORK! ABBY!"

There's a long pause. "Oh! Abby! It's so good to hear from you, dear!"

"Listen, Gertie," I say, "I was wondering if I could ask you a few questions?"

"WHAT?"

I grit my teeth. "Can we meet somewhere Gertie? I'll come to any restaurant you like."

"Oh, that's so sweet, but I just ate lunch, dear!"

"Gertie," I say patiently. "I just need to talk to you. Coffee, maybe?"

"Oh! Well, that would be lovely!"

I breathe a sigh of relief. It's a long shot, but maybe

Gertie remembers seeing Monica in the stairwell that day. I don't know if anyone at work will believe it, but maybe Sam will. I'm desperate to get him on my side. I'm not just being paranoid about Monica. I'm *not*.

———

Gertie selects a small coffee shop just down the block from her apartment. I arrive before she does and order myself a black coffee, although what I really want is a stiff shot of whiskey. Probably better not to get drunk in the middle of the afternoon though. Also, I suspect this coffee shop doesn't stock whiskey. They probably don't even have a liquor license.

I settle down at a small round table between a guy with a goatee typing furiously on his laptop, and an older woman who's staring wistfully out the window. I take a long sip of my black coffee, shuddering at the bitter taste.

Gertie arrives at the coffee shop a few minutes later, leaning heavily on her four-pronged cane. She is limping so badly, it makes me want to burst into tears. Prior to her spill on the stairs, Gertie was always bustling around the office, a little ball of energy. Her injury clearly took a lot out of her. I wonder if she'll ever be the same again.

When she makes it to our table, I get to my feet and we hug. Probably for far too long. Long enough that Gertie feels a need to comment: "Is everything all right, Abby dear? You seem so sad."

I take a deep breath, struggling not to cry. These are

the first kind words I've heard all day. "I'll be fine. How are you doing?"

"Oh, you know…" Gertie smiles and pats her puffy white hair. "Retirement has its benefits. I've been getting to spend more time with my little grandson. What a handful he is!"

"That's wonderful."

"We spent three hours yesterday playing with Legos!" she sighs. "I never thought I was capable of playing with Legos that long! They're actually sort of fun though. What a great idea for a toy. Although I'm not entirely sure how they managed to make so many movies about them. I mean, they're just blocks, aren't they?"

I force a smile. "Yes."

"Anyway, you're going to have your hands full with that new baby, Abby! I'm so happy for you."

A lump rises in my throat. *Don't cry. Don't cry, Abby.*

"And how's your husband Samuel?" she asks. "He was such a sweet man. He must be very excited too."

I know she thinks she's being polite, but I can't do this anymore.

"Listen," I say, "there's something I need to ask you."

"Of course, dear." Gertie places her wrinkled hand on mine. "What it is?"

I take a deep breath. "Do you remember the day you fell down the stairs at work?"

She winces. "Of course I do. It's hard to forget something like that."

I feel a stab of guilt. The last thing I want to do is dredge up bad memories for her. But I need to know. "You told me you thought someone pushed you."

"I didn't mean that though. It was just, you know, the usual pushing and shoving." She laughs lightly. "Show me a young person who *isn't* pushing or shoving!"

"If I show you a photograph," I say, "could you tell me if that person is familiar to you?"

Gertie never had the opportunity to meet Monica. If she recognizes the photo, then that means there's a chance Monica was in the stairwell that day. And maybe it will jog her memory about other things too.

Like that Monica was the one who pushed her.

I pull out my phone and bring up the one photo I've got of Monica, taken in the waiting room at our first OB/GYN appointment. I wanted to take a photo to commemorate the whole thing. In retrospect, it seems so stupid. Who knew it would all go so horribly wrong?

Well, aside from Sam, Shelley, my mother... well, everyone but me.

I slide the phone across the table to Gertie. Who then takes out her reading glasses. God, I forgot all about Gertie's reading glasses. She has this pair of purple-rimmed giant reading glasses that she always keeps stashed away in her purse. Whenever she's asked to read anything, she takes about five hours to pull out those stupid reading glasses. I'm beginning to remember how annoying Gertie used to be.

Finally she gets out her reading glasses and peers through them at the image on my phone. She squints a bit, then lifts the phone up in the air to get more light. Then she turns it around. After about sixty seconds, I'm ready to shake her.

"Well?" I say.

"She *does* look a bit familiar," Gertie admits.

"So you think you've seen her before?"

"Yes, I think I have."

My heart speeds up. "Do you think she's the person who pushed you down the stairs?"

Gertie looks up sharply. She pulls off her giant reading glasses and her eyebrows bunch together. "Abby, are you all right?"

"No!" And now I can't hold it back anymore. I really am sobbing. I had so much hope for this meeting, but that was stupid. How could Gertie remember something that happened a year ago, when she couldn't even remember you had to press "send" on the fax machine before a fax would go through? "I'm *not* all right. Somebody slipped drugs into my coffee at work and I got fired and my husband thinks I'm a drug addict and…"

Her eyes widen. She gawks at me for a moment, but then she pulls me in for a hug. "This is going to be okay, Abby. I promise you."

"No, it's not! How can it be okay?"

"Trust me," she says so convincingly, I almost believe it. "You're a good person, Abby. Everyone knows you didn't do anything wrong. It will all work out in the end."

While Gertie is hugging me, I hear a buzzing noise coming from my purse. I pull away from her embrace and find my phone in my purse. My eyes widen when I see the name on the screen.

Denise Holt is calling.

# CHAPTER 29

Why would Denise Holt be calling me? It doesn't make any sense. The woman already fired me. Does she want to fire me *again*?

No, it's probably something stupid. Like a complication with my final paycheck. Yet…

"Excuse me," I say to Gertie, who has a perplexed expression on her face. "I… I'm going to take this call outside."

I race out of the café with my phone, swiping to take the call just as I get outside. My heart is already racing. "Hello?"

"Abigail?" There's no mistaking Denise's clipped voice. I can only imagine her ice-blue eyes shooting daggers at me from across town. "This is Denise Holt."

"Yes," I say. "I know."

"Right," Denise says. Then she hesitates, which is very un-Denise-like. Denise never hesitates. She has never questioned any decision or thought she has ever had in her entire life. Or so she'd like the rest of the world to believe. "Listen, Abigail… I… we may have made a mistake…"

I almost drop the phone. A mistake? Denise Holt made a *mistake*? And she's *admitting* it?

This can't be real. It's got to be some sort of meth-fueled hallucination. I should pinch myself to make sure I'm not dreaming.

"All I know is I never took drugs, Denise," I say. "I swear on my life."

"Yes…" She heaves a sigh on the other line. "It's gotten a little more complicated than that, I'm afraid."

My breath catches in my throat. "How so?"

"Well," she says slowly, "I took Monica as my own personal assistant after you left, and… well, this morning I caught her going through my desk when I was out of the room. I couldn't believe my eyes."

"What did she say?"

"She said she was looking for tape, if you could believe that!" Denise snorts. "I didn't say anything, but the entire exchange made me incredibly uncomfortable. So while she was out at lunch, I searched her desk."

I almost laugh at the thought of Denise doing a search of Abby's little cubicle. Not that any of this is funny. "What did you find?"

"Well," she says, "the part that pertains to you was the prescription bottle."

I frown. "Prescription bottle?"

"She had a bottle of a medication called Adderall. I

looked it up and it's basically a form of amphetamine." She clears her throat. "Didn't Monica bring you coffee every morning? And she brought you your lunches too, didn't she?"

"Yes," I breathe.

Up until now, it was all just speculation. But it turns out, I was right. The drug test wasn't a mistake. Monica drugged me to make sure I'd get fired.

"This whole thing is an HR nightmare," Denise groans. "I don't know what we're going to do, given her pregnancy and your little arrangement with her. She could sue the pants off of us."

"Sorry," I mumble.

She's quiet for a moment. I hold my breath, wondering if she's going to give me one of her famous Denise Holt lectures.

"No, I understand," she finally says. "You were… you were going through a lot. And I… I might have handled it better. As your employer." She pauses. "And as your friend."

My shoulders sag. I would never have called Denise my friend in a million years. I *hated* her. But before our fertility struggles carved a wedge in our relationship, we were friends. No—more than friends. She was my mentor. She was the person I admired most of everyone I had ever met.

"Listen," she says, "I want to talk to you about this in person. We need to strategize how we're going to handle this situation, and your help would… well, I'd appreciate it."

"Yes, of course," I breathe.

"Could you come to the office tonight?"

"Sure. What time?"

"Eight o'clock will be fine—you know everyone will be gone by then." I can almost hear the smile in her voice. "Those slackers are always gone by seven."

I remember all the late evenings in Denise's office with a feast of Chinese food spread out along her desk while we worked. "That's for sure."

"So I'll see you tonight?"

"I'll be there."

Denise hesitates for one more moment before saying: "Don't worry, Abigail. We're going to make this right."

———

As soon as I got off the phone with Denise, I made excuses to Gertie and got out of the café. My mind was spinning.

Of course, maybe my mind was spinning because Monica had been slipping amphetamines into my coffee.

When I got home, I sent off a text to Sam: *We need to talk when you get home.*

He wrote back: *Okay.*

I wanted to relay to him everything Denise had told me, but not over the phone. I wanted to tell him to his face. Except by seven-thirty, Sam still wasn't home yet. I didn't know where he was. I didn't want to think about where he was. I figured I'd deal with him after my discussion with Denise.

I need him to believe me. More than anything.

It's nearly eight when I get to the office building, and most people have gone home for the day. It occurs to me for a moment as I hover outside the building that since I was escorted out by security, there may be some sort of note not to let me in. And on top of that, I'm not really dressed for work. I'm wearing a nice shirt and slacks, but it's not a typical Abby Adler power outfit.

Oh well. Here goes nothing.

I stride into the building confidently. Like I've said, confidence goes a long way. I immediately recognize Patrick from all my late nights at Stewart. He's the security guard on most nights—a gangly guy with an easy smile. I wait for him to challenge me, but instead he flashes me a big smile.

"Hello, Abby!" He waves to me. "Working late again, are you?"

"Yes, I am," I say.

He winks at me. "Well, don't stay *too* late."

I used to think Patrick had a crush on me, back before my self-confidence was shattered by the woman trying to steal my job and my husband. Maybe I can get it back though. Denise is finally on my side again for the first time in a very long time. I've got hope I might come out of this with my career and my marriage intact.

When I get up to the floor for Stewart Advertising, it's

very quiet. Everyone has gone home for the day, which is no surprise. As she pointed out, Denise and I were the only two people who regularly worked late. My heels click against the ground as I make the familiar journey to her corner office.

The door to Denise's office reads "DENISE HOLT" in shiny gold letters. I usually keep my door partially ajar, but Denise always keeps her door shut tight. So I knock.

No reply.

She wouldn't have left, would she? No, never. If there's one thing you can say about Denise, she's conscientious. She wouldn't tell someone to show up for a meeting and then flake. That wouldn't be like her at all.

On a whim, I try the doorknob—open. She probably went to the bathroom. I push the door open to wait inside.

Except Denise isn't in the bathroom. She's sitting at her desk, her head in her arms. Like she's napping or crying or something.

"Denise?" I say.

She doesn't answer.

What the hell is going on here? There's no way Denise is napping at her desk. I'd sooner expect a pig to go flying past the window. But why isn't she lifting her head? Why isn't she acknowledging that I'm standing in front of her.

"Um, Denise?" I say again.

No answer.

I approach the desk and put my hand on her shoulder, but she doesn't even flinch. I shake her this time, but instead of sitting up, she falls to the floor.

And that's when I see all the blood.

———

There's yellow tape around Denise's office, which has been cordoned off by the police that are now swarming the office. I'm sitting in somebody's desk chair, hugging myself, unable to stop shaking.

Denise is dead. I don't entirely know what happened to her, but when I rolled her over on the floor, trying to help her, I found her lifeless blue eyes staring into nothingness. I'm no doctor, but at that moment, I knew it was too late for an ambulance.

It probably sounds terrible, but for a moment, I considered making a run for it. After all the bad blood between me and Denise, the last place I wanted to be caught was at her murder scene. But Patrick had seen me come in—nothing would look guiltier than running. Also, there was the small matter of having her blood smeared all over me.

But more than all that, I couldn't leave her like that. Denise was my idol at one time. She had been trying to help me. I couldn't let her body lie there all night, rotting on the floor of her office. She deserved better than that.

"Mrs. Adler?"

It's the voice of a female detective, who told me her name but I promptly forgot it. She's standing in front of me, holding up a plastic bag containing a shiny, metal object.

"Yes?" I manage.

"Does this object look familiar to you?"

"Not really," I mumble.

"Could you take a closer look?"

I squint at the blood-soaked object inside the bag. It takes a second for me to make out what it is. It's a letter opener.

With the name "ABBY" engraved on it.

"That's mine!" I gasp.

Well, this is looking worse and worse. I'm starting to long for when my only problem was an alleged meth addiction.

The female officer goes back to talk to the others. I don't like the way they keep looking at me when they talk. And now they're pointing at me. Great.

Oh my God, what if they arrest me?

The female officer comes back over to me. My heart is pounding in my chest. This is so bad. "Mrs. Adler, we'd like you to come down to the station to answer some questions."

"Am I under arrest?" I croak.

Long pause. "No, we'd just like to ask you some questions."

"Should I…" I swallow hard. "Should I get a lawyer?"

"You can if you wish," she says. "But we're just going to ask you some questions. We'd like to find out who killed Ms. Holt as quickly as possible, so we'd appreciate your cooperation."

"Okay," I say dully. "I'll go."

"Is there anyone you'd like for us to call to pick you up at the station?" she asks.

"My husband," I say.

As I recite Sam's number, I can't even imagine what he's going to say to all this. It was bad enough when it was just drugs. Now there's a possible murder charge thrown into the mix.

It's obvious I've been set up. If there was any doubt about it in my mind, that letter opener confirmed my fears. Someone wanted me to be set up on murder charges. Someone who was worried Denise knew too much.

And I'm afraid that someone is going to get their wish.

# CHAPTER 30

At the police station, the female officer introduces herself again as Detective Sweeney. She gets me set up in an interrogation room, which, besides the name, isn't nearly as scary as it sounds. It's a small room painted sky blue with a metal table in the middle and a plastic chair on either side. I'd rather not be in here a long time, but it doesn't frighten me.

I sit down in one of the chairs and Detective Sweeney sits across from me. She has a pleasant face with a disarming smile, which I suspect might be the point. They're hoping I'll tell them something to incriminate myself. But I won't.

Because I didn't kill Denise.

"Mrs. Adler," Sweeney begins. She hesitates. "May I call you Abby?"

"Yes."

"Great. Abby." She flashes that disarming smile again. "I was hoping you could clear up a few things for me."

"Uh, okay."

She folds her hands in front of her. "You were fired by Ms. Holt yesterday, weren't you?"

I nod.

"What was the reason for your termination?"

I consider lying, but that would be stupid. It would be easy enough to find out the real reason. "I took a drug test that came back positive for meth. But it was a false positive—I don't take any drugs."

"I see." Sweeney nods, but something changes in her expression. "So given you were fired, why were you in the building?"

"Denise asked me to come by."

"For what purpose?"

"She said she thought someone had tampered with my drug tests and she wanted to discuss it."

Sweeney raises an eyebrow. "She called you and said that?"

"Yes."

"Did she say who she thought had tampered with the test?"

I hesitate for a moment before nodding. "Monica Johnson. My former personal assistant."

"I see. And why did she think Ms. Johnson tampered with the drug tests."

"She found a bottle of Adderall in Monica's... er, Ms. Johnson's desk. That's an amphetamine. She believed Ms. Johnson had spiked my coffee with it."

"Why was Ms. Holt searching Ms. Johnson's desk?"

I squeeze my hands together. "She told me she saw Monica snooping around her desk, and... I think she wanted to make sure she wasn't stealing stuff."

Sweeney cocks her head thoughtfully. "You know, Adderall is a medication prescribed for ADHD. Why did she jump to the conclusion that Ms. Johnson was poisoning you? Couldn't it have been a prescribed medication?"

"I... I'm not sure..."

"And are you aware," she continues, "that Adderall is very unlikely to result in a urine drug screen being positive for methamphetamines?"

I was not.

Sweeney doesn't wait for my response. She quickly jumps to an entirely new line of questioning, which makes me nervous the other line didn't go very well for me. "So you say Ms. Holt called you on your phone..."

"She *did* call me. I have the call in my history."

"Can I see?"

I nod and pull my phone out of my purse. At least I have proof of the call from Denise. I bring up my call record and hand it over to Detective Sweeney, who studies it thoughtfully.

"Did anyone else witness this call?" she asks me.

"No." I think about how I raced out of the café the second I saw Denise's name on the screen. "But she called me. You can see it on the screen."

"Right." Sweeney nods. "The question is, what did she say?"

"I told you what she said."

"Yes," she agrees. "You did."

What is *that* supposed to mean?

"And did Ms. Holt tell her suspicions about Ms. Johnson to anyone besides you?"

"Well, no," I admit. "I don't think so, at least."

"Don't you think that's odd though? If you believed one of your employees was poisoning another, wouldn't you speak to HR?"

My palms feel very sweaty all of a sudden. "Well, she thought it might be an issue because, you know… Monica is pregnant."

I know it will come out eventually, but I can't tell the detective that Monica is our surrogate. I can't even imagine how that revelation will make me look. I don't want to think about it. I'll deal with it when it happens.

"Now Abby," Sweeney says, "when is the last time you saw that letter opener?"

"A few weeks ago?" I feel my eyebrows bunch together. "I thought I lost it."

"Lost it?" She cocks her head at me. "Would you have taken it out of your office?"

"No. But… it wasn't in the drawer where I usually keep it. Maybe someone borrowed it."

Or stole it because they wanted to frame me for murder.

"Prior to your termination yesterday," she says, "how would you categorize your relationship with Ms. Holt?"

"Um, it was fine."

"Did you get along with her?"

"More or less." I'm finding it hard to swallow and I feel like I'm choking. "Everyone has their differences, right?"

She smiles at me. "That's true."

How long will it take for her to hear the story about the "bitch" email?

"Is it typical for Ms. Holt to stay at work that late?" she asks.

"Uh, yeah. Usually."

"Is the office usually otherwise empty at that time?"

"Mostly. That's why she wanted to meet at eight."

"Did you ask Ms. Holt if she would meet with you?"

I frown. "No, I told you. She asked *me*."

"So you didn't send her an email, requesting to speak with her?"

"No…"

My heart is pounding as Detective Sweeney reaches into the inside pocket of her jacket and pulls out a folded piece of paper. She carefully unfolds it and examines the contents. "So you didn't send Ms. Holt an email saying, 'I have information about you that could ruin you. If you don't want it to get out, I suggest you meet with me tonight at eight.'"

I stare at her. "No. I definitely didn't."

She pushes the printout across the table so I can look at it more carefully. I see the return email address at the top as my own, addressed to Denise. And then the words Sweeney just read to me. Threatening words. Words I never wrote.

Unless I'm going crazy.

"I didn't write that email," I say with as much conviction as I can muster.

"Would you give us access to your work email account, so we can look for it?"

"Yes, of course."

But I have a sick feeling what they'll find when they check my email. Because it occurs to me now that I'm not the only person with access to my email account. My former assistant also had access to my email. Monica.

I'm about to tell Sweeney this detail, but then she leans forward, as if to tell me something in confidence. She flashes me that disarming smile of hers. "Listen, Abby," she says. "I know it was very hard on you losing your job yesterday. That's devastating for anyone. And when something like that happens, people can do desperate things."

I freeze. What is she saying?

"I get it," Sweeney continues. "It's tough enough to find another job in this economy even without the drug accusations hanging over your head. And even if it wasn't their fault, you tend to blame the person who swung the ax."

"I… I didn't blame Denise…"

"Didn't you?" She raises an eyebrow. "I'm going to be honest with you, Abby. The evidence is overwhelming right now. You are going to go to jail for this—I guarantee it. But if you confess now, maybe we can work out a deal."

I stare at her. "I didn't kill her."

She gives me a pitying look. "I've been doing this a long time, Abby. I'm telling you what's going to happen. You seem like a good person who made a really bad mistake, and I want to help you."

"I didn't kill her," I say again.

"Now we both know that's a lie." Her eyes connect with mine. "If you confess now, I can offer you a deal. But the second you leave this room, that deal goes away. And when we arrest you, it will be for first-degree murder. That's life in prison."

I feel sick. I literally feel like I'm going to throw up all over this nice, clean table in front of me. She thinks I'm a murderer. All the police think I did this. And so will everyone else in the world.

"I want to speak to a lawyer," I say.

———

It's nearly midnight when I get out of the police station. They haven't arrested me, which I'm taking as a good sign. They must not have enough evidence, if that's the case. And maybe that's why they were pushing so hard to get me to confess. After Sweeney, another officer came in to talk to me, then a third after that. But I kept my mouth shut. I wasn't saying one damn word without a lawyer.

An officer leads me into the waiting room in the station, where there are two long rows of plastic uncomfortable-looking chairs. I'd imagine during the days that the chairs would be mostly filled, but right now, there are only a few people there, including one guy who looks like he's passed out drunk. In the middle of the second row, I see a familiar figure, slumped forward, his head in his hands.

Sam.

"Mr. Adler?" the officer calls out. "Here she is."

He lifts his head from his hands. There are purple circles under his eyes like the ones I had this morning. He doesn't smile when he sees me. He doesn't even look at me—not really. He struggles to his feet, fumbling with his jacket.

"I parked down the block," he says in a hoarse voice.

"Okay," I mumble.

I follow him wordlessly to his Highlander. I have no idea what they told him exactly, but by his reaction, it's clear he's heard a lot of the details. I wonder if they questioned him. If they did, I wonder what he told them.

*My wife has a drug problem. I tried to get her help, but she's refusing to admit she has a problem. She hated her boss and probably killed her.*

We don't say another word to each other on the entire walk to the car. When we get inside, I expect Sam to start up the engine, but instead, he drops his head against the headrest, his eyes glassy.

"Sam," I say.

He rubs his face with his hands. "What?"

I don't know what I want to say. I want to ask him if he thinks I killed Denise, but I'm afraid of the answer to that question. So instead, I say, "Did the police question you?"

He shakes his head no. "They just told me what happened. They wanted to question me, but I told them no. I'm not talking to anyone without a lawyer and I wish you hadn't either."

"Yeah," I breathe. "I didn't realize how bad it was till I was in there."

"We'll find you a lawyer tomorrow," he says.

I feel a twinge of hope. He's saying "we" will find me a lawyer. That means he's still on board. He's not packing up my belongings and throwing them out the window.

"I didn't kill her," I say. "I swear to you."

He doesn't say anything.

"I *didn't*. Do you honestly think I did?"

He shakes his head. "If you had asked me a few months ago, I would have said no. Definitely not. No way in hell. But now…"

"Sam!" Tears spring to my eyes. "You're saying you think I'm a murderer? You really think I'd do that?"

He's quiet for a moment. He rubs his face again. "No. I guess not."

My shoulders sag with relief. He believes me. "I think I was framed, Sam. Apparently, someone sent an email that—"

"I don't want to talk about it."

"But you need to know that—"

"I don't want to hear it right now." His Adam's apple bobs. "I just want to go home, okay? We'll talk about it tomorrow."

Silence fills the car. I don't say another word. Even though Sam claims he believes me, I'm not so sure. At the very least, there's doubt in his mind.

I always felt like Sam was a man who would stay by my side no matter what. Somehow, in eight short months, we've lost that.

# CHAPTER 31

"These charges are absolutely ridiculous. What you need is a good lawyer."

My mother, in stark contrast to my husband, is absolutely convinced of my innocence. So much so that she thinks if they do arrest me, the police will have a wrongful arrest lawsuit on their hands. My mother is very into lawsuits. Last year, she got a pants suit she didn't like from Saks Fifth Avenue and she called her lawyer to see if she could sue. (The answer was no. But she *was* able to return it. It's unclear why she didn't do that in the first place.)

We're sitting in the bistro a block away from my apartment building, where my mother is treating me to lunch. The place is packed from the lunch rush, but my mother slipped the hostess a bill of some denomination, and we got a table pretty quick. I'm glad for the low buzz of conversation in the restaurant, because I don't want anyone to overhear what we're saying.

"Sam already got me a lawyer," I say.

"Oh, did he?" she snorts. In her eyes, Sam is still that twenty-six-year-old kid who backed into her mailbox with his clunky old Honda and knocked it over. I'll never forget the crestfallen look on Sam's face when he did that—it was as if he knew that single act had cemented her dislike of him forever.

"The lawyer is really good," I say. And I add, because I know it will garner her respect: "He's costing us a bundle."

"You mean he's costing *you* a bundle," she corrects me, peering at me over the rim of her water glass.

"Sam and I don't think about our money that way."

She laughs. "Well, that suits him, doesn't it?"

"Stop it. You *know* Sam doesn't care about money."

"Abby, *everyone* cares about money."

I grit my teeth and scrunch up the napkin on my lap between my fingers. I'm not about to have a tantrum in this bistro, but it's tempting.

"So," my mother says, "tell me about this 'wonderful' lawyer Sam got for you."

I pretend like I didn't hear the scare quotes in her question. "He's been a criminal lawyer for thirty years. He has an incredible trial record. Sam says he's the best there is."

My mother isn't listening though. She's distracted by something across the room. I follow her gaze to where an attractive man in a pin-striped business suit and red power tie is seated alone at a table for two, his eyes pinned on his smartphone.

"What do you think of him?" my mother asks.

I raise an eyebrow at her. "What do you mean?"

The man straightens out the collar of his pin-striped jacket. Brioni, I believe. Pricy. He lifts his eyes and catches me staring, and my cheeks grow warm. Before I can look away, he winks at me.

"He winked at you!" my mother cries triumphantly.

"So?"

"So you should go talk to him."

I gape at her. "I'm not going to do that!"

"Why not?"

"Because I'm *married to another man*?"

"Yes, well, it's good to have a backup, isn't it?"

I wish I could say this is the first time my mother has said something like that since Sam and I tied the knot. I don't get it. And honestly, I'm sick of it.

"Why do you hate Sam so much?" I blurt out.

She blinks a few times, taken aback. "I don't hate Sam."

"Then why are you suggesting I date another man?"

My mother considers this question. She takes another sip from her water glass, still thinking it over. Finally, she says, "I always thought you could do better. You're wealthy, you're beautiful, and you have an amazing career. You could have had any man you wanted."

"But I wanted him. And he's been a great husband."

"Has he?"

"He absolutely has." I suppress the urge to pound my fist on the table. "And he got me a great lawyer. He's going to help me fix this terrible mistake."

"Well," my mother says. "I hope you're right."

# Chapter 32

"Fifteen years would be a gift, Abby."

The words of my attorney, Robert Frisch, echo in my ears. The walls of his office feel like they're closing in on me. Obama's smile in the photo is mocking me. This can't be happening. Fifteen years. No. No way.

"I didn't do it," I say for what feels like the millionth time.

Frisch sighs. He so clearly doesn't believe me. I know he's one of the best criminal attorneys in the city, but right now, I'd trade him for a newbie lawyer who at least believed my story. But nobody believes me. Sam doesn't. Frisch doesn't. Even Shelley, my best friend, isn't returning my calls.

And Monica... well, she's the only one who knows the truth.

She killed Denise and planned to pin the murder on me—the final nail on my coffin. It wasn't enough that she got me fired for the drugs she planted in my urine. It wasn't enough my husband texts with her morning and night. None of that was good enough for her. She wants me behind bars, where there's no chance I can take back what's mine.

"I think you should take the plea," Sam says. "This is your best chance."

"I'm not spending the rest of my life in jail for something I didn't do!"

"It's not the rest of your life."

Is he kidding me? "It's fifteen years!"

I'm thirty-seven now. In fifteen years, I'll be fifty-two. Any chance of becoming a mother will be gone forever at that point. My career will be gone. And my marriage…

Sam is staring straight ahead at Frisch's desk, refusing to look at me. If I go to jail, it's over between us. Some people make marriage work behind bars but we won't—he thinks I'm some kind of monster. If I take this plea bargain, he'll end up moving in with Monica. Maybe not right away, but eventually. The two of them will raise their son together. Happily ever after ending for both of them.

Maybe I should let them have their happily ever after. Sam stuck with me through all the infertility, even knowing it was all my fault. He's a good guy. He deserves to be happy.

But not with Monica.

Forget everything she's done to me, even though that's pretty damn hard to do. If I care about Sam at all, I can't let him get involved with Monica. She's a psychopath.

She's a *murderer*. The second he burns her toast, she'll probably stab him in the chest.

"Think about it, Abby," Frisch says to me. "This option won't be around forever. The police have a really solid case against you."

My head is spinning as I sit in Sam's car, riding back to our apartment. He has to go to work now, but I'm home for the day since I'm home every day now. He waits until we're halfway back before he says, "I think you should take the plea."

"Yes, I know what you think."

"Frisch knows what he's talking about."

I stare out the window, at the storefronts whizzing by. I'll miss this if I go to jail. If that happens, all I'd see around me are bars and the prison courtyard and guards and…

Oh great, now I'm crying.

"Abby." His voice softens. "Don't cry."

Nope. Still crying. I don't think I can stop.

It's funny because I'm not a crier. I never cry. Maybe once a year, I have one big epic cry just to get all my frustration out of my system, then I'm good for the next three-hundred-and-sixty-four days. I hate the loss of control I feel when I'm sobbing. But lately, I feel like a leaky faucet. All I do anymore is cry.

Sam probably thinks it's from the meth. And maybe it is.

"Listen," he says gently, "if you want to go to trial, then… let's do it. Okay?"

I wipe my eyes with the back of my hand. "If I went to jail, you'd move in with Monica."

"No, I wouldn't."

"You would."

"Stop it. I wouldn't."

I don't believe him though. I can see in his eyes that he's done with me. All the kindness is gone. Who could blame him—he thinks I did something horrible.

I wipe my eyes again with my shirt sleeve. I stare out the window again, trying not to think about what's likely going to happen in the next few days. Jail. I can't wrap my head around it.

I wonder if they'll handcuff me. Do they always do that? If I agree to go quietly, do they have to put the handcuffs on? I really don't want to be handcuffed. It seems so… medieval. Maybe I should just go to the police station and turn myself in. In fact…

Wait.

Holy crap.

"Sam!" I cry. "Stop the car!"

"What?" he says. "Why?"

Fortunately, he's already slowing to a stop at a red light. The second he comes to a complete stop, I unlock the door and leap out of the car. I don't even give him an explanation. At this point, I'm sure he's chalking this up to my erratic drug-fueled behavior. Whatever. This is more important than the possibility of Sam thinking slightly less of me. You can't get lower than zero, after all.

Or maybe you can. Negative numbers and all. Sam would know about that one.

Once I'm out of the car, I'm tearing down Broadway as fast as I can run. It's not easy because I'm wearing heels, but if I lose sight of this girl, I'll never forgive myself. This is my only chance to clear my name.

"Chelsea!" I cry out when I'm within earshot.

The girl doesn't turn. Her blond hair gets tossed by the wind as she strides down the street, clutching a Hot Topic bag. I'm getting seriously out of breath chasing her. Also, my heel gets jammed in a crack in the pavement and I nearly go flying, but I miraculously manage to right myself. It takes me another second, but I finally draw close enough to seize her arm.

"Chelsea," I gasp.

She turns, blinking her blue eyes in surprise. It's the same girl, all right. Same one who talked to me about what a wonderful, selfless person Monica Johnson is. And then her phone line inexplicably got disconnected.

"Excuse me?" she says.

"I…" I'm still gasping to catch my breath. Wow, I'm really out of shape. Good thing I'll have fifteen years to get buff in prison. Isn't that what people mostly do in prison? Work out and get tattoos of skulls? "I'm Abby Adler. We… we talked a while ago about Monica Johnson."

She blinks a few more times. "Who?"

*What?*

"Monica Johnson," I say again. "Your *roommate*."

She shakes her head at me, her brow furrowed like she's really trying to figure it out. And now I really think I'm losing it. Did I imagine the whole conversation? Was this entire thing a meth-fueled fantasy?

But then her eyes light up. "Oh! You're that lady who wanted the baby!"

I'm not insane. Thank God.

"So how'd it go?" she asks me.

"I'm assuming you don't live with Monica anymore."

"Uh…" She scratches her upturned nose with the hand not holding the Hot Topic bag. "The truth is…"

I raise my eyebrows at her.

She smiles crookedly. "Monica and I were never roommates. She just asked me to say we were."

*What?*

"So…" I narrow my eyes at her. "How do you know Monica?"

She shrugs. "We were sort of friends in college. Not really though. Mostly, I used to be close with her roommate."

"So why didn't she give me the number of her *actual* roommate so I could talk to her?"

She laughs so loudly, a few people on the street turn to look at us. "Oh, she wouldn't want you to do *that*."

My stomach churns. This was the whole purpose of Sam's plan to vet Monica—to find out if she was a wack job. But then she gave us all made up friends and family. I never tried calling her mother again, but now I wonder if the woman on the phone was even really her mother.

Maybe that's why Monica said she was a Red Sox fan. Because the story of her being from Indiana was total bullshit.

"So Monica's roommate didn't like her?"

Chelsea snorts. "That's an understatement."

"But you didn't like her either. Did you?"

"No, but…"

"But what?"

She hangs her head. "Monica paid me two-hundred bucks to say I was her roommate and that she was awesome."

Oh my God. This isn't a matter of Monica falling in love with Sam after she got pregnant. She was planning to deceive me all along.

Was Monica the one who pushed Gertie down the stairs? Was she trying to get my assistant out of the way so she could worm into my life?

What the hell? Why would she do that? Why *me*?

Chelsea—or whatever her real name is—sees the look on my face and flinches. "Hey, I'm sorry about this. I didn't think anything I said that day would make a difference one way or another. Also, I'm, like, a starving actress, and I *really* needed the money."

"It's not your fault," I say, even though I'm actually quite irritated with this girl for what she did. My whole life is destroyed over two-hundred bucks. Couldn't she have at least held out for five-hundred? "But I do need your help."

"Sure," she says. "Whatever you want."

# CHAPTER 33

The first thing I extract from Chelsea, whose real name is apparently Taylor Reynolds, is her real phone number. Sam doesn't believe one word I've told him about Monica, but maybe he'll believe another person. More than anything, I'm determined to convince him I'm innocent. I can't get through this if Sam isn't on my side.

The second thing Taylor does for me is she gets out her phone and places a call to Cynthia Holloway, the girl who used to be roommates with Monica. Taylor's information may be damning, but it sounds like Cynthia's got a whole lot of other things to say. If I could prove Monica is certifiably crazy, which I'm convinced she is, maybe I can save myself.

Maybe.

"I really appreciate this," I tell Taylor, as she searches for Cynthia's number in her phone. I remember the days when I would have all my friends' numbers memorized. Now I'm lucky I know my own number.

"No problem," she says, flashing me a smile. She's fascinated by the whole thing. I'm probably giving her a story she'll tell all her friends at happy hour tonight.

We stand on Broadway together, stepping aside to allow all the people by with their shopping bags. She locates the number and presses the green button for the call to go through. I stand there, a blister throbbing in my big toe. This is the last time I run in heels. If there's any chance I'm going to be doing hard labor, I need my feet in good shape.

No. Can't think that way. I'm going to fix this.

"Cynthia?" Taylor's face brightens. "Hey, it's Taylor! What's going on?"

Then—I swear to God—the two of them chat for like five minutes. Like I'm not standing right there next to Taylor, with my whole life hanging in the balance. I'm convinced she's forgotten I'm even there. When she launches into an account of everything she got at this great sale at Anthropologie, I finally tap her on the shoulder and clear my throat loudly.

"Oh!" Taylor says. "Hey, listen, Cyn, you remember Monica Johnson?"

Even from a foot away, I can hear the female voice on the other line say, "Oh *God*."

Taylor giggles. "So I've got this lady here who is having some major issues with Monica, and she was hoping to talk to you."

"In person, if possible," I add.

"Yeah, in person," Taylor says. She listens for a moment, then looks me over. "No, she doesn't look nuts. I mean, she seems nice. Sounds like Monica's done a number on her."

I wait, shifting between my feet. I hope this woman is willing to talk to me. If I can get an old roommate of Monica's to talk about how crazy she is, at least Sam might be willing to consider I could be right. I know it's hard for him to think ill of her, considering she's pregnant with his child, but he's got to see reason if there's enough evidence staring him in the face. He's *got* to.

Taylor pulls the phone away from her ear. "Cynthia says she's got to go to work in an hour, but she's available till then. She lives in the village."

I nod. "Give me her address."

———

It's a half-hour cab ride to Cynthia's apartment, and I make the driver speed the whole way, promising I'll foot the bill if he gets a ticket. Everyone I know seems to think Monica is a saint—it'll be vindication to meet someone else who recognizes she's not what she seems.

I hope that's what this is, anyway. If all Cynthia's got are stories about how Monica ate all the Frosted Flakes and didn't buy a new box, I'm going to be disappointed.

Cynthia lives in a brown brick building in the west village with fire escapes zig-zagging back-and-forth across the front of it. I find the last name Holloway and press the button. After a moment, a loud buzzer sounds off and the door to the building unlocks.

The apartment is on the fourth floor and it would be too much to hope for an elevator. I huff it up the stairs, the blisters multiplying on my poor toes. I ignore the pain though. I need to talk to this woman. She's the key to everything—I'm sure of it.

Cynthia Holloway turns out to be a petite girl around Monica's height with a funky black pixie cut and a nose ring. She smiles broadly at me when she opens the door, revealing a crooked incisor. "So you're a victim of Monica's, huh?"

"Abby," I say, as I struggle to catch my breath.

"Right." She nods, and glances at the back of the apartment. "My other roommate Ellie is here too. She wants to get in on dishing on Monica too."

"Are we doing Monica stories?" Another voice rings out from the back of the apartment. A girl with light brown hair swept into an effortlessly messy bun comes into view, wiping her hands on her skinny blue jeans. "Can I go first?"

Cynthia winks at me. "Why don't you have a seat, Abby?"

I sit down on a bean bag chair in the middle of their living room. I don't know if I've ever sat in a bean bag chair before. I gingerly settle down into the middle of it, clutching my purse in my lap, and I immediately sink down amongst the beans. I don't know how I'm going to get up from this stupid thing. It is pretty comfortable though.

"So how do you know Monica, Abby?" Cynthia asks me as she settles into a Papasan chair.

The whole story would take more time to tell than the time I've got. Better keep it quick. "I worked with her. Until she got me in trouble with our boss, and I lost my job."

The two girls exchange looks. "Sounds like a Monica special," Ellie comments.

I cough into my hand. "So, um, what was your experience like with her? She was… a difficult roommate?"

Cynthia laughs bitterly. "'Difficult' doesn't even describe it. She was a psychopath. Honestly, by the end, I was scared she was going to murder us in our sleep."

My heart skips in my chest. Okay, this sounds promising.

"She wasn't going to murder us in our sleep." Ellie rolls her eyes. I suppress the urge to tell her what I know. "But yeah, she was nuts."

"It was our senior year of college and I rented this place with Ellie and another friend of ours," Cynthia explains. "But at the last minute, our other friend decided to move in with her boyfriend. I put an ad in the college paper, and a week later, Monica was moving in."

"And…" I bite my lip. "She was… bad?"

"She was fine for a couple of weeks," Cynthia says. "And that's when the crazy started." She scratches at her knee thoughtfully. "She'd, like, accuse me of finishing her yogurt or something dumb like that. No big deal, right? I hadn't, by the way—I hate that stupid yogurt that makes you poop. But anyway, she'd get so angry. She'd start sifting through the trash, looking for the containers. And then she'd storm out, leaving the trash all over the floor. Tell me—who *does* that?"

"Oh, and she'd accuse us of going through her room." Ellie leans forward, getting into the story. "She put a lock on her door, so how could we, right? But she was convinced. She said she was putting a camera in there, so she'd know if we went in." She shakes her head. "She'd get *so* angry over it. I mean, we'd be sitting out here with some friends, and she'd just come out and start screaming at us at the top of her lungs."

"Not to mention that she called the police on us," Cynthia adds. "Repeatedly. Like, she thinks we're being too noisy, so instead of knocking on our door and saying to turn the music down, she'd call the cops and puts in a noise complaint. I almost had a heart attack when the police showed up at our door. More than once!"

"Or the building manager," Ellie says.

"Right." Cynthia shudders. "Oh, and she almost got *me* fired too. She called my boss and told him I was stealing office supplies."

Ellie grins. "Well, you *were* stealing office supplies."

"Yeah, but she didn't need to tell on me!" She pounds her fist on the coffee table. "Who does that, seriously? I confronted her about it, and she's all like, 'Stealing is wrong. You deserved to get caught.'"

"Crazy Monica."

"Yep, Crazy Monica." And then Cynthia's eyes widen. "And what about the smell?"

Ellie gasps. "Right, I totally forgot about that!" She turns back to me. "So here's the creepiest thing ever. She was dating this guy for a couple of months, but it was a sort of tumultuous relationship—like, they'd always be yelling at each other. We could all hear it through the walls. And then one day, they're having a really loud fight, and we hear this huge 'thump' and the fighting suddenly stops."

"And then," Cynthia continues, "over the next week, we start to notice this awful smell coming from her room. Like, really, really bad. Like something rotting in there. I was convinced she murdered the guy and he was rotting in her room."

"He totally wasn't."

"He was!"

If I were a neutral third party hearing this story, I would have said they were being ridiculous. But knowing what I know now about Monica, I bet she killed the poor guy. He's probably at the bottom of the Hudson River.

"We tried to look for him in the papers," Cynthia says. "But we didn't know his name, so… you know, we couldn't. But I'm sure she must have killed him."

Ellie rolls her eyes. "She was nuts but she wasn't a

murderer."

"Yeah, well, what about that stake we found under her bed?" Cynthia turns back to me. "After she moved out, I found this broomstick she'd whittled into a stake hidden under her bed. I swear, she was planning to impale both of us. We're lucky to be alive."

I chew on my lip, trying to decide if this is enough. Yes, it makes Monica sound loony, but it's nothing definitive. I don't know if these two flaky girls will be enough to convince Sam of anything. And that's the point of being here—to get him on my side.

"Oh, and the worst part," Cynthia says, "was Monica's mother. Oh my God, that lady was *so* creepy. And she was here all the freaking time."

"Yeah, she was the worst!" Ellie agrees. "Cyn, did I tell you about that night I left my room to get some water, and Monica's mother was just… like, standing in front of my door. It was two in the morning!"

"She was a good cook though," Cynthia says. "Did you ever try her brownies?"

"Um, no. I wouldn't eat anything that woman cooked! It was probably spiked with, like, cyanide!"

My head is spinning. I talked to a woman on the phone named Jean Johnson, who claimed to be Monica's mother. But I suspect Jean Johnson was just as fake as Chelsea Williams. "So Monica's mother *didn't* live in Indiana?"

"God, I *wish*," Ellie laughs. "Monica was originally

from Boston, but her family moved to the city, and they have a place uptown. Or at least, they did back then."

Monica's mother. Her *real* mother—not that phony I talked to last year, who probably had been reimbursed a couple of hundred bucks. I bet whatever her mother has to tell me will be a lot more convincing than the word of these two young girls.

"By any chance," I say, "do you have her parents' phone number?"

"No," Cynthia says. My heart sinks. "But I have their address. We had to forward Monica's mail there for a while."

Well, that would work.

# CHAPTER 34

My phone was buzzing inside my purse during the entire ride to Cynthia Holloway's apartment, but I was afraid to look at it. I ditched Sam while he was stuck in traffic and never told him why—he had to be freaking out. After I get out of Cynthia's apartment, I finally dare to pull my phone out of my purse. Unsurprisingly, there are six missed calls from my husband, as well as several screens full of text messages:

*Where are you?*

*Abby, where are you??*

*Can you tell me where you are?????*

*You jumped out of a moving car. Can you at least let me know you're okay???????*

It wasn't a moving car. We were stopped at a light, for God's sake.

I bring up Sam's number on the screen. I'm itching to hit the green button to place the call, but something stops me. If I tell Sam what I'm up to, he'll think it's nuts. Just like he thought it was nuts when I accused Monica of spiking my coffee. He'll say, "So what if Monica had a couple of roommates who didn't like her?" And he wouldn't be entirely wrong.

That's why I've got to get more information. The fact that Monica didn't want me to talk to her parents is a good sign they've got plenty of juicy details to clue me in on. I have a feeling Mom and Dad Johnson are the key to everything.

The Johnsons live all the way uptown, which means I need to hop in another taxi to get there. I can't call them and give any sort of warning I'm coming, but that could be a good thing. I'm sure they're not going to love me showing up to tell them I think their daughter is a murderer. Especially since it sounds like from what Cynthia and Ellie said, the fruit doesn't fall far from the tree.

The Johnsons' building is a modest-looking apartment building with a green awning and a doorman at the entrance. The lobby is dotted with marble tables and tacky bright red sofas. I smooth out the blouse I put on this morning for my visit with Frisch, and put on my best, professional smile.

"Excuse me," I say, using the same confident voice as I do with our clients. "I'm looking for the Johnsons."

I must look important because the doorman doesn't seem at all suspicious of me. "They're in 6B. May I ask your name?"

"Abigail Adler," I say. "Please tell them I'm their daughter's boss."

I had been debating in the taxi ride over what I should say. Ultimately, I decided to stick with something close to the truth. I have no idea how much Monica tells her parents. If her old roommates are to be believed, she may be very close to her mother. But I suspect most people would allow their daughter's boss upstairs, especially if she looks respectable.

I hold my breath, waiting for the doorman to call upstairs. Even if my story is solid, it's the middle of the afternoon—Monica's parents aren't even necessarily home. This could all be for nothing.

But fortunately, the doorman gets through to someone on the other line. He repeats what I told him, listens for a moment, then smiles and waves me upstairs.

This time there's an elevator, at least, but my stomach is doing somersaults the entire time I'm riding upstairs. I have no idea what to expect. Monica's parents could be anything from completely normal to batshit crazy. For all I know, Mrs. Johnson is going to pull a knife on me at the door. Probably not, but who knows?

So I'm not feeling great about the whole thing by the time I knock on the door to 6B. My knees are weak and I feel queasy.

Mrs. Johnson is the one who opens the door for me. She's an inch or two taller than I am, with plain brown hair swept back from her face into a simple ponytail and rimless glasses. She appears to be roughly in her fifties based on the patterns of lines on her face. She looks...

Very normal.

When she sees me, a weary look comes over her face. She peers at me over her half-moon spectacles. "Sorry, I didn't catch your name?"

"Abigail Adler," I say. "Monica works for me at an advertising agency."

She thrusts out her hand in my direction. Her handshake is firm. "Louise Johnson."

Just as I had suspected—Jean Johnson was another piece of fiction.

"So," Mrs. Johnson sighs, "what has Monica done this time?"

Her words catch me off-guard. Somehow I thought she'd be more defensive about Monica. "Um, could I come in?" I ask.

Mrs. Johnson lets out another sigh and waves me into the small apartment. It's modest—the living room is smaller than our own, and the furniture looks worn. I settle down on a threadbare sofa, and Mrs. Johnson sits about two feet from me. She doesn't offer me a beverage.

"Things had been going so well." Mrs. Johnson pulls off her glasses and rubs her eyes. "I hadn't heard anything about Monica in over a year. I thought...well, maybe the bad period was over." Bad period? "But I knew in my heart it was just a matter of time. People don't change."

I don't know what to say to that.

"So tell me," Mrs. Johnson says, "what has she done? What do you need?"

I hesitate, debating how much to say. It's very clear from speaking to Monica's mother that she has no idea about the arrangement we have together. "When is the last time you spoke to Monica?"

"Like I said, over a year." She shakes her head. "These days, my husband and I only intervene when it's required. Not like when she was younger."

"There have been some thefts at work," I say. Better not to mention the murder. I don't want to put this woman on high alert. "We're trying to get to the bottom of it."

"Monica's always at the bottom of it," she sighs. "Sorry, I shouldn't have said that. But it gets to the point where you just get exhausted by it all. Ever since she was a teenager…"

Mrs. Johnson stops, clearly realizing it would be in her daughter's best interest not to go on.

"Mrs. Johnson," I say, in my most professional voice. "I like Monica very much. She's an excellent employee. I want to help her. And it would help *me* to know what she's going through, because… well, it's all going to come out soon anyway."

I hold my breath, waiting to see if the woman will believe my lies. She narrows her eyes.

"An excellent employee?" Mrs. Johnson snorts. "*That's* hard to believe."

"It's true. She's very skilled and organized and—"

"Yes, but she's crazy!" The woman's brown eyes are wide, and for a moment, she looks a bit crazy herself. "I'm sorry if this hurts Monica, but it's probably in your best interest to let her go. Before she does even more damage. Take it from someone who knows."

"What do you mean?" I ask carefully.

"It's not entirely her fault, you understand." Mrs. Johnson's shoulders sag. "I think she tries to do the right thing. Well, sometimes, at least. But she's... well, the psychiatrists have disagreed on the diagnosis a bit..." Psychiatrists? "Most of them agree she has severe borderline personality disorder."

My mouth falls open. We checked out Monica's medical records so thoroughly. How did we miss a major psychiatric disorder?

"Borderline personality disorder?"

She nods. "Like Glenn Close in *Fatal Attraction*? That movie where she murdered the rabbit?"

Oh great. I picked a rabbit-murdering psychopath to be the mother of my child.

"The doctors have tried so many medications to try to help her," she goes on. Medication*s*? Like, plural? "But none of them have worked. Sometimes they help a little, but not enough to matter."

I flash back to Dr. Wong's office, when she asked Monica if she was on any medications. Monica said no. Of course she wouldn't be. She's *pregnant.*

"What makes her dangerous though," Mrs. Johnson says, "is her intelligence. She has a genius-level IQ on testing. Did you know that?"

"I... I'm not surprised."

"A math genius." I see a twinge of pride for the first time. "If she could focus, I bet she could win a Nobel Prize. But... well, that's out of the question now."

There's no Nobel Prize in math—a fact I know thanks to Sam. Instead, there's a Field's Medal, which is only given every four years and rarely given to mathematicians over the age of forty. Sam is realistic about his chances of winning one, especially now that he's thirty-eight, although he admits he was never a true contender. *I think my Field's Medal is out the window,* he sometimes jokes.

"You said she's dangerous." My heart speeds up in my chest. "Dangerous in what way? She seems perfectly normal."

"Oh, she's good at playing the part." She lets out a joyless laugh. "But don't be fooled. My husband and I started locking our doors at night, if you know what I mean."

I stare at her. "You did?"

"Oh yes." She stares off into the distance. "I knew she had problems but I never thought she was dangerous until her sophomore year of high school. She and her best friend Sandy were fighting over the same boy. Silly stuff, you know? But girls are so emotional at that age, and they had a falling out, and then..."

I get a horrible sinking feeling in my chest. I don't know if I want to hear the end of this story, but how can I not hear it? "Then what?"

She shuts her eyes for a moment. "Sandy went missing."

I squeeze my knees so tightly, my fingers hurt. I can't believe I invited this crazy person into my life. How could I have been so stupid? "Maybe she just ran away? Girls do that."

"No, she didn't run away." Mrs. Johnson's eyes grow distant, staring off into nothing. "They found her floating in the Charles River a week later."

I clasp my hand over my mouth. I think I'm going to be ill. I really do. "Mrs. Johnson, can you... can you tell me where the bathroom is?"

She points a long, skeletal finger down the hallway, and I grab my purse and run. I make it to the toilet in time, but all I can manage is a dry heave. I skipped lunch because I was so anxious about my appointment with Frisch, so there's nothing in my stomach.

My head spins as I straighten up and look in the mirror. My face is deathly pale and my black hair is disheveled. I run my fingers through my hair and splash water on my face, but none of it helps. I consider freshening up my makeup, but what's the point?

When I come out of the bathroom, Mrs. Johnson is fiddling with her phone. She looks up when she sees me, her expression flat. "I brought up an article about Sandy if you'd like to see it."

I hold up a hand. "No, uh… that's fine."

She raises her eyebrows at me. "Are you all right, Ms. Adler?"

I nod, attempting a weak smile as I sit back down on the sofa. "Yes. Of course."

She shrugs and puts her phone down on the table. "The murder was quite a big deal, as you'd imagine. And most everyone believed Monica had something to do with it, even though they could never prove it. That's why we left Boston and moved here."

A chill goes through me. Monica killed someone as a teenager and got away with it. Not only is Monica a killer, but she's apparently good at it. She was good at it when she was a teenager, so she must be great at it by now.

Mrs. Johnson leans back against the couch. "I'm sorry. I shouldn't have told you all this. I should be advocating for Monica—I know. I used to see a therapist myself, and all we'd talk about would be Monica. Monica, Monica, Monica…"

Sounds like what I'd be talking about if I had a therapist.

"Can I ask you a question, Mrs. Johnson?" I say.

She nods. "Of course."

"How did you lose touch with Monica?"

"Oh." She shakes her head. "We started fighting over the affair. That was about three years ago. And things just deteriorated from there."

"Affair?"

She rolls her eyes. "She started having what I thought was a quite ill-advised affair with her math professor in college. I told her so, but she didn't want to hear it."

Her words make me freeze up. "Math professor?"

"Oh, yes." She nods. "Well, you should have seen the guy. He was very attractive—I almost couldn't blame her. But of course, he was quite a bit older than her. And married, of course."

"Married…?" I swallow a lump in my throat. "Where did Monica go to college again?"

When Mrs. Johnson names the university where my husband teaches, it's like a punch in the gut. No. *No.* It couldn't be.

*It couldn't be.*

"The professor was clearly taking advantage of a very young girl," she goes on. "But Monica didn't see it that way. She was absolutely in love, and she took all my criticisms of him as a personal attack."

I bunch up my skirt with my sweaty fists. "You don't… do you remember his name?"

"Steve," she says thoughtfully. She frowns. "No, that's not right. Simon? No…"

"Sam?" I squeak.

She snaps her fingers. "Right. Sam. That was it. I'd never seen her so infatuated with a man before. Apparently, they were *in love.* Can you imagine?"

I can't even pretend she's not talking about my

husband. A math professor named Sam? There's no way this is a coincidence.

"Do… do you know what happened with them?"

She shakes her head. "As I said, our relationship deteriorated after that. I have no idea what she's been up to. I imagine she moved on when she couldn't get him to leave his wife. Or else maybe she got him fired. It would serve him right."

Or maybe…

Maybe the two of them figured out a way to finally be together.

# CHAPTER 35

Sam and Monica are having an affair.

The timeline Monica's mother gave me means the affair has been going on for *at least* three years. Three years of him sneaking around behind my back—easy enough to do with his flexible schedule and my long hours. That ratty couch he has in his office at the university was probably a great place for him to hook up with her.

It seems impossible in some ways. Sam has been my rock for the last ten years. But at the same time, some parts of it make so much sense. After all, he's had attractive undergrads throwing themselves at him for years—he's not made of stone. It's understandable he would have cracked at some point. Well, not understandable. But *conceivable*. This thing he had with Monica was surely not his first dalliance.

My mother was right—he's much too good-looking. What a mistake.

Sam always seemed like he loved me for me. If

anything, he always seemed to resent the fact that I had so much money—he never let me spring for things we could afford, like a spot in the parking garage. Then again, he loved the condo that we could never have afforded without my money. So in summary, he clearly didn't *just* love me for me.

And if he really wanted a child, it must have been frustrating as hell for him to look at all those young, fertile girls in his classes and know any one of them could give him the baby I couldn't. I'm sure that's what Monica pointed out to him when they were first together. When they were hatching this diabolical plot.

Janelle—the girl who had promised us her baby—never seemed like she would back out. She was gung-ho on giving us the baby. But now that I think of it, I never spoke with her. Sam told me she had backed out, and that was that. I trusted him.

And of course, Sam was the one who did the background check on Monica, which I'm sure he never actually did. He was the one who gave me the numbers for "Chelsea" and Monica's "mother." He claimed to have checked everything out. Yeah, right.

I'm sure Sam and Monica had a lot of fun plotting to keep me from her OB/GYN appointments. Messing with the times in my calendar—either one of them could have been responsible for that. Or spiking my food with drugs—that could have been a joint effort as well. Oh, and the crystals of meth that Sam "found" in my drawer—that solves *that* mystery.

That letter opener that killed Denise... that was a present from Sam. I thought it was a sweet and thoughtful anniversary gift. But as it turns out, he was providing me with a murder weapon.

And now Sam is pushing to get me to plea bargain. Who knows what he told Frisch to get him to advise me in that direction. All he wants is to get me out of the way with as little cost as possible. And then he can finally be with Monica.

There's only one problem.

If Sam did all that, he's not just a jerk. He's not just a cheating husband. He would be an outright psychopath. I mean, he could have divorced me if he wanted. It would have been rough and he would have lost out on my money, but it's not like he's some unemployed loser—he could have supported himself post-divorce. Even if he didn't personally kill Denise, setting me up on murder charges is the work of someone seriously disturbed.

I've known Sam for over a decade. Yesterday I would have told you I know him better than anyone else in the world. I don't think he's like that. I'd never think he'd be capable of something like that.

Then again, you can't underestimate the influence of an evil woman. And my big bank account.

And sex. That's a pretty big influence too.

I walk home from the Johnsons' apartment to clear my head. When I get back to the apartment, the first thing

I do is go through Sam's dresser drawers and his closet. I don't know what I'm looking for exactly. Lipstick stains that don't belong to me? Love notes from Monica? Monica's lavender-scented perfume clinging to his boxers? I have no idea. Whatever I'm looking for, I don't find it. All I find are shirts and pants and underwear, all of which smell like our laundry detergent and a little like his aftershave.

After I complete my exhaustive search of our bedroom, I collapse onto our sofa and sob. Yes, I'm crying yet *again*. I can't believe my husband would do this to me. I *love* him. I thought he loved me. When he held my hand that day in front of the judge, looked into my eyes, and told me he would love me till death did us part, was that all a lie?

I remember the way he said it. So seriously. The way he was so serious about everything in our relationship. Like once he said those words, he meant them with his very soul.

Shit.

I reach for my phone. I bring up my list of Favorites and see Sam's name topping the list. I put him there after our third date. But I can't call him now. I'm not ready to confront him yet. Instead, I press Shelley's name.

It rings three times and I'm certain she's not going to pick up. She's been avoiding me since Denise's murder, which can only mean she thinks I did it. But then I hear her voice on the other line. She sounds subdued, but at least she answered.

"Hi, Abby." Her voice is wary. "How are you doing?"

Against my will, my eyes fill with tears again. "Shelley, can you please stop acting like I'm a murderer?"

There's silence on the other line. My stomach twists as I wait to hear what she's going to say. I don't think I can take being rejected by one more person I care about.

Finally, she lets out a sigh. "I'm sorry, Abby. It's just... well, you have to admit, it looks bad."

"You think I don't know that?"

"And you hated Denise more than anyone..."

"I didn't hate her," I say honestly. "We just... we had a falling out. But I didn't hate her." I pause. "And anyway, there's a difference between hating someone and stabbing them with a letter opener."

Shelley lets out a strangled laugh. "Yeah, I guess that's true."

"Listen," I say, "is there any chance you could meet me for coffee? I really need to talk to you."

"Sure, Abby. Just tell me when and where."

———

It takes about half an hour to fill Shelley in on the entire story from beginning to end. By the time I finish, culminating in my visit to Cynthia's apartment, her mouth is hanging open. I don't know if she's shocked or if she thinks I'm nuts. The former, I hope.

"Wow," she breathes. "That's..."

I hang my head, staring into the depths of my mug of coffee. "I know. You always used to say Sam was a little too perfect. Guess you were right."

"Well," she says thoughtfully, "he wasn't *that* perfect. He was *nice*. But…"

I frown. "But what?"

"Well, he was boring sometimes, wasn't he?" She takes a sip of her foamy drink. "I mean, sometimes he was fine, but other times, you'd ask him some innocent question, and he'd turn it into some big mathematical problem. Like that time we were getting soft-serve ice cream and I told him to be careful not to fill it too high because it would fall, and he started trying to calculate to what height you'd have to fill the cone before it would tip over."

I smile to myself. Shelley got so pissed off when he got out his pen and started making calculations on a napkin at the yogurt place. "Monica would probably love that."

"And the math jokes? Ugh."

"She likes those too." I squeeze my coffee cup so hard, it burns my hand. Monica is so perfect for Sam in so many ways—I can't even blame him for falling for her.

No, that's not true. I can blame him. Cheating asshole.

I stir the coffee listlessly with my spoon. "So you think it's really true? About Sam and Monica?"

Shelley hesitates. "Honestly?"

"Of course honestly!"

"Yes. I do."

My heart sinks. Shelley knows Sam very well, and if she believes it could be true, it's a bad sign. "Really?"

"Well," she sighs, "I don't know. There was always something about him I couldn't put my finger on…"

"You never said that before!"

"I don't know. I thought it was all in my head."

My phone buzzes within my purse. I pull it out and see a text message from Sam:

*Where are you? I think we should talk.*

I look up and Shelley has her eyebrows raised. "Was that Sam?"

I nod. "He wants to 'talk.'"

She takes a sip of her coffee, peering at me over the rim of the glass. "Are you sure it's safe to be in the apartment with him?"

"What do you mean?"

"I mean," she says, "if he and Monica plotted to kill Denise, he's capable of anything. What if he and Monica are in the apartment right now, armed with a knife and duct tape?"

"Oh my God, he wouldn't do that!"

"Wouldn't he?"

I look down at the text message from my husband. I don't know what to think anymore. I hesitate before typing back:

*I'll be out late tonight. Let's talk tomorrow.*

# Chapter 36

Shelley and I end up staying out very late. After coffee, we go to a restaurant to grab dinner. And after that, we go to a bar and have a few drinks. Well, more than a *few*, if I'm being honest. I keep telling myself that I need to stop, that it's more important now than ever to have a clear head, but alcohol is the only thing that numbs the pain of Sam's betrayal. By the time I stumble home, it's after midnight and all the lights are out in the apartment.

I creep into the dark bedroom, swearing softly as I trip over one of Sam's shoes that he left lying in the middle of the room. He's *always* leaving his shoes in a place where I can easily trip on them—it used to drive me crazy. How hard is it to throw your shoes in the closet, for God's sake?

I remember when that used to be the worst of our problems.

Sam is passed out in bed. He's wearing an undershirt and boxers, and has thrown the covers mostly off him in his sleep. That's another thing he always does. He starts out with two covers neatly covering him, then within an hour, ends up coverless.

His glasses are on the nightstand next to the bed, and he's breathing deeply in an almost-snore. He's got that five o'clock shadow, and as I look down at his features, it's hard to blame Monica for falling for him. I couldn't resist him either when we first met. I still can't. Even now that I know the truth.

My eyes fall on his cell phone, which is plugged in on the nightstand. He told me his phone password and I don't think he's changed it. Presumably, I should be able to get into his phone. And then I'll see what he's been talking about with Monica all this time. I know I said I didn't want to violate his privacy, but that was before there were murder charges involved.

I have to know the truth.

I snatch the phone from the table before I can change my mind. I punch in the six numbers that make up Sam's code, and to my surprise, the phone unlocks.

I quickly click on the icon for text messages. Monica's name is right at the top—he's made no effort to hide it. I click on their texting thread, reading the last few lines of their back-and-worth.

Sam: *I really don't know what to do about Abby. This is bad.*

Monica: *I know.*

Sam: *She wouldn't come home tonight. So that plan is*

*off.*

Plan? What plan? What had he been planning if I had shown up tonight like I was supposed to? Did it involve duct tape?

"What are you doing?"

I nearly drop the phone. Sam has woken up and is peering at me through the darkness. In the light of his phone, I can make out his brown eyes. My heart starts to race in my chest.

"Um," I say.

He frowns. "Is that my phone?"

"Yes…"

He sits up in bed, blinking at me as he slides his glasses back on. "Are you snooping through my phone?"

There's no point in denying it. It's painfully obvious what I'd been doing. I should have at least taken the damn phone in the other room instead of looking at it one foot away from him—what the hell is wrong with me? I'd be the worst spy in history. "I… I guess so."

"Why?" He sounds genuinely baffled.

He doesn't know what I know. He thinks I'm still completely in the dark. I hesitate, not wanting to give away my hand until I have more information. But in the end, I can't help myself. "Are you having an affair with Monica?"

His eyes grow huge. He gapes at me for a moment, then he stands up from the bed and yanks his phone out of my hand. He stands there for a moment, and I'm suddenly aware of how much bigger he is than I am. I wouldn't have called Sam a "big" guy, but he's pushing six feet—a full six inches taller than I am—and he's got tight muscles standing out in his arms from all those hours in the gym. As he stands over me, his eyes darken and I take a step back.

If he wanted he could throw me across the room like a rag doll. He could do whatever he wants to me.

But instead, he yanks his pillow off the bed and pushes past me.

"What are you doing?" I ask.

"I'm going to sleep on the couch," he says. "I don't want to share a bed with you right now."

"Oh," I mumble.

As he gets to the entrance to our bedroom, he hesitates and turns to look at me. "I don't even know you anymore, Abby," he says.

"Likewise," I say.

He narrows his eyes at me. "Also, you smell like whiskey."

Well, that could be accurate.

"Good night," he says, as he slams the door shut behind him. If he wasn't having an affair before, I think I've remedied that.

But on the plus side, at least he hasn't duct-taped me to a chair.

# CHAPTER 37

I sorely regret my alcohol intake last night when I wake up the next morning with a throbbing headache and a mouth that tastes and feels like sandpaper. I roll over in bed and see the empty spot next to me. It's the first time in our entire marriage that Sam went to the couch to sleep. I have a bad feeling it won't be the last.

While I'm lying in bed, the doorbell chimes sound throughout the apartment. I rub my eyes, wincing at the noise. I can't even imagine who would be coming here on a weekday morning. I'm certainly not expecting anyone.

Oh my God, is it the police coming to arrest me?

My heart is slamming in my chest as I race out to the door in my bare feet. I lean in to look through the peephole, and I nearly faint with relief when I see my old assistant Gertie standing there. She's clutching a shopping bag from the grocery store in one hand, her cane in the other, and beaming at the door.

I fling the door open and her face breaks out in a

smile when she sees me. Well, until she gets a closer look at me. It's disturbing the way her eyes widen and she takes a step back. I wish I had checked a mirror first before I ran out here.

"Abby!" she gasps. "You look like you haven't slept in weeks."

No, I'm just hungover. But I don't say that. "Yeah, it's been rough lately."

"Well, that's why I'm here!" She holds up the shopping bag. "You were so sad last time I saw you. I wanted to make you some breakfast."

"That's really sweet, but…"

Apparently, Gertie is not taking no for an answer. She pushes past me and quickly makes herself at home in our kitchen. Within seconds, she's running water and clanging pots.

"Can I do anything to help?" I ask.

She waves me away. "Of course not! You go, um… freshen up."

I can take a hint.

I stumble in the direction of the bedroom to check out the damage. I almost gasp when I see the circles under my eyes and my hair sticking up in defiance of gravity. When I was in my twenties, I could throw back a bunch of drinks and still look gorgeous in the morning, but not so much now. I run a brush through my black hair, and dab on some makeup.

There. Better.

When I return to the kitchen, I smell frying eggs, which makes my stomach growl in spite of my semi-hangover. It reminds me of Sam's attempt to cook an omelet for breakfast a few months ago. He put too many eggs in the pan, and the center of the omelet was completely raw while the outside was dark brown. We nicknamed it "Salmonella Surprise." We laughed a lot that morning. (And had corn flakes for breakfast.)

I can't believe Sam is sleeping with Monica. How could he?

"Have a seat, Abby dear," Gertie says. She's wearing Sam's "I ate some pie" apron and moving eggs around the frying pan. She picks up the pan and scrapes the eggs onto two plates. She brings my plate out to the dining table, then limps back to bring out a glass of orange juice. "Breakfast is served!"

I don't know if I'm hungry, but I don't want to seem ungrateful so I sit down. At the very least, I'm incredibly thirsty, so I down the orange juice in three big gulps. It makes my pounding headache feel ever so slightly better.

I dig into the eggs a little more reluctantly, but after the first bite, I'm shoveling them into my mouth. They're actually really good. Much better than Salmonella Surprise.

"What do you think?" Gertie asks, grinning at me across the time.

"You need to show my husband how to make this," I say. Although I suspect Sam will never try to make me eggs ever again. Those days are over.

"I'd be happy to." Gertie winks at me, and I can't help but notice that up close she doesn't have as many wrinkles around her eyes as I'd expect her to. I always thought of Gertie as pushing seventy, but now I think she's likely closer to sixty. It's a shame that she hurt her hip so badly at such a young age. I still wonder if Monica was responsible—I'll probably never know the truth.

I've nearly cleaned my plate of delicious eggs when the doorbell rings again.

Gertie looks up from her own plate of eggs. "Are you expecting someone, Abby?"

I shake my head no. Maybe this time it really is the police. I wipe my mouth with the napkin Gertie brought me, then get to my feet to check the door. When I see Monica standing in front of the door, I nearly pretend not to be home.

I don't want to be alone with Monica. Mrs. Johnson's terrifying stories are still ringing in my ears. I don't trust that woman for a second. She almost certainly killed Denise in cold blood.

But then again, Gertie is here. She wouldn't try anything in front of a witness.

Would she?

I turn the locks on the door and crack it open, but keep the chain in place. Monica looks stunning in a bright red dress, with her black hair silky and loose around her shoulders, but my eyes are immediately drawn to her belly. God, she's gotten huge. She's got to be ready to have the baby any day now.

"What are you doing here?" I snap at her.

"Could you please let me in?" She clutches her belly with both hands. "We need to talk."

"Oh, do we?"

She hesitates. "Sam asked me to come here and speak with you."

"Who is it?" Gertie calls from the dining table.

I stare through the crack at Monica, who looks like she's just struggling to stay upright at this point. Monica might be dangerous at her worst, but I don't think she is right now. I could probably take her, even if she had a knife. Or a letter opener. And anyway, Gertie is here—it would be two against one.

"Fine." I close the door, unhook the chain, then throw it open for her. "Come on inside."

Monica waddles into the apartment. Well, she sort of waddles. Even though she's very pregnant, her gait is not entirely ungraceful. I wonder what Sam thinks of it all. I'm sure he thinks she looks incredibly sexy. He's clearly having sex with her, because he and I haven't had sex in a month.

Monica notices Gertie sitting at the dining table and stops short. "I didn't realize you had company."

"Oh!" Gertie struggles to her feet. "I could go if you'd like, Abby."

"No," I say quickly. It makes me feel safe that Gertie is here, even though she's an old woman with a cane. "Please stay."

Gertie glances at Monica, hesitating. Maybe it's selfish of me to ask Gertie to stay, especially if Monica is the one who pushed her down the stairs. I don't want to put Gertie's life in danger. But no, it will be fine. Monica won't try anything with both of us here.

"I'll tidy up in the kitchen," she finally decides.

Monica settles into one of the chairs while Gertie hobbles into the kitchen, out of earshot. Monica flips her black hair over her shoulder, and once again, I catch a glimpse of her pale roots. Her dark eyes meet mine and I shudder involuntarily.

"Sam had an early class this morning, but I promised him you and I would have a heart to heart." Her smile doesn't touch her eyes. "Things have gotten a little out of control, don't you think?"

I stare down at my plate of eggs. "I don't know what you mean."

"I don't have to tell you that your behavior last night was very upsetting to Sam, Abby." She clucks her tongue against the roof of her mouth. "Searching through his phone? Not very classy."

I lift my chin. "I had just cause."

She's quiet for a moment. "Yes," she finally says. "I suppose you did."

Her answer doesn't make me feel any better. "What do you mean by that?"

"I think you know the answer to that," she says

quietly.

I raise my eyes. "What?"

"Abby," she says. "It's over."

I stare at her. "Excuse me?"

"You and Sam. Your marriage. It's over."

The orange juice and eggs in my stomach threaten to come back up. "What are you talking about?"

"Think about it, Abby." She gives me a pitying look. "You're a mess. *Look* at you. You're a drug addict. You're about to be arrested for *murder*." She shakes her head. "Sam and I feel it would be best for you to find another place to live, so we could live here and take care of the baby."

With those words, she puts her hand protectively on her belly. That was the baby I was supposed to raise with Sam. Now he'll still raise the child, but I'll be out of the picture.

"I…" I look down at my empty plate, feeling ill. "I'd like to hear it from him."

"Sam doesn't have the heart to tell you. This is very difficult for him."

"Oh, really?"

She snorts. "Honestly, you never should have been with him in the first place. You're hardly even attractive, and intellectually—well, there's no comparison. You don't know real numbers from the *Real Housewives of Orange County*."

Yes, I do. I know what real numbers are. They're all

numbers that are… well, real. Like, not imaginary.

I better not say that though. I could be wrong.

"Sam married you for money," she says. "Your trust fund. Pure and simple. And now you've outlived your usefulness."

Is she right? Did Sam really just marry me for my money? I wouldn't have believed it if someone told me that a year ago. But now…

There's a buzzing sensation in the back of my skull. I shake my head to clear it, but it doesn't go away. I look at Monica, and for a second, I see two of her. But then when I blink, she becomes one again. I rub my face.

Monica frowns. "Are you okay?"

"I…" I squeeze my eyes shut, then open them again. "I feel sort of… dizzy."

She looks down at the plate of eggs in front of me, then she leans back in her seat to glance into the kitchen. She calls out, "Was it in the eggs?"

Gertie comes out of the kitchen, drying her hands on one of my hand towels. Weirdly, she's not holding her cane, even though she barely seemed able to take a step without it when she arrived. "No," Gertie says. "It was in the orange juice. She drank it about ten minutes ago."

My mouth falls open. "Gertie?"

"And you put the whole bottle in there?" Monica asks.

"Every last pill."

Monica smiles at Gertie—this time a genuine smile. "Thanks, Mom," she says.

# CHAPTER 38

My head is spinning. I don't know if it's from whatever was in the orange juice or the fact that Gertie and Monica are suddenly co-conspirators, and possibly even mother and daughter. Is this a dream? Am I hallucinating this? It certainly can't be real!

"You..." I make my gaze focus on Gertie, which is becoming increasingly difficult. "You're Monica's mother?"

"Oh, you're quick," Gertie laughs. "Maybe you *are* smart enough to be with Sam."

"But," I sputter. "I *met* Monica's mother. I was at her apartment the other day. She... you're not her."

Monica sneers. "That was my *step*mother, Louise. How could you think *that* was my mother? She's nothing like me!"

I look between Monica and Gertie, and now I finally see it—the resemblance. It's in the eyes and the chin. But I'm starting to get the feeling there's more of a similarity than just the superficial. I remember what Cynthia said, about Monica's "crazy mother" always showing up.

"I should thank you, Abby," Gertie says, her eyes glinting. "When Sam first came to work to see you and he told me he was a math professor at the same school my daughter was attending, I told her right away this was someone she needed to get to know. Didn't I, Monica?"

Monica nods. "I signed up for his class the very next semester. And… well, my mother was right, as usual. Sam and I fell in love instantly."

"After I engineered my early retirement, I told Monica just what to say to get hired," Gertie says proudly. "I told her to mention the fiber yogurt commercials and you'd be falling over yourself to hire her."

They played me like a violin. A wave of dizziness washes over me, and I have to grip the table to keep from falling out of my seat.

"I knew how desperate you were for a baby," Gertie continues. "After you managed to arrange that adoption, I was worried you'd pin down Sam permanently, but… well, we found a way to take care of that. And after the adoption fell through, you were willing to do… well, anything. And if you had any doubts, I knew I'd be able to dispel them when we talked on the phone."

My vision blurs for a moment, and I blink until it comes back in focus. "On the phone?"

Monica's lips curl into a smile. "You asked to speak with my mother." She nods her head in Gertie's direction.

"So you did."

The woman with the out of state area code was Gertie. How could I have failed to recognize her voice?

"But then Denise figured you out," I say. "So you had to get rid of her."

Monica snorts. "Please. Denise didn't figure me out. I'm so much smarter than her—than either of you. I *wanted* her to catch me rifling through her desk. Then I took a long lunch so she could search my cubicle and find those pills."

"But… why?"

"Because I knew she'd call you." She rolls her eyes. "You might not have known this, but Denise thought the world of you. Whenever you weren't around, it was always, 'Well, Abigail does it this way, so why can't you?' Or, "Abigail never leaves early—why are you going home to your family?' I could tell she regretted what happened."

Hearing her say those words about Denise is a jab in the chest. Denise never hated me. Even when she was disappointed about my life choices, she still thought I was one of her best employees.

And Monica murdered her for it.

"Those Adderall were completely legal, by the way," she adds. "Any police officer could confirm that. And they're not what made you fail your urine test. That was straight-up meth."

Monica has thought of everything. Her stepmother was right—she really is a genius.

"Why are you doing this?" I manage.

My head is swimming, but at least I'm still conscious, so that's something. The full effects of the pills haven't hit me yet. Maybe I can make myself throw up. I feel like that might happen anyway. But in case I can't, I'm hoping she'll at least tell me what she drugged me with.

"Isn't it obvious?" Monica says.

"No," I say. "You've already set it up so I'll be in jail for the next fifteen years. Why kill me?"

"This is so much cleaner." Monica folds her hands together and smiles as if pleased with herself. "You're depressed about everything you've done and don't see a way out, so you overdose on the entire bottle of your sleeping pills."

My sleeping pills. Damn. No wonder Sam wanted me to get a refill so badly.

I wiggle my ankles, noting my legs still feel intact. Could I possibly make a run for it? Monica is pregnant, for Christ's sake. And Gertie is—well, she's in better shape than I thought. But still. Maybe I could do it.

"We need to tie her up." Gertie's eyes are narrowed at me. She must know what I'm thinking. "I don't want any chance of her trying to make a run for it."

"No." I grit my teeth. "You're not going to tie me up. I won't let you."

Monica laughs. "Oh, I think you will."

Monica rifles around in her purse hanging off the edge of the chair. My mouth drops open when she pulls out a handgun. A *gun*. She doesn't point it at me, but just its presence makes me freeze. It looks so *ominous*.

"We had a firing range right by my house growing up," she says casually. "I'm actually quite a good shot. Not that I'd need to be at this distance."

I look between Monica and Gertie, my heart pounding. If she shoots me, it's over. I have no chance.

Monica sifts through her purse again and pulls out a piece of white stationery. She slides it across the dining table so I can see it. I stare at the words on the page, written in a perfect replication of my handwriting done by someone who's had a year of studying my handwritten notes and practicing. The signature is perfect—only a handwriting expert would be able to tell the difference, and I doubt one would ever be called in.

It's a full confession to everything. My drug problem that got out of control. Murdering my former boss when she wouldn't go along with my blackmail scheme. Culminating in an apology to Sam, in which I give him my blessing to go on with his life.

"Your last words." She smiles at me and I shiver. "It's poetic, isn't it? Aren't you glad that's how you'll be remembered?"

I nod at the gun in her hand. "If you shoot me, that will mess up your suicide plan, won't it? If you shoot me to death in my own home, how will you explain that?"

"Oh, I'm prepared." She rests her right hand protectively on the gun. "I've still got access to your work email account. This morning you sent me an email inviting me over to 'talk.' And then when I arrived, you pulled a gun on me because jealousy had gotten the better of you. There was a struggle and... well, unfortunately, I got the better of you. And poor Gertie here was a witness to the whole thing."

"Yeah, but how would *I* have a gun?"

She doesn't bat an eye. "I don't know—maybe you needed it around because you had so many dealers coming to your apartment. Who knows? It's unregistered— probably stolen. You probably bought it on the black market."

I'm speechless. She's thought of everything.

"I think suicide would be far more respectable though, don't you?" She points the gun in my direction, which scares the hell out of me. I've never had a gun pointed at me before. I've never held one in my hand. Honestly, I don't even know if I've been this close to one. "Speaking of which, let's move this to the bedroom." When I don't budge, her eyes narrow. "Unless you want to go for option number two."

My legs feel like rubber as I get to my feet. I don't know if it's the sleeping pills taking effect or if I'm just scared out of my mind. But I practically fall on my way to the bed, gratefully collapsing against the mattress.

"Stay there," Monica commands me, shaking the gun in my face.

As I'm lying there, she holds her belly and winces. For

a moment, I wonder if I would have any chance of trying to get the gun away from her. She's large and her balance is probably terrible. Maybe she's even in labor—who knows? It's not ridiculous to think I could do it. Either way, I'm going to die. It might be worth the risk to go down swinging.

But then again, I had trouble walking to the bed. It's clear I'm in no position to fight. And even if I overpowered Monica, I've still got to get through Gertie. I can't imagine being successful at that, considering how I'm feeling.

And then Monica whips a roll of duct tape out of her purse, and starts taping my ankles. Damn, I knew duct tape was going to be in my future. I recognize it as the cheap duct tape from the supply closet at work—she probably swiped it. How ironic. Keeping me subdued apparently wasn't even worth the price of a roll of tape.

When she tapes my wrists, I realize any chance I had to escape has gone out the window. I never even tried. I've read all these books and newspaper articles about people who rose to the occasion when they were in danger, and then stories about people who just sat there and let themselves be killed. I always believed I'd be in the former category. If it came down to it, I believed I'd be a hero.

Maybe it has to do with the will to survive. Even if I survive this, what do I have? My career is destroyed. I've got murder charges hanging over my head. And I'm married to a man who got his girlfriend to make it look like I killed myself.

I may as well just let go.

"It's the right thing," Gertie tells me as Monica secures my limbs. "You've been keeping Sam from being happy. This is what he's wanted all along. A child. A woman who shares his passion. You kept him from all of that. I felt so sorry for him when I was working for you."

*But I loved him.*

*And I thought he loved me.*

"It's so selfish," Monica practically spits at me. "Any decent woman would have stepped aside."

"As if you're any better," I mutter under my breath.

Her eyes widen. "*Excuse* me?"

"I'm just saying," I say. "There are plenty of younger, prettier girls in his classes. What do you have that they don't have?"

"I'll be the *mother of his child*," she hisses at me, getting her face up in mine. Which is frightening, considering I currently can't move my arms or legs.

"Right, that's true," I concede. "But you'll probably be too busy and tired from taking care of the baby to give him the attention he deserves. And I hear it's awfully hard to lose that baby weight…"

Monica looks like she wants to slap me. I hope she does. If she hits me hard enough to leave a mark, then there will be some evidence my death isn't a simple suicide. I deserve that. Redemption after death.

But before I can say anything else to provoke her, I hear the lock on the front door turning.

# CHAPTER 39

"Shit," Monica says under her breath.

"Who is that?" Gertie asks.

"How should I know?" Monica replies irritably.

I'm as clueless as they are. Who *is* that? The super? The police, come to arrest me? Any of the above would be great. But I assume if it was one of those people, they would knock before simply barging into the apartment.

Before I can ask who's there, Monica rips another piece of duct tape off her roll and slaps it over my lips. And then she shoves me so hard, I roll off the bed, into the foot-wide space between the bed and the wall. My shoulder hits the floor hard and I gasp under the duct tape. The radiator sticking out of the wall is sharp, and I can feel the cold metal slicing into my forearm.

"Abby? You home, Abby?"

It's Sam. Sam's voice.

What the hell?

Monica leans over the bed, where I'm wedged

between the mattress and the wall. Her face is bright pink. "Don't move a muscle. Or else."

For good measure, Monica tosses a blanket on top of me. It dulls the sounds and makes it sort of hard to breathe, but I can still hear through it. I hear Monica say to Gertie: "Mom, you hide in the closet, okay?"

I hear the door to the closet right next to the bed swinging open, then shutting soundly. But I'm confused now. Why is Gertie hiding in the closet? It's not like Sam doesn't know she exists.

Doesn't he?

"Hey, Sammy." Monica's voice, traveling through the thin walls of our apartment.

"Monica?" He sounds baffled. "What are you doing here?"

"Abby called me to come over to talk," she says. "But then she was just… ranting and raving. And she finally ran out."

"She… ran out?"

"What are you doing here, anyway? I thought you were giving a lecture?"

"I canceled it." I can hear him sigh. "I sort of had it out with Abby last night, and I couldn't stop feeling shitty about the way we left things. I really need to talk to her. We've got to figure this out."

My heart swells. Sam isn't plotting against me with Monica. He's on *my* side. And even after all the things he believes I've done, he wants to try to work things out with me. Of course, it would be nice if he believed me in the first place, but I have to admit, the evidence was pretty damning.

"Do you know where she went?" Sam asks.

"I have no idea. Honestly, she was almost unintelligible. Probably high out of her mind."

Sam is quiet. *Don't believe her. Please don't believe her.*

Monica's voice again: "She said something about getting out of town. She was calling the airport."

"The *airport*?"

I calm my heavy breathing so I can hear them better. The radiator is really starting to hurt my arm—I wouldn't be surprised if it's bleeding.

"Yeah, she ordered an Uber to LaGuardia, so…?"

"Jesus Christ. All right… I, uh… maybe I'll see if I can get over there and find her. You don't have any idea where she might have been booking tickets for?"

"I'm sorry, no."

"All right."

Oh my God, he believes her. He's leaving! *Please don't leave, Sam! Don't believe her!*

"Let me just call her phone real quick though," he says. "Maybe I can talk some sense into her."

"No, Sam." There's an urgency in Monica's voice. "You can't talk sense into her. You *can't*."

And that's when I hear it. The ringtone. *My* ringtone.

"Monica?" He sounds so confused, I want to run over and hug him. "Why are Abby's purse and phone still here?"

"Um…" I hold my breath, waiting to hear what she'll say. "She was in such a state, Sam… she just left everything behind."

"Even her *phone*?"

"Apparently…"

"I'm sorry," Sam says. "If there's one thing I know about Abby, she would *never* leave the house without her phone. Where is she, Monica?"

"I told you—I don't know!"

"Abby!" He's shouting now. "Abby! Are you here?"

*I'm here! I'm here!*

"Abby!" His voice is louder now. He's coming toward the bedroom. "Abby! Where are you?"

"Sammy, she's not here…"

"Abby!" The bedroom door is open now. His voice is much louder. "Abby!"

With all my might, I kick against the side of the bed. The noise makes Sam go quiet. I hear bedsprings creak. A second later, the weight of the blankets lifts off my body, and Sam is staring down at me, a look of growing horror on his face.

"Abby," he gasps, bending over me. "What… what's going on?"

*Call the police!*

But it's too late for that. Much too late.

# CHAPTER 40

"Get up, Sam."

I can't see Monica, but I can imagine what she looks like. Stomach bulging under her striking red dress, black hair falling loose around her face, eyes flashing. Gun pointed at my husband's face.

"Monica." His voice is hoarse. "What are you doing?"

"I said *get up.*"

His face disappears from view. I lift my head just enough to see him standing there, his hands raised in the air. I can move a little by squirming, but not very much. I shift over to the side so the radiator edge isn't slicing my forearm anymore. Stupid radiator. That thing is so sharp, it could cut through…

Oh my God, could it cut through the duct tape?

"You're unbelievable, Sam." Monica's voice is filled with venom. "Here I am, offering you *everything*, and all you want is *her.*"

"But she's my *wife*," Sam says. And he says it so

simply, like it's an immutable fact that once a person is wed, they are mated for life. As he says those words, I don't understand how I ever could have doubted his fidelity. That is Sam all over—undyingly faithful.

"But she can't give you anything you want!" Monica is practically shouting now. "She doesn't fulfill any of your needs!"

"Trust me, Monica. She fulfills my needs."

I squirm again, moving my body upward until the sharp edge of the radiator is against my wrist. It's difficult, considering my wrists and ankles are bound, and also, the sleeping pills are starting to hit me. Keeping my eyes open is an effort and my body feels really heavy.

Painfully heavy.

"I can give you more though," Monica says. "I'm ready to give it to you."

Sam lowers his voice a notch. "We talked about this in your apartment the other night, Monica. I told you *no*."

I can't even focus on what they're saying anymore because my wrists have made contact with the radiator. If I know anything about the duct tape from work, I know it's cheap crap. If I can just get the right angle…

"I'm not talking about the other night, Sam." And now her voice has softened. "I'm talking about three years ago. At the university."

"The university?"

"I was in your linear algebra class," she says. "I came to every single one of your office hours."

"Oh."

He doesn't remember her. I'm not even looking at his face, but I can hear it in his voice.

"My hair was blond then," she says. "I dyed it when I saw that picture of Abby you've got in your office. But I was there every week. You said you thought I was really promising."

"I… I'm sure I meant it, but…"

"And we had coffee that time after class," she adds, her voice rising in volume. "At Starbucks. You bought me a cappuccino."

He coughs loudly. "You and I… had coffee together? *Alone*?"

"Well…" She hesitates. "It wasn't *alone* exactly. I was with two other students and… you treated all of us. But you couldn't take your eyes off me the whole time."

"I… I'm not sure if…"

"And then one day," she goes on, not waiting for a response, "when we were alone during your office hours, I tried to kiss you, and you just…" Her voice is wrenched with emotion. "You jumped out of the way. Like you were *dodging* me."

Sam is quiet.

When she speaks again, Monica sounds furious. "You really don't remember *any* of that?"

"Well… um… stuff like that… it kind of happens… a lot."

"And you're never even *tempted*?"

He snorts. "Of course not. I'm *married*."

My husband deserves a medal. I want to jump up and hug him, except for the fact that I'm completely immobilized.

But then I feel the tape ripping under the sharp edge of the radiator. And a second later, my wrists are free! I can move my arms again! My legs are still bound, but I'm halfway there. As long as Monica keeps her eyes on Sam and not me. And also, as long as I don't fall asleep, which is becoming a distinct possibility right now.

"Sam." Her voice softens. "It isn't too late for us. Look at me—I'm having your baby. And I can tell you're attracted to me."

"Monica, come on…"

I grit my teeth. Would it kill him to pretend to be interested in her for a few minutes, just until we can get the gun away from her? People do that in movies all the time, and it seems to work at least occasionally. I just need another minute. One more minute to get my ankles free.

"You wouldn't have to even do anything," she says. "Abby's already taken a bottle full of sleeping pills, so she's probably already unconscious."

No, I'm not. I'm getting my damn ankles loose. Although to be fair, if I didn't have a ton of adrenaline pumping through me right now, I probably would be unconscious.

"A bottle of sleeping pills?" Sam gasps. "You… you poisoned her? Abby…"

"It's for the best," she says. "Don't you see? She's all wrong for you. It would be so easy to let her go…"

"Jesus Christ…"

"You know this is the right thing to do, Sam. You don't have to feel guilty anymore. I've done the hardest part."

And now my ankles are free. Except it doesn't help me as much as you would think. I'm wedged in this tiny little space, I'm half-asleep from a bottle of sleeping pills, so I'm not sure how I'm supposed to leap out and overpower anyone. I don't think I can.

"Monica." Sam's voice is calm but I know him well enough to hear the underlying panic. "We've got to get Abby to a hospital. I swear, we'll figure out a way to help you with… well, everything. But please, Monica. Don't…" And now his voice breaks. "Please let me take her to a hospital."

"*God.*" Monica's voice is filled with disgust. "You're pathetic. Even when something a million times better is staring you in the face, you don't want it. My mother was totally wrong about you." She snorts. "Well, too bad it doesn't matter. It's too late for her. For both of you."

In the entire time I've known Sam, I've never seen him throw a punch. Correction: we've never been in a situation where him throwing a punch would make even remote sense. He's not some drunk who gets into bar fights. Yes, he's in good physical condition thanks to that insurance-lowering gym membership, but he doesn't go around punching people.

But I manage to sit up just in time to see him lunge at Monica.

As he's doing it, the gun goes off, the shot echoing through the apartment. Wow, that's loud. I don't know if she got him or not, but he's got his left hand on her right wrist, and she's screaming. It takes him a few seconds, but between his much greater strength and her abdominal girth, she falls to the floor.

But she's still got the damn gun.

I manage to sit up, but it takes every ounce of my strength. I feel like I'm moving through molasses. I don't know how I'll be able to do anything at all to help Sam. And what's more, now that I'm standing, I can make out the blood on the floor. Actually, quite a lot of blood. And now I can see the crimson seeping through Sam's shirt.

And that's when I see the door to our walk-in closet crack open.

Gertie.

I watch in horror as she ventures out and sees all the blood on the floor. She probably has no idea it's all Sam's. I see the panic growing on her face. She's going to try to get Sam off Monica. If she gets involved, it will be two against one. And Monica still has the gun in a death grip in her right hand.

I don't care if I have only one ounce of strength left in my body. I can't let Gertie and Monica win. I've got to stop this.

*Move, Abby. Move!*

My body obeys. Reluctantly at first, but then I'm propelling myself across the room, at Gertie. I feel like I don't even entirely have control over my arms and legs anymore, but against all odds, they're doing what I want them to do. I lunge at Gertie, knocking her against the wall. And just before I do, my eyes lock with Monica's for a split second, and she lifts the gun in her hand...

The sound of gunfire echoes through the room for the second time. My heart pounds as the same crimson on Sam's shirt leaks from a hole in Gertie's left temple. Gertie's lips form a shocked O, two seconds before she collapses to the ground.

"Mom!" Monica screams.

Sam, startled by the gunshot, somehow allows Monica to scramble out from under him. We both watch in silence as Monica rushes to Gertie's side, as fast as she can, given the load she's carrying. She bends down beside her mother, the tears forming in her eyes. "Mommy..."

Sam looks shell-shocked—he's as pale as I've ever seen him. He lifts his left hand to touch his forehead, and he's shaking badly. His shirt sleeve is drenched in blood. "Holy shit," he breathes.

"Sam," I manage.

My head spins seconds before I collapse like a rag doll against the floor. I'm so out of it that I don't even realize it's happening until I'm on the floor. I can't keep my eyes open much longer.

"Abby?" He drags himself across the room to me in a half-crawl. He grabs my clammy hand in his. "You're awake."

"Yes," I manage. "Barely."

"Hang in there," he says, "we're going to get you to the hospital." He brushes a few sweaty strands of hair from my face. He looks white as a sheet—I wonder how much blood he's lost. "I promise. I just need to go to the living room and get my phone. Okay?"

"Don't leave me alone," I whisper.

"It'll be for only half a minute. I'll be right back."

"No," Monica's voice interrupts us. "You won't."

I use every last bit of strength to lift my eyes to look at Monica. She's glaring at us, her eyes moist and red-rimmed. The gun—she still has the gun. I forgot all about it. I can't keep track anymore. I'm so tired. I'm so, so tired…

"She's dead," she hisses at us. "My mother is dead."

"You're the one who shot her," Sam points out.

"I was aiming for *her*." Monica's eyes are like daggers as she lifts the gun in the air. "And this time, I won't miss."

Sam's eyes widen when he sees what she's doing. Honestly, I don't know how I ever doubted his loyalty to me, because the first thing he does is hurl himself in front of me, so if Monica does fire a bullet, it will have to go through him first. I want to tell him not to sacrifice himself for me, but I can't. My eyes are drifting shut—words would be far too much effort for me.

"You'll have to kill me first," he says to her.

"Don't be stupid, Sam."

He doesn't say a word, but I feel his hand squeeze mine.

"That's really what you're choosing?" she says incredulously. "*Her*?"

"That's right," he says. "I'm choosing Abby."

My hero.

I'm going to die knowing how much my husband loves me. That's worth something.

My eyelids are too heavy to keep open. I hear the click of a gun being cocked. And then the explosion of gunfire for the third time.

# CHAPTER 41

I wake up in a white room.

At first, I think it's possible I've died and I'm in heaven. But no, heaven wouldn't look like this. There wouldn't be so many cracks on the ceiling in heaven. There wouldn't be a clanging air conditioner next to my bed in heaven. And I probably wouldn't have an IV in my arm either.

I'm thinking I might be in a hospital.

I struggle to swallow, but it's hard with my throat so parched. The last thing I remember is the gunshot. Monica had the gun and she pulled the trigger. She shot at Sam.

Oh no…

He's got to be dead. She shot him point-blank.

Except if Monica killed Sam, how did I get to the hospital? *She* sure wouldn't have called for an ambulance.

I hear a groan and look to my right, which sets off a throbbing pain in my temple. There's a blue recliner next to the bed, and lying inside it, covered in a light blanket, is my sleeping husband. He mumbles something in his sleep and shifts, trying to get comfortable.

He's alive.

Oh my God, he's *alive*. And he's not on life support either. He's doing well enough that he's sleeping in *my* hospital room.

"Sam," I whisper. He stirs but doesn't open his eyes. "Sam!"

This time his brown eyes fly open. He sits up in the recliner, a smile creeping across his face. "You're awake."

"Yeah." I nod. "I'm awake."

He reaches over and takes my hand. His is warm and comforting, which makes me self-conscious about how clammy mine feels. "Thank God you're okay. I'm was so worried, Abby..."

I rub my eyes with the arm that doesn't have an IV. "What happened?"

"What do you remember?"

I look at his left arm, which seems more or less intact. "You got shot."

"Oh, that?" He pulls his hand from mine to rub at his arm. He winces. "It was a superficial wound. They bandaged it up in the ER. I'm fine."

"But Monica..." I bite my lip. "She was pointing the gun at you. She was going to shoot you again."

Sam lets out a long sigh and drops his head. "She didn't shoot me. She..."

I frown at him. "What?"

"She shot herself."

My mouth falls open. "She shot *herself*?"

He looks down at his hands. "I thought she was going to shoot me. I thought she was going to *kill* me. I figured that was it. But then… she turned the gun on herself. Put it below her chin and pulled the trigger. I guess when she realized her mother was dead, she just… I don't know… lost it."

In spite of everything Gertie did to me, I feel a jab of sorrow over her death. She was my assistant for years—I knew her only as a sweet older woman. I have to believe that couldn't have all been an act. I'll miss her smile and her cookies.

I'm not so sure Gertie's death was the reason Monica shot herself though. I saw the look on her face when Sam tried to protect me. She was heartbroken over her mother, but that wasn't what pushed her over the edge. She shot herself because she knew I had won.

"I just need you to know," he says quietly, "nothing ever happened between me and Monica. *Nothing.* I never touched her. I swear to you."

"I believe you."

His shoulders sag. "You do?"

"Of course I do."

He rakes a hand through his hair. "Well, you're the only one then. The police looked at me like I was a piece of shit, your mother threatened to take me "for everything I've got," whatever that means because I've got nothing, and Monica's stepmother actually slapped me in the face. Apparently, nobody thinks it's plausible that I wouldn't have slept with her." He shakes his head. "Is it really so crazy that I wouldn't want to cheat on my wife?"

I manage a smile. "Apparently, yes."

"She really set me up. Told everyone I was her boyfriend or her husband. I had no clue—I feel like a moron for letting it happen."

"Well," I say, "she was pretty good at manipulating people. You were the one who didn't want to go through with the whole thing in the first place. I was the one who talked you into it."

"I know, but…"

I reach out for him, and he grabs my hand in his again. "I heard everything you said to Monica in our bedroom. I know you weren't sleeping with her. And…" I swallow, feeling an ache in my dry throat. "I know you jumped in front of me to stop her from shooting me."

He ducks his head down as he squeezes my fingers. "You're my whole life, Abby. If anything ever happened to you…"

"Yeah," I say. "I know what you mean." The thought of losing Sam was what propelled me forward to hurl myself in front of Gertie back in our bedroom.

He shifts in his seat. "And I'm sorry I didn't believe you about the drugs. I should have known you'd never do anything like that."

I nod, although the sting is still there. I wish he had

believed me.

"I never thought you killed Denise," he says. "Honestly. I didn't know what the hell was going on, but I didn't believe that." He shakes his head. "You know, Monica was the one who told me to buy that letter opener for you. I ran into her when I was picking you up at the office and asked her for anniversary gift ideas. I can't believe she was planning it even then…"

"She and Gertie were planning it for *years*…"

When I think of it, I feel sick. All those years when I thought Gertie was a sweet old woman who was doing her best, all she was doing was targeting a husband for her daughter. She knew early on that Sam and I were having fertility problems, and she knew how badly I wanted a baby. She planned to get me out of the way, then have my money and my husband for her daughter.

And then a thought occurs to me. My brain was so foggy when I woke up, I didn't even think of it. "Sam, the baby…" I feel like I'm choking. "Is the baby… dead?"

A ghost of a smile touches his lips. "No, they managed to deliver him safely. He's in the neonatal ICU. Doing okay."

"Oh."

I exhale, thinking of our tiny baby, hooked up to monitors in an incubator. I dreamed of that baby for so long. I already love him a little bit, even though I've never even seen him. But after what Monica did to us…

"It's okay," Sam says suddenly.

"What's okay?"

His brown eyes are sad. "If you don't want him. I get it."

"Sam…"

"No, really," he says. "After everything that happened, I'd understand if… well, you know. Anyway, we'll work something out."

I try to sit up in bed, but my head throbs. I lie back down again, knowing I'm going to be chained to this bed for at least another day. "Do you want him?"

"Of course I do."

Of course he does.

He's quiet for a moment. When he speaks again, his voice has a tinge of excitement: "Do you want to see a picture?"

I nod.

Sam whips out his cell phone and it takes him seconds to bring the image up on the screen. He holds his phone up for me, and I squint at the newborn baby on the screen.

He's tiny. Painfully tiny and helpless and adorable, like the newborn I always dreamed of. He's got oxygen prongs in his tiny nose and he's wearing a little white hat and sweater that are really small, yet still impossibly big on him. I can make out five perfect little fingers on his left hand.

"He looks like you," I say to Sam.

I always thought it was ridiculous when people said babies look like adults. All babies look like little old men.

(Yet the converse isn't true—old men don't look like babies.) But actually, this baby really does look like Sam. Something about his nose and his lips.

"I thought so too." He grins at me. "They let me hold him this morning. Just for a minute, but it was…"

He turns his head away. He's trying not to get too excited. The mother of this child tried to murder us both, after all. But really, there's only one right thing to do.

"I want him too," I say.

Sam's eyes light up. "Yeah?"

"Of course I do. He's adorable, he's beautiful, and he looks like you."

I don't say the last thing I'm thinking: *And he doesn't have a mother.*

"As soon as you're feeling better," Sam says, "you have to come with me to see him. Okay?"

I can't suppress a smile. "Okay."

"Also…" He winks at me. "We have to come up with a name."

Right. We get to choose a name for this baby that is now ours—we will be taking him home. Something that seemed like an impossible dream only days earlier.

"I'm so happy we finally have our child," I sigh.

He nods. "I know what you mean."

"This is what we wanted for so long."

"Yeah…"

"It's just… it's hard to know we're only getting him because his mother is dead."

Sam is quiet. He has an odd expression on his face that's making me uneasy.

"What?" I finally say.

He rubs at the back of his neck. "I never said Monica was dead."

# EPILOGUE

## *One Year Later*

David is learning to walk.

I know—I didn't want him to be named David. But Sam really pushed for the name—it was his father's name, after all. Sam doesn't talk about how much he missed his father after his heart attack took him away from their family, but it meant a lot to him to name his son after the man. And the name is also meant partially to honor Denise, who made me the woman I am today.

And now David is one year old, pulling up on the coffee table, and taking those first cautious steps into the abyss of our living room. He's cautious and serious—just like his dad. He's also sweet like his dad. In so many ways, David is a clone of Sam.

I adore him. I love him more than I thought it would be possible to love another human being. I loved my parents and Sam, of course, but this is different. I spend hours marveling at his perfect little hands. When I hug him, I feel like I can't squeeze him tightly enough. When I have difficulty sleeping at night, all I have to do is go into his bedroom and peer down at his sweet little sleeping face, listen to his deep, even breathing, and all the tension drains from my body.

He has changed my life.

Sam comes into the living room with a plastic container of baby food. After all the complaining I did about how awful baby food tasted, Sam decided he was going to cook his own. And believe it or not, even though Sam couldn't cook adult food to save his life, the little meals he puts together for David are absolutely delicious. Even I think so. It's like he's got a talent. I told him he needs to start his own company, but he says he's going to stick to math.

David loves the food too. As soon as he spots the container, his chubby little cheeks stretch into a smile. That smile tugs at me every time.

Sam ruffles David's hair affectionately before lifting him into his high chair. That's something David's got that isn't like either of us—blond hair. Sam claims he was blond as a kid, but I've seen pictures and he's lying. His hair was a lighter shade of brown than it is now, but he's not towheaded the way David is. That hair is all Monica.

Thanks to my son, there isn't one day that goes by when I don't think of that woman. There isn't a day when I don't search his face for traces of her features. I will never stop watching his behavior, wondering if he'll end up crazy like she was.

I was lucky in that when the police searched Monica's apartment after she shot herself, they found plenty of evidence linking her and her mother to the murder of Denise Holt. They also found out she'd been stealing money from the company—something I worry would have been attributed to me, if things had gone differently on that fateful day. This is surely why they wanted to wrap things up neatly by making it look like I killed myself—she knew if she were ever under investigation, the truth would come out.

We also discovered that prior to offering to be my surrogate, Monica had been in contact with Janelle and had convinced her the two of us would not be appropriate parents. She was the one responsible for taking away the baby that was supposed to be ours.

Also, she's still alive.

"Yum, yum," Sam is saying as he holds the little plastic spoon out for David. "Yummy mashed turkey."

David gobbles it up like it's poached lobster. And honestly, it is pretty good. I sample everything Sam makes, because there's still part of me that doesn't trust him after Salmonella Surprise, but everything is great.

"Yum yum," David babbles.

Sam laughs. He's so good with David. He adores him more than I could have imagined. And David adores Sam. It sometimes makes me sad we had to wait so long for this. And we'd still be waiting if not for Monica.

So yes, Monica is still alive.

Alive but in a vegetative state. The last time I saw her, she was lying in a hospital bed, breathing with the aid of a ventilator, drool sliding down the side of her chin. Her scalp was crisscrossed with staples. Severe brain injury, they said. Unlikely to have a meaningful recovery.

I heard recently that she was off the ventilator, at least, but still not eating or talking or walking. She doesn't know what's going on around her. Still in a vegetative state. After a year, it would be considered permanent.

Sam finishes feeding David the container of baby food, and he's gotten it absolutely everywhere. There's baby food on his bib, but it's also on his chubby little arms, his hair, his cheeks, and there's a glob on his eyelid.

"How does he always get so messy?" I muse.

"He takes after you."

"Oh, really?"

"Yeah." Sam nods, wide-eyed. "I'm always picking food out of your hair after you eat dinner. Honestly, it's such a pain, Abby."

I smack him in the arm, and he grins at me. Everyone says having a baby kills your sex life, and… well, I can't say we're as hot and heavy as we were before. We're both tired a lot more than we used to be—David hasn't been the best sleeper in the world. But at the same time, we still make time for each other. We have regular date nights. We still make out on the sofa while David's asleep in his crib. There are times when having a demanding baby has put a strain on our relationship, but for the most part, it's made our family complete.

"Do you want me to give him a bath?" I ask.

Sam shakes his head. "Nah, I'm on it." He turns to David. "You ready for a bath, big guy? What do you say?"

David throws up his arms excitedly. "Ba!"

That kid loves baths as much as he loves Sam's baby food.

Sam lifts him out of his high chair, doing his best to mop off some of the baby food, but it's a hopeless cause. The two of them disappear down the hallway to our bathroom. I can't help but smile. Maybe David's technically got Monica's genes, but I've seen hardly any traces of her in him, aside from his hair. He's all Sam so far.

While I work on cleaning up the disaster David left in his high chair, the buzzer rings to alert me there's a visitor downstairs. I go to the sink to quickly wash the mashed turkey dinner off my fingers before I press the button on the wall to see who's there.

"Mrs. Adler?" The doorman's metallic-sounding voice pipes out of the intercom. "You've got a visitor to see you. Louise Johnson."

Louise Johnson. Monica's stepmother.

What is *she* doing here?

"Send her up," I say before I can overthink it.

I've spoken to Louise Johnson a handful of times since Monica shot herself. She and Monica's father agreed to take Monica home when it was clear she wasn't going to get any better. I'm surprised they did it, after all she put them through when she was growing up. They seemed like nice people, and against my better judgment, Sam offered to let them visit David from time to time. But Mrs. Johnson told me kindly but firmly that they weren't interested. I was relieved.

I wonder what she wants. I wonder if Monica's okay.

What if she woke up? What if she opened her eyes, sat up in bed, and demanded to see her son?

Well, that's very unlikely. They told me Monica would never wake up. No chance, the doctors said.

But you never know…

By the time Louise Johnson rings our doorbell, I've worked myself into a state of absolute panic. I fling the door open and find her familiar face, with several more gray hairs than before and deep lines between her eyebrows. It must be hard caring for Monica.

"Hello, Mrs. Johnson," I say, as calmly as I can muster.

"Hello, Mrs. Adler," she replies.

Apparently, we're not on a first-name basis.

"How are you?" I ask stiffly.

"Fine, thank you." She manages the thinnest of smiles. "And you?"

"I'm well." I swallow a lump in my throat. "How is, um… how is Monica?"

"The same." She averts her eyes. "No change."

Is it awful that my first thought is "thank God"? Am I a terrible person for not wanting the woman who nearly killed my entire family to be walking around again? It's a relief that Monica Johnson is one thing we won't have to worry about anymore.

But then she adds, "Except…"

My heart skips a beat in my chest. Except? Except *what*? Monica is in a vegetative state. They told us it was permanent. That she would never, ever wake up. She is "as good as dead," the doctors said. *Except what?*

I clear my throat. "Except what?"

"Oh." She seems surprised by my question. She shakes her head. "Nothing. Never mind."

Nothing? *Never mind?* I want to shake the woman until she tells me exactly what she meant by "except," but I somehow manage to get control of myself before I do something stupid.

"So, listen…" Mrs. Johnson lowers her eyes and starts rummaging around in her purse. I flinch, remembering the way Monica pulled a gun from her purse the last time she was here. But Mrs. Johnson isn't like that—I have nothing to worry about. Although I don't relax until she retrieves a small, frayed yellow blanket from within the purse. "I was going through some old boxes at the back of the closet yesterday and I found… well, this was there. It was… it used to belong to Monica."

I stare down at the blanket as if she told me it's covered in scabies.

"It was her favorite blanket as a child," she sighs. "Even as a teenager, she used to keep it in her bed. It... meant a lot to her."

"Oh," I say, because for God's sake, what else can I say to that?

"Look, Abby." Mrs. Johnson lifts her eyes to meet mine. "I know how you must feel about Monica. I... I've gone through a lot of the same emotions. But she gave you the greatest gift you can give a person."

I don't disagree with her.

"I know Monica would want her son to have this blanket." Her eyes flit down to the worn yellow fabric, then back up to me. "Obviously it's your decision, but I hope you'll give it to him. So that he's got at least a tiny part of his biological mother with him."

*He's already got her blood running through his veins!* Isn't it enough that every time I look at my son, I'm searching for traces of that evil woman? I love David so much, but I can never erase the fact that half his genes belong to *her.*

But when Mrs. Johnson thrusts the blanket in my direction, I take it from her. There's no point in arguing. Let her believe I'll give David the blanket if it gives her peace. Except the only place this blanket is going is the trash bin.

Just as I'm closing the door behind me and throwing the deadlock into place, Sam emerges with David, who is now sparklingly clean and snuggled up in a green towel.

Sam always brings him to me after his baths because he knows how cute I think he is when he's all wrapped up like that. David is beaming at me, showing off his six tiny teeth.

"Who was at the door?" Sam asks.

"Monica's stepmother." I shudder as I say the words.

Sam's face pales in what I'm certain is a reflection of my own. "How is Monica?"

"The same," I say.

*Except...*

"Oh." His shoulders sag. "That's comforting."

"Also," I add, "she brought us this blanket that used to belong to Monica."

I hold the blanket to my nose and jerk my head back at the smell. Monica's lavender-scented perfume is clinging to it, intermingled with the faint smell of laundry detergent. As if I needed another reason to hate this blanket.

"Christ, why does she think we'd want that?" Sam also shudders as he holds David tight to his chest. "Get rid of it. Now."

"Banka," David says, pointing to the blanket with a chubby hand.

"That's right," I say. "It's a yucky blanket and we're going to get rid of it."

I turn to throw the blanket in the trash, but just as my hand hovers over the bin, David's face crumbles. "Banka!" he wails.

"No, buddy," Sam says patiently. "That's not for you."

"Banka!" Tears are running down my son's face. He's flailing his body around to the point where Sam is having trouble hanging onto him. He's quickly growing inconsolable. "Banka! Banka, Mama!"

My fingers are still gripping the blanket. I step away from the trash and David's face fills with relief. "Banka," he pleads with us.

"Don't give it to him," Sam says. "I don't want it in my house."

David's hand is outstretched, trying his best to reach the blanket. He didn't even get this excited over the toy truck he got for his first birthday (although to be fair, he liked the box the truck came in significantly more). He's really upset. All this over a *blanket*?

"I'll just let him have it for now," I finally say.

"Abby, no…

"Within a day, he'll lose interest in it," I say. "I guarantee it."

Sam is shaking his head, but it's hard for me to say no to David when he gets like this. He's my only child and I spoil him. So instead of throwing it away, I hold the yellow blanket out to him. He takes the blanket happily, burying his face in the lingering scent of Monica's perfume.

**THE END**

# Acknowledgements

Considering that writing appears to be a solitary process, it's amazing how many people I get help from before I complete a novel!

I'd like to thank my mother, for being the first person to read *The Surrogate Mother*, and the first person to say "wow" after reading it. Sometimes we all need a wow.

Thank you to Kate for plot advice and careful, brilliant editing. I'm very grateful to Catherine for lending me your expertise with the advertising industry and for help with the tricky last scene. Thank you to Rhona for your insightful advice on the cover, and to Zack for marketing advice. Thank you to Jenna for the beta read, and for cluing me in that Christian Louboutin is now trendier than Jimmy Choo. (Who knew?) Thank you to Jessica for your always bitterly honest feedback over the years. Thank you to my other, newer beta readers—Kate, Laura, Sarah, and Liz—your advice and thoughts were incredibly helpful. Thank you to my new writing group for your awesome feedback.

Also, sometimes you also have to thank people who didn't have anything whatsoever to do with the writing process. So thank you to my husband, for being a good-hearted mathematician on which I could base my protagonist's good-hearted husband. (We will all assume you got mono that time through completely innocent means, such as riding the monorail.) And thank you in advance to my father, for not complaining I didn't mention you in the acknowledgements.

And thank you to all my readers. You guys are why I do this, so please keep reading!

Made in the USA
Middletown, DE
29 March 2023

27900202R00203